SWORDS OF FIRE 2

RAGE m a c h i n e Books
Canada
Copyright © 2021 RAGE m a c h i n e Books Canada
© David A. Hardy, Michael Ehart, M. D. Jackson (writing as Jack Mackenzie) and
G. W. Thomas
Artwork © by M. D. Jackson

ISBN: 978-1-927089-92-7

First Edition July 2021

Editor's Note

For a complete catalogue of RM Books visit www.gwthomas.org

Contents

This book is dedicated to
Charles Gramlich

SWORDS OF FIRE 2

EDITED BY

G.W. THOMAS

RAGE MACHINE BOOKS

Introduction

IT SEEMS odd to be writing an introduction for a sequel to a book that was published in January 2010. Eleven years is a long time to wait. But if nothing else it has proven that Sword & Sorcery is always around, going in and out of style for some. (For others like myself, it is a state-of-mind that never really goes away.)

We are offering more of those 15,000 word novellas for your enjoyment, just as Lin Carter did back in 1972. The novella is a perfect length for a heroic fantasy tale. It is long enough to do some world building but keep things moving. There is room for a little character development along with the thrills and chills of swordsmen and swordswomen taking on the creatures of darkness.

Now we could have asked for different writers this go-round but in eleven years Jack, David and I have written a few new pieces so this wasn't really necessary. We are very happy to invite Michael Ehart to the series, though he is hardly a newcomer to RAGE machine Books. His "The Tomb of the Amazon Queen" appeared in *Dark Worlds Magazine* in Winter 2008. Michael received a nomination for a prestigious award for that novella, and well deserved. Ninshi, the hero of that tale, appears here, a most welcome addition.

Jack Mackenzie and I have been publishing books together for a long time now, but not even half as long as we have known each other. You might think there is no competition between us, admiring when the other sells a book or two. But sometimes little things creep in that make you wonder if we really are as close as those two rogues, Sirtago and Poet. If you read Jack's tale "Through Dungeon's Deep" as well as the stories in *Heralded By Blood* you will find Sirtago often curses things like *"By Gwut's hairy ass!"* The sharp-eyed among you might notice that if you remove the "u" you get GWT. Those initials are not unknown around here...

So pull up a bar stool, fill that flagon with cool ale, give the bar keep's daughter a wink while we settle down for a rousing tale or two.

G W. Thomas

Gladiator King

David Hardy

THE awnings were spread over the seats in the amphitheater of Capua. The Italian sun was warm and that meant the wine vendors would make a nice profit. There was to be a prize distribution of tickets good for an extra ration of government bread and a special show in honor of a Flavius Varro, the Roman prefect. All in all, it should have been a fine day to watch gangs of barbarous thugs battle to the death.

It should have been, but it wasn't. The people of Capua were in ferment, at odds with the Romans. Up and down the peninsula, the Italians complained that they fought all of Rome's wars, but gained none of the rewards of victory. The patricians and merchants of Rome waxed richer, while the Italians got poorer.

There had been riots and brawls, thuggish battles without the benefit of seats, awnings, or bread lotteries. Rebellion was in the air, and Rome's "allies" hinted darkly at throwing off Rome's yoke.

Even Cingetorix the gladiator could sense the undercurrent of desperation in the town. Wealthy citizens had been talking to Titus the lanista, seeking to hire his gladiators as guards.

And here was another sign of a time out of joint. A beggar girl standing by the arch, a little apart from the throng of fans and gamblers who were there for fun or profit. Dressed demurely, she was not at all like the harlots the lanista provided for the gladiators, nor yet like the disreputable matrons who showed up at the gates of the amphitheater, looking for a thrill with the killer slaves.

Cotys the Thracian was walking ahead of Cingetorix, his helmet was off, and he leered at the girl. "*Mentula me, saluta te.* See me after the show." The girl did not even bat an eye. Cotys kept walking. The Thracian never let setbacks bother him.

Cingetorix drew near the girl. She looked up at him, seeming to recognize the face beneath the helmet's grill. "King of one hundred battles, son of the drowned north, heed me."

Cingetorix kept walking. "Maybe later, baby." Another thrill-seeker. They bored Cingetorix.

"You bear the sacred bough, the mistletoe the druids revere. Man of the Cimbri, today you shall see the god you serve."

Cingetorix stopped. "How do you know my tribe?" He fingered the amulet of mistletoe he wore about his neck.

"I know you are of the blood of the druids and that she that bore you was counted a wise woman where the heavy sea washed the fens of the Cimberland." She had drawn back her shawl, revealing a delicate, olive-skinned face, and eyes of ancient blue.

"Those people are all dead. I am but a slave who kills other slaves to amuse crowds."

"You are a priest enacting an old rite. The Romans have forgotten its meaning, but in the countryside of Italy, we still remember."

"Get moving," Titus the lanista shouted. "Can't you hear the music? This is Capua, boy. They are the toughest audience this side of Rome."

"Remember the words of Vestinia," the girl said, a strange ringing in her voice. "The World Tree holds up the heavens, and the king shall walk under it, defending his rule, sword in hand."

Cingetorix turned away from the strange girl, the girl with the eyes that saw too much, and hurried on to fall in with the troop. Titus was still talking. "You're up against the best Thrax in Umbria. Win this and we can set up a match with Cotys. Just think of the money riding on that!"

Cingetorix was up soon. Armed in Gallic-style, long sword and big shield, Cingetorix was to fight a Thrax armed with a razor-sharp curved knife and a small shield, the classic pairing of heavy versus light. The betting would be heavy. Capua was where the best gladiators learned their brutal craft and the locals loved the sport.

Outside the band was blowing trumpets and beating drums in warlike style. Cingetorix had little inclination to wonder about the strange girl. Public entertainment always brought out crazy people, attention-seekers, groupies, and worst of all, people who wanted to mix gladiator battles with politics. Yet, Vestinia had spoken of Cingetorix's people. He remembered the slaughter ten years ago when the Cimbri were defeated in a great battle with the Romans. The river ran red with blood as the Romans broke the shield-wall and stormed the wagon-laager. Cingetorix saw the Valkyries scream over the field, gleaning the sword-harvest. That day saw the start of ten years of slavery for Cingetorix. The only token that remained was the little amulet given him by his father, carved from mistletoe in the form of hammer.

He pushed the memories aside. The important thing was to win today, to keep winning, to amass money, to earn the rudis, the wooden sword of freedom, to be a freedman with a Roman citizenship. He began to stretch his muscles and called for the attendant-slave to give him a pre-battle rub-down. And then he touched his amulet for luck.

"Hey, 'Rix!" Cotys said. "Don't lose today. I'll be busy crushing some Gaul who's supposed to be hot. Honestly, I think he's better than you. Not that you're bad, just not in the same rank. Good luck anyway."

Cingetorix ignored Cotys. The man liked to talk big. The band finished and the show was on. The ritual of the salute to Flavius Varro, the Roman governor, was perfunctory and accompanied by some booing which put Varro's legionnaires on edge. First up was a pair of veterans showing off expert technique, but not trying for bloodshed. It was the sort of thing that enthralled sword-enthusiasts but bored crowds. Next up was a pair of tyros, clumsy and brutal. One got in a lucky hit and the other went down, bleeding heavily. It looked like his career was finished before it started.

Cingetorix felt a cold draft and a shadow fell across his shoulder.

13

He turned and saw the man dressed as Charun, the old Etruscan demon of death. At the games there was always a slave dressed in this guise, whose task it was to drag off the slain.

The slave had a bristling beard, a vulture's beak of a nose, face smeared black, a blood-rusted hook in one hand, hammer in the other, and dead eyes that seemed to bore into Cingetorix's own, an abyss that fell all the way to Hell. Cingetorix turned away in revulsion. When he looked back, the man was gone.

Cingetorix was a child of the barren north, raised on tales of trolls and Samhain night when Hell opened wide. He knew the breath of the Otherworld when it fell upon him. And yet he was a seasoned fighter, keyed to a fighting pitch, the scent of unexpected blood in his nostrils. This was just the way the gods told him to fight like a demon.

"You're on! You're on!" Titus bellowed. They were dragging away the fallen tyro, pouring clean sand over the blood as the band played to cheers. The fellow impersonating Charun no longer looked so fearful. Just the same, Cingetorix touched his amulet, to renew the luck.

Cingetorix wasted no time but paired off with his man. The referee held his staff between the fighters. "Give 'em a good show. If I call a break, you break. No shirking, or you get whipped. Hold up a finger to yield. If you go the limit, Prefect Varro gives thumbs up or down."

Good gladiators were seldom killed, but a fight was a fight. Cingetorix won some and lost some, but he never put up a finger and he never needed to be whipped.

"Let's go," Cingetorix said.

"My pleasure," the Thrax replied.

The Thrax was fast. He feinted with his little knife and whipped his buckler to block Cingetorix's long sword. But Cingetorix was used to such tricks and stalked the Thrax with pantherish speed. The Thrax hovered on the edge of his reach and Cingetorix stepped in, whipping his sword in an arc that would have flayed the Thrax had he not leapt backward.

The Thrax was game and came back with a vicious slash of his knife. The Thrax struggled to get in close while Cingetorix tried to keep his distance, each one looking to gain the best ground for their fighting style. Neither man had more than a scratch and they were growing winded.

"Break," the referee commanded.

Cingetorix stepped back just as the Thrax lunged in, driving his knife toward his belly. Cingetorix snapped his shield across his torso, deflecting the blow that surely would have disemboweled him had he lowered his guard. "The tree of Nemi is mine!" the Thrax hissed. Cingetorix spared a glance at the referee, but the official was looking at Varro. The Roman scowled in disappointment, and Cingetorix knew it was not because of the Thrax's poor sportsmanship. He felt a cold chill in his gut and the shadow of Charun danced across the sand.

Titus was at Cingetorix's side, rubbing oil into his weary shoulders. "That cheating bastard!" Titus whispered.

"What in hell is the tree of Nemi?" Cingetorix asked.

"Damned if I know," Titus replied. "Now take that Thrax apart like a rag-picker does a cheap toga."

"Ready!" the referee yelled. Titus trotted back to the sidelines. "On guard! Fight!"

The battle was on in earnest. There was little craft or strategy, no effort wasted on a mere wound, no attempt to win cheers from the crowd, only a grim determination to slaughter the other. Cingetorix did not pause to wonder why the battle had turned vicious, he only sought to win, to live, and to slay.

The crowd roared as sparks flew from the clashing weapons, and the gladiators evaded death by inches. Then they roared louder as the Thrax drew blood from a slash that missed severing Cingetorix's jugular by a hair.

The Thrax put Cingetorix on the defensive, attacking furiously in an effort to get inside Cingetorix's guard and use his Thracian knife in a killing stroke. Cingetorix stumbled and the Thrax charged in for the finish. Cingetorix shifted his shield and punched the edge directly into the Thrax's face. The Thrax's helmet rang like a bell and he staggered back. But he was a warrior of superb resilience and he brought up his shield and knife overhead to block the descending arc of Cingetorix's sword.

It was of no avail and Cingetorix smashed through, cleaving the Thrax from shoulder to breastbone. The crowd went wild. For once Cingetorix was too weary to acknowledge a hard-won victory.

Now came Charun to drag off the fallen gladiator. Charun snarled, "Dog, kneel before thy master." Cingetorix knew this was not a slave in a player's mask, but the dread demon himself.

"You are not my master," Cingetorix said, showing a bravado he did not truly feel.

"Fool! I am the god of this temple and you are my least worthy priest. Seest thou the offering thou hast laid? Kneel I command!"

Cingetorix swayed, eyes wide with horror as Charun pointed with his bloody hammer at the dead Thrax. Yet his knee would not bend and words poured out in an unexpected defiance. "Foul demon. Get back to Hell, ere I send you there." Cingetorix whipped up his shield into a guard and rushed Charun.

Charun laughed and raised his great hammer like a toy. He swatted aside Cingetorix's thrust with ease and cracked Cingetorix's shield with a tap of the hammer that sent the gladiator staggering.

"You blaspheme, dog," Charun hissed. He raised his hammer to strike down Cingetorix. Involuntarily, Cingetorix reached for his amulet.

Before the hammer could descend, Cingetorix heard a strange wailing song. It was a woman's voice singing, and its sound was like sweet honey, laced with poison. Charun swung his hammer, but Cingetorix parried with his sword. The demon's great strength was gone.

And then the demon was gone too. Cingetorix looked about in wild surprise. The crowd was still cheering, though some were laughing. Titus hurried forward as the band struck up a tune. "What in Hades was that? Making passes in the air over a dead man? Prefect Varro was not pleased. Get a move on, the next bout is up."

A slave masked as Charun dragged off the dead Thrax, casting a nervous glance at Cingetorix's hostile glare and bloody sword. Other slaves dumped sand on the bloodstains and smoothed it out. Cotys was swaggering into the arena amidst the throng's cheers, his opponent doing likewise. And the show went on.

After the show, in the tunnels below the amphitheater, Cingetorix paced uneasily outside the gladiators' chambers. He still bore his sword. From a dark side-tunnel Vestinia emerged.

"You saw the demon," she said.

Cingetorix nodded.

"You have the second sight. You were born with it. It was a birthright from you father."

"How do you know my kin? You are a Roman."

"I am no Roman. I am Vestinia of the Marsi. My tribe is Italian, but not Roman. My mother was a cunning woman, and my grandsire read the future in the entrails of the sacrifices. And your father was a druid and your mother a wise woman."

Cingetorix nodded. "My father was Catuvolcus, a druid of the Volcae and my mother was Astrid a volva of the Cimbri. He read

16

doom in the auguries the night before we battled the Romans at Vercellae. Yet he went out to fight and die nonetheless, for what many may escape his doom? My mother died too. She stabbed a Roman soldier to give me a chance to flee. They caught me anyway. I saw what they did to her before she took her life." He shuddered, the horror still living in memory.

"Enough!" Cingetorix shouted. "What of it? They are dead and gone. I am a living man and my business is with…"

"Those about to die." Vestinia glanced down the tunnel.

In the flickering lamplight, a lictor, axe and rods in hand, strode towards Cingetorix. Behind him were two legionnaires. The lictor raised his hand in command. "Cingetorix the gladiator, by order of Prefect Gnaeus Flavius Varro, you are under arrest. Drop the sword and come quietly. You and the girl are coming to the prefecture."

Two thoughts raced through Cingetorix's mind. One, that he would never emerge from the prefecture alive. The other that he could cross the space and plunge his sword into the lictor's heart before the legionnaires could react.

Cingetorix was right. The lictor died instantly and the legionnaires fell back in surprise. They were used to inspiring fear, not being subject to it. Cingetorix leapt on the man to his left like a starving tiger. He swatted aside the soldier's shield and sheared off the man's head. The other dropped his shield, not to flee but the better to seize Vestinia.

Sword at her throat, the surviving Roman growled, "One step more slave and the girl goes to hell."

Cingetorix hesitated. What was Vestinia to him anyway? But he was unwilling to see her die. She had come to warn him, though of what was not clear. Cingetorix would not throw Vestinia's life away. "Roman, hurt that woman and you die like a dog." She was under his protection now.

"Then back away," the legionnaire growled.

Vestinia was whispering, the legionnaire darted his eyes at her, but Cingetorix could not hear the words. As a shadow—a shadow like a vulture that walked like a man—fell across Cingetorix's shoulder the soldier's snarl of defiance turned to one of horror. His sword drooped in a nerveless hand. Instantly Cingetorix struck, stabbing the soldier in the neck above his mail corselet.

Cingetorix paid no heed to the falling Roman. He whirled to face the demon he expected to find at his back. But there was nothing.

"Charun can be seen by those who are close to death," Vestinia said.

"And how did the Roman know he was close to death?"

Vestinia gave no reply.

They ran to the outer gate of the amphitheater. Titus stood there in the gathering gloom.

"Running off?" Titus shook his head. "For a woman, gods above. I thought you had better sense."

"I've got to go, Titus," Cingetorix said, hand on the hilt of his sword. "Sorry."

"For this you give up show business!" Titus shouted at their backs.

But they paid no heed. Already crowds were forming in the streets, shouting, "Down with Varro! Down with Rome!" More than once Vestinia led Cingetorix down a side alley away from marching soldiers. "I know this city well, it was old ere the Greeks arrived. There is many a passage, both above and below ground, that not even most Capuans know of, let alone the Romans." They entered an alley, only to find a patrol of Romans blocked one end. They turned to go back, but a mob of Capuans, armed with swords, cudgels, and stones entered the other end.

Vestinia pointed at a section of wattle and daub. And as rocks and javelins began to fly Cingetorix pried it away to reveal a crude stairway leading downward. They hurried in as the shouts of enraged fighters and the cries of the injured echoed overhead. At the base of the stairs Vestinia pulled a lamp from a niche and struck a light. The entrance led to a foul-smelling tunnel that dipped below ground to catacombs and sewers.

The lamp cast its flickering shadows across the lightless niches where the dead moldered amid benighted streams of unutterable filth. On all sides Cingetorix heard things moving, and whispered sounds that never came from mere vermin. There was even the rustle of a vulture's wings.

"Quickly!" Vestinia said. She pointed upwards, at a block of stone set in the low, vaulted tunnel roof. Below it was a large flat boulder, just big enough for a man to stand on. "This must be pushed aside. As you value your life and sanity, you must push that aside before *they* come."

Cingetorix eyed the stone in the uncertain light. "Was there ever a woman who could not find a heavy thing for a man to lift?"

"This is no time for jesting," Vestinia said. The rustle of wings drew closer. Cingetorix mounted the boulder, bracing himself against the upper stone. He stretched, pushing with arms, legs, and back. It was like pushing at a mountain.

"Hurry!" Vestinia hissed.

Cingetorix's breath came heavy in the foul air. He tensed to push again. This time he felt something move. Cingetorix kept pushing, but the stone moved no further. The sweat poured off him. Voices whispered in the dark. The foul tunnel was a tomb, where Cingetorix's bones would lie forever in the filth and darkness. The stench of death rose as vulture wings flapped. Cingetorix sensed unnatural things gathering in the dark to destroy him.

"The lemures come," Vestinia whispered. "The spirits of the evil dead follow Charun."

Cingetorix's strength was failing him. The stone remained frozen in place. He touched his mistletoe amulet and prayed for strength.

"A warrior of the Cimbri does not surrender," a voice like Cingetorix's father said.

Cingetorix gathered his strength, then attacked again. Neither the stone nor Cingetorix would yield. Cingetorix gave a heave, at the limit of his might.

The stone broke free. Sweet clean air washed over Cingetorix. He tumbled the great stone aside and saw stars. He turned and gave a hand to Vestinia, lifting her up to freedom, then followed. Cingetorix spared but a backward glance as he rolled the stone back in place. In the sputtering light of the discarded lamp he saw a vulture-winged form surrounded by a horde of thing that might have been men and might have been maggots.

"Capua burns," Vestinia said. She pointed at the city, where flames were shooting up against the nighted sky. This was the beginning of the Social War, the great struggle between Rome and the Italians. No longer content to be allies in name and servants in fact, the Italians demanded an equal share of rights in the Republic and the empire it had carved from the Pillars of Hercules to the Pontic Sea.

Neither Cingetorix nor Vestinia gave the matter much thought. The task of obtaining food was more on their minds as they fled from the seat of war. Vestinia knew the countryside and pointed out the best roads to take. Though they traveled together, Vestinia kept to herself, granting nothing to Cingetorix save her company and directions.

They stayed away from towns and the Romans' well-guarded roads. Though they glimpsed marching soldiers from afar, the pair avoided all such, Roman or rebel. They approached the country folk warily. The hill-dwellers were mostly free farmers, though wealthy *latifundistas* had made inroads too. The free farmers had no love for escaped slaves such as Cingetorix. The slaves on the latifunda would never turn in a runaway, but they would happily rob and murder a stranger. But in unsettled times there was no authority to report an escaped slave to, and none wished to trifle with an armed gladiator at any time.

But at one crossroads hamlet, they found a dozen wooden crosses, each with a man nailed upon it, a grove of grisly fruit, reared in the Roman style. A gray-bearded elder told them, "Thus Rome punishes rebels. Marcus Papius Mutilus of the Marsi is fighting the Romans, and those were some of his troops. When the soldiers were done, their centurion bade us give him word did we see a barbarian gladiator traveling with a woman. The right word would reap a golden reward. Hiding the fugitives would put a man up a Roman tree."

Cingetorix loosened his sword. "And what word will you give the Romans?"

The gray-beard shook his head scornfully. "None. We Samnites are not filthy rats for the Romans. May Mutilus smite the Roman dogs!" Cingetorix and Vestinia left, for neither thought it wise to test the Samnite code of silence unduly.

They went deeper into the hills, rising up toward the Apennines. As they tramped a dusty road above a valley filled with olive trees, Cingetorix said to Vestinia, "Witch, with all your cunning knowledge, tell me why a Roman prefect wants my head? And why a vulture-winged death-demon pursues me as well?"

"You are not the only one with second sight. Your foes have divined where your steps will take you."

"And how do they know that when even I don't know where I am bound?"

"Was there ever a Roman who did not keep a diviner close by?"

"Well, from what I've seen, the wisest course with any diviner is to hear him out and do the opposite. Where does Flavius Varro think I'm going?"

"On the shores of Lake Nemi there stands a grove where in is a very ancient oak. Under that oak is the King of Nemi. He is a runaway slave and holds that office until he is slain by another runaway."

"Sounds like a comfortable spot if you can stand the competition."

"He that is the priest of the sacred tree is more than a king in name. It is no hollow rite, enacted for show. The king is the king of the life of the land. He guards the world tree whose unseen branches stretch to heaven and whose roots form the roof of hell. You are a fugitive slave Cingetorix, go there and you shall be a king."

Cingetorix cast his mind back to the tales he heard as a boy. He said, "My father, Catuvolcus, was a druid of the Volcae and my mother, Astrid, a wise woman of the Teutons. They were both deeply versed in the lore of the Gauls and the Germans. Father told me of the bloody rites enacted among the sacred groves of the Gauls, and mother told about the bloodgrove at Uppsala where nine of all that is male is drowned or hanged. They told me of the World Tree that the Northmen called Yggdrasil and the Cimbri called Irminsul and how the tree stands by the Well of Wisdom. Yes, and that Odin himself gave an eye to drink of the well and suffered himself to be pierced and hung like those rebels we saw that he might grasp the runes of knowledge. And I learned that the Norns weave a man's fate such that the threads bind him ever so tight."

"I know my father spoke truly." Cingetorix scratched his chin. "That being the case, we'll go anywhere but Nemi." Cingetorix pointed to the Apennines. "We can cross the peaks, away from the war, come down to the Adriatic and take a ship for the east."

"What?" Vestinia snapped. "But the Sacred Tree, the King of Nemi, you can't! No! You've got to!"

Cingetorix laughed at Vestinia. "I'm pretty certain I don't. If some devil out of hell and a mad Roman are going to be waiting for me at Nemi, then it's the last damn place I want to be. If the Fates decree that I go to Nemi, I suppose I'll have to. But why not wait until I can go without being set upon and crucified or worse? The Fates may order this or that, but right now my legs answer to my will and my will is to go to the sea, or Gaul, or Thrace, or any damn place but Nemi." Cingetorix set off briskly down the road. "Come on if you're coming woman. It isn't safe in these parts."

Vestinia stood in the road, protesting and sputtering, until Cingetorix reached the nearest bend at which point she grabbed up her bundle and ran after him.

That night Vestinia complained that the wind blowing from the mountains made her cold, so she begged leave to share the warmth of Cingetorix's bedroll.

The next day the sun shone brightly on the land and the road rose gently toward their destination, big and beautiful in the distance. Cingetorix allowed himself to relax and let his feet eat up the miles. He was so relaxed that when the Romans stepped out into the road he was surprised. Yet not so surprised he couldn't get his sword out.

There were six of them. Cingetorix was vaguely aware of Vestinia taking to the brush. Maybe she'd go summon a demon or not, this was a matter of muscle and steel and skill and nerve. That and luck. Cingetorix touched his amulet.

The first soldier was slow and careless and Cingetorix hamstrung him. The others were taken aback, but not so much that they forgot their training. The five remaining ones stalked Cingetorix like wolves while the wounded one raved and cursed for he'd be a cripple for life. Cingetorix let a sneer cross his face. "Some of you will envy your friend soon. And whatever happens, my woman has escaped."

The nearest Roman's brows knit. Cingetorix could see he would rather be chasing down a helpless woman for sport than fighting a gladiator to the death. "Take him quick boys, so we can get the woman."

The first one that moved lowered his shield just a little and nearly lost his head. Cingetorix broke through the Romans' ring, slashing another Roman, and then put his back up against a tree, ready to sell his life dearly. "Come on you bastards, who wants to taste my sword?"

They came. Cingetorix fought as he had never fought before. His sword was a flickering flame as the Romans tightened their ring of steel. No longer were they taking chances, this time they would bear in and crush Cingetorix by weight of numbers.

Cingetorix was breathing hard and sweat beaded on his brow when he heard pounding hooves. The Roman before him leapt a little forward and a lance point was sticking out of his chest. The remaining Romans broke in fear, but strange warriors on foot and horseback swarmed over them. In moments the Romans were butchered and the victorious fighters were stripping the dead.

Cingetorix stood apart, watching warily. They were Italian soldiers, rebels Cingetorix assumed. A centurion shouted, "Make way for the praetor!" The soldiers saluted as their commander arrived. He was a stocky man, with a round face and beak of a nose, dressed in Samnite-style armor. At his side was Vestinia.

"Hail Marcus Papius Mutilus!" the centurion said.

Mutilus swept a sharp eye over the dead Romans before coming to rest on Cingetorix. "You're that barbarian gladiator, eh? I see you've met my daughter."

Cingetorix was so surprised that he did not resist when the centurion took his sword.

The rebels marched Cingetorix to their camp and took him to

Mutilus's tent. Vestinia was there already. Mutilus sat drinking wine, he offered a cup to Cingetorix.

"I thank you for your troops' help with those Romans. It was looking as though the Fates had snipped my thread. I am happy to have been the means by which your honor's daughter was restored to her loving father's bosom. If I may put myself further in your debt, may I beg a day's worth of food so I might be on my way."

Mutilus laughed. "You may eat your fill, but you'll eat it in this camp. You're a runaway slave, a brigand by appearance, and a kidnapper of innocent girls. I could have you crucified."

"Of course, your excellency. No doubt the gods will shine their approval on the way you dispense justice." Cingetorix kept his voice calm, but his eyes were on a sword hanging from its strap. He calculated the odds of fighting his way out, and they were not good.

Mutilus waved his hand. "Don't worry. I don't intend to crucify you. Not today anyway. I'm a fan of yours. Your shows are always great. I remember the match with that Greek two-sword expert. What was his name…"

"Socrates Deuteros."

"He came in second that day!"

"He tried the Socratic method on me. It didn't take."

"What fun." Mutilus gestured at Vestinia, who was watching with a face like a limestone caryatid. "My wayward lamb has been telling me of your adventures. She said you were going to escape to cross the mountains and escape to Thrace."

Cingetorix nodded.

"Strange that she didn't try to lure you to the Grove of Nemi. She prophesied about it when she was Varro's woman." Mutilus looked from Cingetorix to Vestinia, who glared back with naked loathing. "She told him that the high priest of Nemi is an escaped slave, who must slay his predecessor. By some rite known to Vestinia, the priest is also the secret king of Italy, and may sway the fate of all that lies between the toe of Calabria and the snow-topped Alps." Mutilus looked back at Cingetorix. "Or some silly talk like that. Girls love their secrets, almost as much as they love telling them." Mutilus slapped his sword. "This is what sways the fate of men.

"You are no doubt wondering how my daughter came to be in Varro's house. When I was young, I enjoyed roving among the peasant girls of these parts. The expected happened, but by then I'd shipped out for the Spanish Wars. I was a prefect leading a cohort of Marsic 'allies.' Around here the main choices are working the land or going to the wars. I picked the wars.

"I went to Spain. Scipio was pacifying the rebel tribes. Marius and Sulla were junior officers in those days. Varro was a tribune on the proconsul's staff. We got to be friends. We'd go on a mission, torch some barbarian huts, carouse at the wine shops back in Saguntum, then it was up country again fighting the tribesmen. Varro and I were in the thick of it, I saved his life from Celtic headhunters and he got me out of an ambush by Lusitanian desperadoes.

"We lost a lot of good Marsic boys in Spain. After a while I realized the Romans got the plunder and we got the hard knocks. When we came back, Varro used his wealth to buy up lots of Marsic land and run slaves on it. The locals were going broke, selling anything to get out of debt, livestock, seed corn, land, children. Varro bought Vestinia."

Vestinia let out a laugh of derision. "As if you noticed. Life at Varro's villa was much more comfortable than on the farm." She drew herself up. "I could read the messages of the gods in the wind, the clouds, a bowl of milk, or the entrails of a victim. Varro knew my worth. You were only interested in me so you could make political speeches about the greed of Roman rule."

"A father has to look for what is best for all his family." Mutilus frowned. "Enough. Cingetorix, you know that the Romans offer you only a wooden tree and an agonizing death. I respect good fighters and you can serve as my bodyguard. Vestinia, you will have a comfortable place making prophecies of victory to keep up the troops' morale." Mutilus waved in dismissal.

Cingetorix bided his time. Staying with Mutilus's army seemed the best bet. The land was aflame with war. Sulla landed in the south with newly raised troops. With merciless efficiency Sulla left the proud Greek city of Neapolis a charnel house of ash and slaughter. Marius was mustering veterans at Rome, offering thanks to the gods for giving him one more war to wet his sword in the blood of Rome's foes.

Other rebel forces had smashed Roman armies that had taken the Italians' fighting prowess too lightly. A few of these luckless Romans fell to Mutilus's shark-like prowl along the peninsula. Varro evaded him, hanging on the rebel's flanks with wolfish caution. Word came that Cotys was now Varro's bodyguard.

Cingetorix's job was to stand by Mutilus in battle. The general selected the best spot to watch the course of the struggle and to direct forces as needed. It was an education for Cingetorix. Used to the cut and thrust of the arena, he observed how a line of spears acted as a shield, how an infantry charge was like the deadly blow of a secutore's sword, and how cavalry was a flashing knife to finish off a fallen foe.

When the moment called for it, Mutilus would charge into the Romans, sweeping all before him with his bodyguards. Cingetorix was at the tip of the charge, pitting his arena-honed reflexes against the enemy. He won much favor in the eyes of Mutilus.

Before any encounter, Vestinia read the omens. She never failed to predict victory, which gave the soldiers immense confidence, for her predictions were ever correct.

Mutilus left a trail of wrecked Roman cohorts and burned Roman settlements as he wound his way along the edge of the hills. At one stop he studied the map with his officers while Cingetorix stood guard. "Sulla's army of recruits is south of us, taking one stronghold at a time. Marius's veterans are pushing from Rome in the north. Varro has the local garrisons, too few to do much, but they can push us towards the other Roman armies. Sulla is the anvil, Marius is the hammer, and Varro is the tongs."

"What do we do?" a centurion asked.

"Don't get pinched, that's what." Mutilus said. "Too close to the sea and the Romans can catch us in the open. Too far up in the mountains and we starve." Mutilus's finger hovered over the map, tracing a line of march across the hills. "Beyond this ridge is a rich valley where Roman senators nest in there villas, built on the sweat and blood of Marsic soldiers and farmers. What do you say, boys? Shall we let 'em enjoy the fruits of their crimes or shall we root out their lairs and lay 'em in ashes?"

"Ashes!" the rebels roared.

None remarked that the valley of the wealthy senators was very near to a place marked "The Grove of Nemi."

They found the villas and tore them to pieces, the absent owners' slaves joining in the destruction gleefully. Mutilus occupied a retired consul's vacation home and held a feast for his staff, who put their muddy boots on silken couches that cost more than most had ever seen. Cingetorix was drinking fine Falernian wine from a patrician's golden cup when the scouts arrived. "Varro has arrived at the head of the valley with two full legions and cohorts of Numidian cavalry and Thracian foot."

Mutilus raised his cup in a toast. "To Varro! It is time for old friends to meet." The officers roared in laughter, but it rang hollow to Cingetorix's ears.

"Vestinia, let the witch give the omens!" they cried. "Tell us witch, will we beat the Romans like a rented mule or will we smash 'em like eggs?"

Vestinia arrived, with the knife and the victim. She invoked the gods above and below, the wisdom of the snake and the sharp eye of the eagle as a slave kindled the fire. A handful of laurel to appease the Mother of All, then she plunged the knife into the sheep. Her hand came out with the liver and Vestinia stared intently at the bloody thing. Her eyes widened in horror.

"Speak, girl," Mutilus said. "What do you read in that mess?"

Vestinia mastered herself but her voice shook though. "You shall hold the field, but the contest will be a bloody one."

"I never expected less than a rough brawl with Varro," Mutilus said. "So long as it is victory."

The officers agreed, but Cingetorix could see they were affected by Vestinia's prophecy. Mutilus rose to give last minute orders, allowing Cingetorix a bare moment to linger before guard duty.

"What rune did you read?" he asked.

"I read my fate."

"And mine?"

"You are a fugitive slave, at the beck and call of a half-mad rebel. You think you can assert your will against the gods?"

From outside Mutilus called and Cingetorix ran to his general's service.

In the dark before dawn, war drums throbbed in the rebel camp. Men fell in line as centurions barked orders. Scouts came in, reeling in the saddle for lack of sleep, but bearing vital reports for the general. The Marsic cavalry saddled up, their horses catching the men's tension, ready to dash upon the enemy or to flee.

The sun came up over the hills, revealing the Roman advance. Their regular tramp and the metallic clink of armor made a strange paean to the dawn. Mutilus posted himself on a hill between the camp and slightly behind his line. He pointed a cluster of horsemen about an Eagle standard. "Varro."

The Numidians screened the Roman advance. They were barbarous tribesmen from Africa. They rode like centaurs and kept their faces veiled, a strange horde of masked riders. Mutilus had posted his cavalry on the right. He ordered a trumpet call and the Marsic horsemen, scions of the best families, sprang to life to sweep the Numidians from the field.

But the African tribesmen were practically born in the saddle. They gave back before the Marsi, only to turn and hurl javelins that struck down un-armored men and horses. The Numidians were ruthlessly exploited. Soon the rebel cavalry were in flight for the hills, the Numidians in hot pursuit.

Varro's Thracians were trying to work around the flank of the rebels. They were recruited from robber tribes in the Balkans, and were sturdy brigands who were happy to skirmish at a distance with javelins, or mix into close fighting with their curved machaera and two-handed rhomphaia that could cut a man clean in half. Cingetorix's old gladiator comrade Cotys was a Thracian.

Mutilus sent out his velites, skirmishers recruited from among the poor and the young. They wore caps of badger fur and were no less fierce than their totem. They plied the Thracians with javelins and ruthlessly cut off any foes who strayed too far from their comrades. They gave as good as they got and soon the skirmishing bogged down into hurling of rocks and insults.

Meanwhile the rebels and Romans marched resolutely forward. Roman pila and Marsic javelins filled the air, and many a man cast away his shield after it was weighted with deadly darts. The hail of missiles ceased and the lines closed to sword point. A hollow clatter of wooden shields resounded among the hills. Each man sought to punch through the enemy shield-wall and stab a foeman, opening a hole for his comrades to follow. It was a stalemate as both sides struggled for an advantage.

"Jupiter and Hades!" a tribune exclaimed. "Our men are holding on, but the Romans have the weight of numbers. Maybe we should fall back on the camp, praetor."

"We're not falling back anywhere," Mutilus snapped. "Send up the reserve cohorts and keep pressing the Romans."

The reserves went in, but the Romans quickly countered and despite their stubbornness, the rebels were forced back. The rear units were already clustering at the base of Mutilus's hill.

"The enemy is getting closer. Shall we send in your guard, praetor?" a prefect asked.

"Not yet," Mutilus said, his eyes on the hills. Cingetorix looked up from the battle and saw a cloud of dust to the right, beyond the nearest ridge. He could just make out the blare of trumpets over the din of battle. Then the figure of a rider topped the hill, then another and another, and then the riders swooped down towards the Romans.

"It's our cavalry boys!" Mutilus shouted. "They shook off those

Numidian dogs and followed a back trail I knew was up there. They're going to hit the Romans like Jove's thunderbolt!" He raised his sword. "Follow me, praetorian guards!" Cingetorix touched his amulet and charged in, sword on high.

Varro's legions staggered, but held under the shock of Mutilus's guards. The Marsic cavalry smashed a great gap in the Roman ranks. Cingetorix was too busy hewing at the soldiers before him to notice, but two cohorts were slaughtered and put to flight before Varro rallied the rest.

Cingetorix was in his element, fighting hand-to-hand with nothing held back. Even as other men in the guard, Cingetorix hewed a blood-red path to Varro. Striding over the carpet of dead and wounded, a Roman centurion barred Cingetorix's path. He shouted, "Come on you rebel dogs! One Roman is worth any number of Marsic rabble!"

"Is one Roman worth a Cimbric warrior?" Cingetorix asked.

The centurion stared at him a moment, as if an animal had spoken, then smiled. "I was there when Marius slaughtered your kind by the thousand." He sheathed his sword. "For a slave, I don't need a sword, just a sturdy stick of correction." The centurion raised the vine stick he carried as a badge of rank.

"I'll take those odds." Cingetorix sheathed his sword as well. The centurion brought his vine stick down as Cingetorix lunged for his throat. The stick landed with bone-cracking force, but Cingetorix took it across his firmly muscled back. He never slowed as his hands went to the centurion's throat.

The Roman's eyes bugged out in surprise. His face turned purple as Cingetorix began crushing his windpipe. The centurion dropped his stick as he jammed his left hand into Cingetorix's throat. With his free hand he snatched out his dagger. The instant the centurion moved Cingetorix took his left hand from the Roman's throat and grabbed at his dagger-hand. The centurion came within half an inch of burying the dagger in Cingetorix's jugular. Cingetorix struggled to hold the centurion's hand. Both men had iron grips on the other's windpipe. Cingetorix gritted his teeth and squeezed with all his might. Blood thundered in his ears like a thousand wild horses' pounding hooves. The centurion's nose began to bleed and sweat ran in streams down his face. Cingetorix heaved and twisted the centurion's arm, the wrist snapping suddenly.

Cingetorix released his foe's broken limb and fastened both hands on the centurion's neck. The Roman made one last gasping effort to throw off Cingetorix and then his eyes rolled back in his head, dead of strangulation.

"What in hell are you doing?" Mutilus shouted. "Wasting time with one stinking Roman when there's still literally thousands that need killing?"

Cingetorix staggered to his feet. His collarbone felt like it might be broken, his throat burned and every breath was agony. He heard a shout. "The Numidians! They circled back and are looting the camp!"

Cingetorix felt a jolt as he remembered that Vestinia was in the camp. Whatever else she might be, he had taken the girl under his protection. Nearby a dead cavalrymen lay sprawled, tangled in his horse's reins. Cingetorix seized the reins and shook the dead man loose. In an instant he was on the horse's back, kicking the weary beast into a gallop towards camp.

The camp seemed almost deserted, save for the dead and dying. Smoke rose from a plundered house and someone was shouting in a strange language. Cingetorix dismounted and advanced warily.

He found the villa where Mutilus had made his headquarters. The gate to the courtyard hung open. A slave bearing a sack of plunder jumped down from a window and ran off. Warily Cingetorix entered the courtyard.

He heard Vestinia scream, "Look out!" Cingetorix looked up to see Cotys on the upper gallery, hand locked in her hair and his knife at her throat. Cotys snarled, "Drop the sword or the witch dies."

Cingetorix hesitated, unwilling to surrender, yet unwilling to throw Vestinia's life away. He touched his amulet, as if it would grant a way out of the impasse. Suddenly, there was a clatter of hooves behind him. Cingetorix turned to see Numidian riders entering the court. He cut the first from the saddle, hacking through the man's leg. Then the butt of a lance crashed across Cingetorix's head. He staggered as more blows rained down, then collapsed into a pit of darkness and pain..

A nightmare journey, staggering at the end of a rope strapped to a Numidian saddle, was followed by days of beatings while locked in a punishment cell. Cingetorix thought he saw Titus in the legion's camp, but he also thought he saw Charun and his father's ghost. The cell in the ergastula, the plantation's slave pit, seemed real enough.

Cingetorix endured hours of being hung upside down while soldiers battered him with sticks, fists, and boots. A Roman tribune shouted questions at him, demanding this or that about the plans of

Mutilus and other rebel chiefs, few of whom Cingetorix had even heard of. Even if he had known Mutilus's plans, Cingetorix told himself he would not have talked. The Romans didn't seem to care if he talked or not, mostly they enjoyed beating him.

On the third day, the door to the cell opened and Varro entered. In the grip of a cruel-faced centurion was Vestinia. Varro inspected Cingetorix as if he was considering buying the barbarian and was unwilling to pay a sesterce more than he had to. Soldiers brought in a stool and ropes.

"I want answers of you. There will be no more trifling. I will put both you and Vestinia to the question. You will answer, you may resist a shorter or longer time, but you will answer." Varro gestured and the centurion stripped Vestinia of her robes and bound her to the chair.

"What are Mutilus's intentions regarding the Grove of Nemi?"

The centurion twisted the ropes about Vestinia's throat. Cingetorix stared grimly at Varro. "Do you torture her to get information or because you are jealous?'

"Why not both?" Varro said, a cynical smile on his lips. "Tighten the rope, centurion."

"I'll tell you everything I know," Cingetorix said.

That proved to be very little. Varro listened quietly as Cingetorix described how Mutilus had dismissed Vestinia's prophecies, yet had moved closer to Nemi.

"And that is all?" Varro asked.

"Mutilus is a fool, for the prophecy is true."

"I know that," Varro said. "But how do you?"

"The girl, let her go."

"She'll be released from the question, but I am not such a fool as to let go such a one as Vestinia the Prophetess." Varro gestured again to the torturer and Vestinia was unbound.

"I have seen Charun the death demon and his slaves, the lemures of Hades." Cingetorix gritted his teeth. "I'd talk more easily out of these fetters."

"Release him," Varro said. "So you have seen the vulture devil of the games himself. So have I. In fact, it was Vestinia who summoned the Black One. In this very chamber, where a slave had been whipped to death, Charun appeared. The spirit spoke grimly of a fugitive who would fight to the death for the kingship of the land.

"And that this king could be compelled to make obeisance by means of a golden bough, plucked in the sacred grove, transferring great power upon he who receives the slave's homage."

Cingetorix touched his amulet, pondering Varro's words and the memory of druidic rites enacted in forests far to the north. "I knew only that Vestinia wanted me to fight at Nemi," Cingetorix said.

"Someone will fight there," Varro said. "And someone will rule Italy. The Republic reels between the ambitions of Marius and Sulla. Believe me, those old comrades-in-arms hate each other worse than they do the rebels. Our Italian 'allies' demand to be masters. The old rule of the patricians is shaking and may yet go to pieces. Rome needs a strong hand. It will be my hand that saves Rome, from rebel Italians, from rebel slaves, from Rome itself."

Varro gave orders for Vestinia and Cingetorix to be locked in together. "I suspect my need for either one is at an end."

Prodded by spears, Cingetorix and Vestinia entered the cell. The shutting of the door cut off all light save a tiny bit filtering in from a small, barred window set high on the wall.

"Cingetorix," Vestinia said in a small voice. "I beg your forgiveness."

"Ah, it's nothing girl," Cingetorix said.

"No, I roused the demon, just as Varro said. And I read the auguries, and spoke your name. I had heard of you, and that you were the son of a northern wizard. The omens told me the rest. I truly don't know if you are fated to win the victory at Nemi or not, but the Fates have selected you for something different from other men. And I have seen how you are to other men as a gray wolf is to a house cur."

"It can't be helped now," Cingetorix drew a consoling arm about Vestinia. "As for being king of this or that, I don't care about such things. I've won battles, won the adoration of crowds, won gold, and won the favors of many women. You're the only one I've saved from gruesome and painful torture of course. Anyway, I'm content to take life as it comes at me. We just need to find a way out of this pit and back on the road."

But Vestinia was content to linger in Cingetorix's arms for a while before seeking escape. While she slept, Cingetorix tested the bars on the window. They were firmly set and the window was small. Vestinia might have fit through, but Cingetorix would never get his powerful frame through it. With enough time he was sure he could pull out a bar and enlarge the hole, but the noise would certainly rouse the guards, which were as plentiful in a Roman army camp as fleas on a dog. Carefully, he tinkered with a bar, slowly working the slack in the setting. It was growing looser when the sound of the door grating open sent a chill through Cingetorix's spine.

He turned, poised to leap on the Roman he expected to see. Instead Titus the Lanista stood in the doorway, a lamp in hand. "There you are my boy. Time to come back to the troop. No more runaway tomfoolery for you."

Cingetorix stared at Titus.Vestinia woke. "I had to bribe a few guards. I expect there will be some gaps in the ranks come muster call. But never mind that. Let's get going. I'll sort out this Varro stuff with Marius at Rome. He's a big fan, you know." He tossed a bundle of clothes to them and they dressed.

"I'll go, and Vestinia goes with me," Cingetorix said. "But I've freed myself. I'm not going to Rome and you aren't either unless you want Varro to track us down and crucify us all."

Titus shuddered. "I'm a citizen. They'll use the sword on me. Look, you are the best. I've treated you like a son. Don't even mention Cotys, his self-regard is bloated beyond reason. But you, you're an entertainer, an artist, I'm your biggest fan. I can't leave you to die in this hole. Now, let's get going before we're seen."

Cingetorix helped Vestinia to her feet. Titus reached behind the door and handed Cingetorix a sword. "I still consider you a fugitive." They hustled out of the cell, into a corridor that led to underground pits where the estate's olive oil, wine, and grain were stored. The sound of scurrying rats came from the side chambers. Cingetorix followed Titus and his bobbing lamp.

Then he heard another sound, the feathery rustle of wings. Gently he set Vestinia on her feet. "Titus, have you got a weapon?"

"What? Just my old wooden sword." Titus blinked in the smoky light of his lamp.

"Get Vestinia out of here." Cingetorix whipped out his sword as lemures swarmed out of every doorway, hole and nook in the cellar. Cingetorix felt for his amulet, needing its luck, for this was no human foe. The spirits of the dead burst from the earth's womb, lusting for his blood.

With a roar of fury he fell upon them, slicing through gelid flesh that stank of decay. They pawed at him with cold, talon-tipped hands and bit with slavering mouths. For every one that Cingetorix felled two more sprang up, with their dead, hopeless eyes and their unrelenting assault.

"Cingetorix!" Vestinia screamed. He looked up to see Charun looming over Titus. The lanista raised his wooden sword to ward off the blow, but the demon's hammer was faster and Titus was felled. Charun scooped up Vestinia.

Cingetorix swung his sword in a mighty two-handed grip, leaving a clearing of brutally hewn lemures awash in their sickly gore. He charged through the space to get to Vestinia's side, but the lemures came at him again, bearing him back by sheer numbers.

Cingetorix's sword swung a path of destruction again, but Charun was already gone. Cingetorix hewed down the last of his standing foes and rushed to the stairs leading out of the cellar. He reached the open air just in time to see the demon flap away into the night. Vestinia struggled in Charun's grasp, but the demon paid her no more heed than if he held squirming rabbit. He fixed a vulture's eye on Cingetorix. "At the grove my priest. Honor the rites of the king."

Cingetorix seethed in frustrated wrath, hurling curses in Latin, Gallic, and Teutonic at Charun. But Charun was gone, into the black night.

He heard a groan. Titus staggered from the cellar. "Jove and Apollo, was I struck by a thunderbolt? Who was that buffoon? Was that the fellow that drags off the bodies at the Pompeii arena? I swear I'll pay him back for that."

"You'll get your chance." Cingetorix could hear the guard being roused by the disturbance. "But only if we get out of here fast." He raced toward the Numidians' horse lines.

Cingetorix grabbed a sturdy-looking bay, threw a blanket over its back. A rope bridle was slung on a bush. Cingetorix fitted it in place as Titus caught up. The Numidian night guard also turned up, waving a spear and shouting angrily in his Berber dialect. Cingetorix took a vicious swing at the guard. Only a hasty retreat saved him from having his head sheared off, though he was spattered with the gruesome ichor on Cingetorix's sword.

Titus had mounted a horse for himself, then helped Cingetorix scatter the other horses with yelps and blows. More Numidians were arriving, but they had little time to chase the fugitives as they tried to catch their precious mounts.

Cingetorix and Titus rode through the night. Wearily, Titus asked, "Now that I am a fugitive from Roman law for your sake, tell me who is this Vestinia that has made you a fugitive?"

"She's a witch."

"They all are, son, they all are." As they rode, Titus related the time the time a Paphlagonian eunuch tried to interest him in buying twin sisters from Skythia, and the time a senator's wife took him to a villa in Apulia and how the senator had walked in on them while they were taking a bath in a tub of wine. "He was more upset that we'd used the good Alban, than that the matron and I were playing 'where's the naughty piggy.' You see the senator had his own thing with the boy who played Palaestra in *The Rope*. Well, that's show business for you."

Cingetorix had to agree.

Dawn found the riders on a hill overlooking a lake. A great oak dominated a grove by the lakeside, and on it was bough of mistletoe that gleamed golden in the sun's first rays.

"Nemi," Cingetorix said.

He dismounted and left Titus to stay hidden. "Keep an eye on the horses. You may want to make a quick get away."

"Your idea about going to Thrace sounds better all the time," Titus replied.

"Just stay away from senators' wives."

"Senators' wives are about the only friends I have left in Rome."

Cingetorix left Titus on the wooded hillside and crept close to the grove. As he went, Cingetorix listened to the sound of the morning. There was none, save the rasp of metal on metal, and a cough, quickly suppressed. There were men hidden nearby, but not ready to make their move. Cingetorix went forward, for Charun's demand left little room for choice.

He reached the grove by moving from bush to bush and making darting runs. The oak stood proud and ancient, its moss-encrusted bark like the hide of a dragon bursting from the earth, its powerful limbs spreading like a king's command to rule all that existed under heaven.

A lone bough of mistletoe dipped down from a branch that was old when Romulus and Remus were being suckled by a wolf. It was tinted with gold, though autumn colors had yet to emerge. Cingetorix walked directly to the bough and snapped it off.

From the depths of grove a man strode into view. He was stocky and well-muscled, without an ounce of fat, though gray had begun to creep into his hair. There were scars on his limbs, though there was nothing of the cripple about him. He walked with the grace and ease of a panther, at home in his jungle stronghold. At his side hung a well-used sword.

"I am the King of Nemi," he said. "I dreamt a challenger would come." His eyes fell upon Cingetorix's amulet. "You bear the sacred bough about your neck. It brings you back to its temple."

"I am under some compulsion," Cingetorix said. "Charun, the guide of the dead, has taken my woman."

The king nodded. "I've heard worse reasons. Shall we begin."

"There is another challenger." Cotys emerged from another portion of the grove, bearing a sprig of golden-tinted mistletoe.

The king sighed. "One at a time, boys. I'm a king, not an octopus."

"I'll be happy to yield to my old comrade-in-arms, Cingetorix," Cotys said. "First come, first served."

Cingetorix knew that Cotys had out-maneuvered him. Cotys could let Cingetorix and the king fight, and then fall on the winner, a fresh sword against one weary, and perhaps, wounded.

"Let the ritual begin." The king drew his sword.

Cingetorix fell upon him with fury, seeking to end the contest in one swift, overmastering attack. But the king had not survived these many long years by being easy prey. He gave ground before Cingetorix's attack, letting the gladiator's fury expend itself. Then he turned to attack, cool and methodical, in a drive that left Cingetorix bleeding from two minor cuts and one larger one on his thigh.

Cingetorix was breathing hard and nearly wild with frustration. A swipe of the king's blade came within an inch of his exposed throat. Cingetorix felt a chill of fear.

He mastered himself, took a defensive stance. He let the king attack, watching his moves and countering. The king was growing weary too. Though fit he had many long years of battle and wounds on him. He survived now upon sagacity and experience.

But it was an experience that thrived on routine. He made the same passes again and again, complacency underlying the years of victory. Cingetorix looked the king in the eye and saw something else, the knowledge that his time was at hand and a willingness to embrace it.

When the king made a left feint for the third time, Cingetorix pretended to accept it, but instead went right. The tip of his sword flew past the king's guard and buried itself deep in the king's chest.

The king sagged to his knees. "It looks like the dream was true," he said as he collapsed.

Cingetorix looked down at the fallen king. He lay in a pool of blood, cradled between the roots of the great oak, high priest and sacrifice at the same time.

"All hail the king," Cotys said. "Now it is time to fight for your crown."

"Just a minute!" Titus entered the grove. He held an emissary's wand. "Some gentlemen outside the grove want to ensure fair play.

There's a lot riding on this contest, as it were."

"Fair play, it is. I have the right to challenge and be met in combat," Cotys said.

"No!" Titus said. "He's winded and hurt. That's no even match."

As Titus and Cotys wrangled, Cingetorix leaned against the oak, closing his eyes. "Look upon me," Charun whispered.

Cingetorix opened his eyes again. Charun stood before him. "If you want the woman, you must defend your rule. None but the brave deserve the fair. Though you shall surely die. But what is that to one is made to die? Is not death but a gateway?

"But you can refuse. There is a way to transfer this burden to another. You can invoke the gods who rule the grove. Offer them a suitable sacrifice, a witch who has betrayed her patrons. Sacrifice Vestinia, pledge obeisance to Hell, give the kingship to Varro or Mutilus, and you shall live long and reap many earthly rewards. You know that Cotys will take that offer."

Cingetorix nodded. He could fight and die, but Vestinia would live. Or he could submit, take a life of ease, and let Vestinia die. He knew which course he would take. "I'll take your challenge and cram it back in your teeth."

"That is as my priests should do." Charun was gone. Titus and Cotys seem not to have seen the demon.

"I'll fight you now," Cingetorix said. "Titus, if you please, let me have a rub down and something for these cuts."

"Make haste, oh king," Cotys said. "The gods thirst."

While Titus helped Cingetorix ready himself, delegations of tribunes and centurions arrived from Mutilus and Varro. Both sides had come to watch the battle.

Cingetorix and Cotys squared off. They hailed the fallen king. *"Rex, morituri te salutamos."*

Titus held up the wooden sword. "On my signal."

The sword dropped. Cotys came at Cingetorix. He was armed thrax-style, with an inward-curved machaera sword. Cotys opened with a fast attack meant to take advantage of Cingetorix's weariness. But Cingetorix was not so easily taken. He gave ground, parrying defensively, and conserving strength. Cotys grinned like a cat who finds a mouse just beyond reach, then broke off the attack.

Both gladiators went cautiously, making probing attacks, looking for weaknesses. Both men had seen each other fight many times. They knew the other's typical tricks and feints. It was a matter of waiting for the other to make a mistake and exploit it.

Cingetorix was feeling the effects of the battering he'd taken from the king. Cotys's attack had come closer to overwhelming him than the Thracian knew. In a contest of time, Cingetorix was at a grave disadvantage. He had to end the fight swiftly, even if it meant a great risk. Cingetorix glanced at Titus, who was as much a spectator as the audience of military men. His hand went to his amulet, and Cingetorix made his move.

Cingetorix went over to the attack, thrusting and cutting, using his greater reach to force Cotys on the defensive. He made a feint at Cotys's left and went low when the Thracian reacted.

But Cotys was not so easily taken. He parried Cingetorix's longsword with a ringing blow and charged in, slashing at close range. The wound on Cingetorix's leg was bleeding heavily and he was limping. Cotys followed up, attacking Cingetorix's weak side. There was a reason Cotys was rated one of the best gladiators in the games. Cotys drove Cingetorix back and back, until he stumbled among the roots of the great oak. Cingetorix's feet tripped over the dead king and he fell back against the tree.

Cingetorix had enough strength to hold off Cotys, with the great holy tree as his fortress. He would fight as a king, holding out in his royal stronghold. But Cotys came on mercilessly. In a single fluid motion, Cotys drew a curved dagger and made a powerful, killing thrust. Cingetorix never expected it. The dagger plunged into him, passing though his guts and into the tree. Cingetorix writhed in agony, crucified to his royal tree. Dimly, as though from a great distance, he heard Titus crying, "Foul! Foul!" There was a rustle of weapons among the onlookers. Then all was dark and silence. No pumping blood, no beating heart, only death.

FOR eight days Cingetorix hung upon the tree, dying slowly and in great pain. On the ninth day, he beheld the runes and stretched forth his hand to grasp their wisdom. Then he drew forth the knife in his side. Cingetorix tumbled to the ground at the foot of the oak.

TITUS was still shouting at Cotys and the rebel centurions were hurrying away. The Romans were eyeing Cotys, while conferring furiously, making plans to seize the new king and hold off the rebels.

He struggled to his feet with a groan of pain. A shocked silence fell over the grove.

"It can't be. You were dead." Cotys stared at Cingetorix in surprise. He lifted the machaera. "No matter. I'll finish you for sure this time."

Cingetorix waved him off. "No, I was dead. Don't you feel the change? Hail the new king." Cingetorix felt the wound in his side. It was bloody and raw, but not deep.

"I do," Cotys said. "I am the king. I can sell this to whatever devil will bid the most." He seemed to look beyond the grove for a moment. "No! Come back! I'll trade it to you! Damn cowards!" Cotys cursed and raved. "I could have been the best gladiator in Rome! I'm not going to sit around some damned tree playing king!"

"Eh, it doesn't sound like a bad life," Cingetorix said. "Not for me, though. You won, I lost."

Vestinia emerged from within the grove. "Hail to he who was king and is no more."

Titus held out his rudis. "Hail. A king, even a former one, can't be a slave. You have earned the wooden sword." The sounds of battle were echoing from the hills around the grove. "I think Mutilus sneaked up on Varro while he was busy watching this."

"May Varro be damned too," Cotys snarled.

Cingetorix rested in the shade of the oak, while Vestinia tended his wounds. He had done enough for one day. A troop of rebels arrived, spattered with the mud and blood of battle. They were a ragged bunch, runaway slaves who had joined Mutilus's army. Their centurion spoke with an accent that was familiar to Cingetorix.

"The praetor is pulling out," the centurion said. "He's whipped Varro, but Marius and Sulla are moving in. They let Varro take a beating so they could have a chance to pin down Mutilus. We're taking to the hills. You can come with us."

"What's your name?" Cingetorix asked. "How did you come here?"

"Thorolvus," the centurion said. "I was a chief among the Cimbri. I was captured by the Romans while fighting alongside a brave man. He was a druid, wise and good in battle. There's a bunch of us from the Cimbri, Teutons, and Ambrones who escaped from slavery."

"We'll come with you," Cingetorix said, rising to his feet. He put his arm around Vestinia. "The druid?"

"Catuvolcus. He was wed to Astrid the Fair. She was my cousin. It's a funny thing. We were headed deeper into the hills to avoid the Romans when I had a dream about them. Catuvolcus and Astrid stood at the foot of an oak with a golden bough of mistletoe beckoning me forward. I took it as a sign and headed here."

Cingetorix had found his folk. He put his arm around Vestinia and went up in the hills to join them.

Through Dungeons Deep

Jack Mackenzie

CHAPTER 1: THE WANDERING GOAT

"IT'S NOT really a dungeon," the old blind man said, leaning heavily on a gnarled walking stick, his milky white eyes staring upwards. "It's more of a labyrinth."

I tried to hide a sardonic smile, more out of habit than anything else. The blind man surely could not hear the expression that my face adopted at this statement. "That's a fine distinction." I managed. "What difference is there between a dungeon and a labyrinth that would…"

"It's a difference that makes no difference," Sirtago interrupted impatiently. He shifted his bulk in his chair. The wooden seat squeaked alarmingly under his weight. "Dungeon or labyrinth, I care not. What of the treasure?"

The old man sat back and sucked at his long clay pipe. The smoke wreathed about his head, mingling with the cloud of the ale-house's great fire as it made its way out of the roof-hole above.

We had agreed to meet the old man at the inn... *The Wandering Goat*, it was... a neutral place, but one of the old man's choosing. Normally, I would not allow such an occurrence, but this time I let the old man have the advantage of a familiar surrounding in deference to his sightlessness. I was, I believe, getting soft in my old age.

The Wandering Goat was aptly named, for it sat atop a perch along a meandering mountain path. The weather was cold and the air dry. I felt it keenly under my furs and cloak. The chill of the northern climes was becoming more and more egregious to me as I got on in years.

I would have preferred to turn around and head back to the southern kingdoms, but Sirtago's relentless quest to put more and more miles between himself and his family pushed him farther and farther into the cold.

I turned and glanced at my companion. Sirtago was a big man. Not fat, though tending more to fleshiness now than ever before, a testament to his passion for food and drink. He was well over six feet tall and muscled like a true warrior. He wore cloth breeches and a fur lined tunic underneath a cloak pinned at his throat with the single reminder of his home, a pin with the sigil of the Ka, the prince of the Southern Kingdom of Trigassa.

One dark eye burned intently from underneath his shaggy mane. His other eye and the side of his face was covered by a leather mask. The mask hid the scars that marred the left side of my friend's face since he was born.

In his younger days Sirtago faced the world as he was made. As Ka of Trigassa none would dare speak of his deformity. His reputation as he ventured from his home kingdom preceded him. Few had not heard tales of the scarred Prince of the Southern Kingdom. His face, deformed as it was, acted as a kind of currency. Those who knew of such things recognized him as royalty and accorded him such deference as his position deserved. I also believed that the younger Sirtago relished the effect that his features had upon those who were not steeled against such a sight. As we left the Southern Kingdoms farther behind, however, his birthright more often then not went unrecognized. Sirtago soon tired of being treated as a monster without the acknowledgment of his position. It had become harder and harder to convince the stolid Northerners that he was a prince and, among those who acknowledged the fact, very few cared enough about the politics of a distant land to afford him any sort of social status.

Plus the mask gave him an aura of mystery, which Sirtago found he enjoyed, particularly when it came to comely lasses. He found he liked better their attention than their shrieks of horror upon seeing his ruined visage. The sight of his scarred face was made more palatable to the fairer sex once he had managed to cultivate their interest and their sympathy.

"Treasure..." the blind man said around his pipe, clenched between twisted teeth. It was almost but not quite a question. He shook his head. "Gold. Jewels. Plundered relics from all four corners of the globe. There is no telling what riches has been sequestered there."

"Where?" Sirtago asked, an avaricious gleam in his one good eye. "Where is the treasure hid?"

The blind man shook his head. "None can say. None who have ventured into the labyrinth have lived to tell."

"Then how do you know that there even is a treasure?' I asked.

The blind man shrugged. "That there is a treasure is beyond doubt," he replied.

Indeed, we had heard rumors of a great treasure locked up in a mountain as far south as the Golden City. I had not taken the rumors seriously then, nor would I had given them much thought. Our every desire was indulged whilst we were residents of the legendary metropolis. The intrigue, however, that embroiled us in that fine city's downfall and forced us to bid a hasty retreat had put paid to those desires and rumors of riches, no matter how tenuous, once again made our ears prick up.

Sirtago flagged a tavern wench for another tankard. I was still sipping my first carefully. I wanted my head clear enough so as not to miss any statements that might beggar belief.

"Treasure then," I said. "But danger as well? As you said, none who have ventured into the labyrinth have lived to tell. What gives you any hope that my companion and I would succeed where other--perhaps better men--have failed?"

Sirtago let out a guffaw at that. "Better men?" he began.

I held up a hand that stopped his outburst. He hid his frown of displeasure in his newly arrived tankard.

The blind man shifted uncomfortably and then shrugged. "Truth be told, none have ventured into the labyrinth save my fellow villagers." He shook his head, his milky eyes staring off into the darkened corners. "We are a simple folk. Farmers, shepherds. We are not skilled in the arts of battle."

I grimaced and shook my head. "What do you farm in these heights?" I asked. "All I have seen in these passes is moss and some scrubby grass. The only creatures I have seen are mountain goats."

"As the road to the East descends the passes give way to a valley. The valley is lush. There is grain, whose use is made by this very ale-house. The brew you enjoy is made from the grain of the valley."

I nodded and raised my tankard to the old man. "'tis a fine brew," I conceded. "Though we've had better."

"True," Sirtago growled.

"Certainly two well-traveled gentlemen such as yourself would have had finer," the old man said. "I have no doubt of that. But to this humble establishment the grain is a treasure, as is the mutton on which the travelers dine. I highly recommend it to you, good sirs. A mutton roast is a feast not to be missed while staying under this roof, should you have the coin. It also serves a stew well should you find that you do not."

I scratched at my beard. The stew was effusing the shabby inn with an aroma that made a pleasing promise to my gob, gullet and belly. At the moment our coin might stretch to a modest bowl, but would certainly not cover a full roast. However I did not want the impoverishment of our coin purses to be evident to the old man, no matter how blind he appeared to be (a condition I was beginning to have cause to doubt).

"*The Wandering Goat* does a brisk trade thanks to our grain and our sheep, and the cooks work well enough with the ingredients we provide, but... well..."

Here the old man trailed off and for a moment I thought his mind had wandered somewhere far from our current negotiations. "Well?" I asked, trying to retrieve his wandering attention.

"Mint," was all he said.

"Mint?"

"It grows wild in the marshes and near the rivers. The valley is blessed with it. The women of the village gather it when it is fresh and dry and preserve it, to be used at any season. It makes the difference between a passable meal and a sumptuous one."

"I see," I said, though in truth I thought the old man's mind to be addled.

"You can't get that here," he continued, gesturing to his rude surroundings. "We do not provide mint to this establishment, because the cooks have no knowledge of how to use it properly. It would be as lustrous jewels before boars."

"Boars?" Sirtago said. He was not as adept with following conversation at the best of times, especially not after three tankards.

"A waste, is what I mean," the old man shook his head. "Though the valley has wild boar as well for those who are adventurous enough to hunt."

Sirtago drained his tankard. "I like a boar hunt."

I cleared my throat pointedly, scowled at my companion. "Your village sounds idyllic," I said." But what has it to do with the treasure? What bearing does your village have on why we should risk our lives to attain it?"

The old man's features darkened and he sighed heavily. "The wizard threatens it," he said.

"The wizard?" Sirtago asked. "What wizard?"

"The one who possesses the treasure," the old man said.

"The treasure in the dungeon?" Sirtago asked.

"Labyrinth," the old man corrected.

"Whatever," I snapped. I sensed that control of the negotiations was about to be scuppered by my companion. Indeed, it would not be the first time that it had happened. "Who is this wizard?"

Here the old man bowed his head. He was quiet for a moment and when he lifted his head his sightless eyes brimmed with tears. "I will not say his name," he said. "For his name carries a dread power even this far away. Suffice it to say he has made the mountain his home for years beyond counting. When I was a boy he had always lived there. Tales of his fell sorcery made my skin crawl long before it became wrinkled as you see it here."

Sorcerers rely on reputation more than anything else. Fear holds most people in thrall. Perhaps the dread stories were just that: stories, but Sirtago and I had encountered sorcerers before, many times, and each time seemed worse than the last. We could not count the many occasions that we had been threatened and almost lost our lives to sorcery. Even if the treasure could be said with certainty to be real, even the possibility of an encounter with a sorcerer was enough to allow us to move on. We would try our luck in the next settlement.

Or so I had determined in that brief moment between the old man's statement and my reply, that I had but drawn breath to give when Sirtago drained his fourth tankard, slamming it down on the table.

"We have faced fearsome sorcerers," he declared. "Why I have even bedded a sorceress who tried to kill me on an ocean voyage. We have killed dark gods and strange beasts in all corners of the southern kingdoms..."

I could see where this was going. Nothing sets Sirtago to boasting as does too much drink. "What my companion is saying..." I tried to interrupt the coming storm of bravado. "Is that we couldn't possibly..."

"We couldn't possibly..." Sirtago echoed.

"Take on such a hazardous threat on the mere rumor of a treasure," So I would have declared and so the matter would have ended.

Unfortunately, Sirtago's voice drowned out my response "...couldn't possibly leave you under threat of such vile sorcery!"

"What?"

"Of course we will help to rid your village of your wizard. We will save you from the foul threat of dark sorcery... and we will claim the treasure!"

NATURALLY the old man was overjoyed at Sirtago's declaration. He sat in rapt fascination with Sirtago's tales of how he had defeated sorceress, sorcerer, monsters, demons and more.

Needless to say I was less than overjoyed at Sirtago's spontaneous recounting of our past deeds, embellished as they were with imagined heroics. In his inebriated state I'm not sure he realized what it was he was getting us into, but he did and there was little that I could do about it.

That was how we found ourselves in the back of a sheep cart wandering away from our warm and cozy inn with its tankards of passable ale trundling down a mountain pathway. The moon was full above us and lighted the way for the tow-headed youth who was the old blind man's guide. The dray horse was immense but sure of foot and clearly knew the way well enough to make the journey even if the cart were without a rider.

The chill of the night air made me pull my cloak tighter around my shoulders and over my nose, though it did little against the smell of the sheep shit, of which the cart was redolent.

For his part, Sirtago was close to senseless. He drunkenly sang an old Trigassan ditty extolling the virtues of whores with prodigious backsides while the sheep cart jostled its way down the mountain.

I was trying to get the lay of the land as we moved. I reckoned if the dray slowed sufficiently I might take the opportunity to brain the tow-headed boy and flee the rollicking cart. Even if I had to half-carry Sirtago up the path, we could probably make it back to *The Wandering Goat* before morning. In his state I could invent a story that would satisfy Sirtago that he had avoided a misadventure and we could be back on our way North.

The path seemed to smooth out and I expected it to slow, but the nag picked up speed instead. The sheep cart began moving more rhythmically now. The rocking put Sirtago into a drunken slumber. Great rumbling snores came from under his leather mask.

The downward slope was giving way now to a level path. The rocky ground was supplanted by a dirt path. The moon was soon hid behind a canopy of trees. Silvery light shone through the dark leaves making the trunks of the trees appear white.

Soon the cart emerged from beneath the canopy and the moon lighted a grassy plain. The chill was not as bad now and my nose was getting used to the smell of the sheep shit. I sat up in the cart and tried to take in my new surroundings.

The cart path wound itself around a marsh. In the distance I could see the darkened hillside down which we had just come. The lights of *The Wandering Goat* were either extinguished or hidden behind some feature of the rock face. Ahead of us the marshes were fed by streams that glinted as they moved their meandering path along the valley floor.

I could see the lights of the village in the distance. The scene seemed peaceful enough but my senses were on alert. I was halfway expecting an ambush or other sort of attack. My hands instinctively clutched for my blades. One hand found the hilt of my one dagger. My other clutched nothing. I had lost the companion to it in a previous misadventure and had not yet found another to match the one that I still possessed.

Sirtago's broadsword was still in its scabbard at his back. Should the need arise I reasoned that I could pull it free. I could wield it in a pinch but I was nowhere near as effective with it as Sirtago was when he wasn't in his cups and uselessly dreaming. I cursed my companion again under my breath.

The village lights got inexorably closer. I could make out a tall wooden wall encircling the outskirts. The cart path led to an ornate gate made of stone. Beside the gate was a small guard hut made partly of stone but mostly of wood and straw.

The nag slowed as it approached the gate. The trundling cart finally rolled to a stop.

My dagger was out of its sheath and into my hands as I crouched in the cart, ready for any attack.

A cloaked figure emerged from within the hut. My hand gripped my blade as my eyes tried to peer into the gloomy shadows in which the figure stood.

"Who is't?" the cloaked figure hissed in a high register. At first I took it to be the voice of a boy.

"'Tis Yolus," replied the tow-headed ox cart driver. "– and Master Theiss."

"Have you a champion?" the cloaked figure asked.

"We have two," the cart driver replied.

I was out of the cart now, crouched low, my feet ready to spring in the soggy grass. The cloaked figure stepped out of the shadow of the gate. A white hand reached up and swept back the hood of the cloak. The reason for the high register of the figure's voice became evident. She was a young woman. I would have guessed her age at twenty summers, if that.

She moved past the nag to the cart. I moved silently into the shadows beneath. From between the cart's wheels I saw her place her hands on the edge and stand on tip-toe so that she could peer into the cart.

She wore a short camisia beneath her cloak. Her legs and feet were bare and as she stretched up to see into the cart I could see that she was similarly bare underneath.

I was taken aback by the sudden sight of the young woman's quim, but I managed to keep my silence.

"I see only one champion," the woman said. "And he sleeps"

"What?" Master Theiss said, startled. "Which one do you see? The big one with the mask or the little one?"

"The snoring one wears a mask."

The little one held still beneath the cart. I wasn't certain what path I would take to get Sirtago and I out of this situation. My mind whirled in a fever of possibilities, including one where I decide that our companionship is at an end and leave him to his foolishly chosen fate.

The young woman's figure was fine, though, and the sight of her most personal possession made me warm with ardour. I allowed myself a brief fantasy of a pleasurable roll in the soft grass before chiding myself back into the state at hand.

The woman descended to her heels and stepped back from the cart. She bent down and peered beneath the cart.

As our eyes locked I gripped my dagger tight, holding it at the ready in a well-practiced stance. In the moonlight the young woman's skin looked pale like marble, but still I could see the apple red of her cheeks and lips. Her mouth widened in a delighted grin. "I've found the other one," she practically squealed. "What are you doing under there, silly?" she giggled.

I felt my cheeks redden. Here I was ready to strike with the one deadly fang with which I was left, and suddenly I was completely disarmed by this charming trollop.

Feeling right foolish I slid my lone dagger into its sheath and climbed out from under the sheep cart.

The tow-headed boy – Yolus – had jumped from the driver's bench and stood staring at me with a blank expression. The young woman's grin persisted. I could see in the moonlight that she was as lovely as she was shapely.

She dug an elbow into Yolus' ribcage. "Introduce me, Yolus," she said, "be a good lad."

Yolus looked at the young woman as if trying to comprehend her exact meaning. He then looked back at me. "This be Laiese," Yolus said. Then he turned to Laiese "Master Theiss didn't give me no names."

"I am Poet," I said stepping forward. I performed a bow whose knowledge of the skill it took to perform was highly prized in several courts to the south. My mastery of the move had paved my way through several bedchambers. In the young woman it provoked little more than a hearty giggle.

"Did you drop through the boards, Master Poet?" Master Theiss asked from the cart's buckboard. "I heartily apologize for our sheep cart's poor construction. 'Twas meant to hold sheep. We had not anticipated that it would be incapable of transporting a stalwart champion such as yourself."

"Your cart's construction was not to blame," I said through gritted teeth. In truth, I was still not happy with the facts of my situation, though Laiese's comely looks was ameliorating that for me, and no doubt. Nevertheless, I felt short with blind Master Theiss. "I merely wanted to assess my situation before allowing you to take us through the gate."

"Our intentions towards you are nothing but honorable. The words that I have spoken this night have all been true. Even a man as blind as I could have seen that, or so I would have thought."

Here I smiled, though he could not see it (or so that seemed. I was, truly, in doubt about the man's sightless condition). "Had you experienced as many a betrayal as we two have in our many travels, you would not think it so egregious that trust is not freely given."

At this point, Sirtago's snores which had provided rich and rhythmic accompaniment to our banter ceased with start. "Another tankard, Barkeep!" Sirtago said as he sat up unsteadily. He squinted at his surroundings. "*Gw'n'th's Tits*! What hour is it? This Inn smells like sheep shit!"

CHAPTER 2: BEYARGMUNN

AFTER Sirtago woke he insisted on more ale, so naturally we had to press on. The cart trundled through the portal and Laiese closed the gate behind us. She climbed a set of narrow steps up to the gate's guard tower and reluctantly I watched as her form disappear into the stone structure.

The cart trundled along until Yolus reined the nag to a stop in front of a longhouse. Master Theiss hopped off the buckboard with a well-practiced step. He led the way through the wooden door. Sirtago and I followed.

The inside was a great hall. Longer than it was wide and the ceiling tapered above to a spine. Like the hull of a great ship, it inverted above us. A fire roared inside a stone chimney. Smoke wreathed its way up into the darkness of the tapered roof. There was a long wooden table in the center of the hall surrounded by rough-hewn chairs covered with skins.

Two chairs were dragged from a corner and set in front of the fire. Here Master Theiss bade us sit.

The fire was warm, the seats comfortable, but I still retained a sense of unease, even when two plump kitchen girls appeared with tankards of ale. Sirtago greeted the ale and the girls with great pleasure. The girls appeared dimwitted to me, but I could see that they were sufficiently intrigued by Sirtago's masked features.

Hopefully Sirtago would refrain from doffing the mask. I did not relish the piercing screams that would surely follow.

For Master Theiss' part his garrulousness of earlier in the evening was replaced with whispered commands to the house's staff. All around I could hear villagers being hastily roused from their beds and exhorted to the kitchens where the clatter of cutlery grew more and more pointed.

Where Sirtago swallowed, I sipped. I had to admit the ale's quality was a good deal better than that which we had been served at *The Wandering Goat*-- and that ale I had rated as above average. Clearly it was a pale reflection of the source that I was enjoying in spite of myself.

Still I clutched vainly at my grim mood. Something about this whole thing smelled off, but hunt as I may I could not find the source of it.

Then the door of the hall opened. I turned to see Laiese standing framed in the open space. She wore her cloak again, but beneath was a longer tunic and below that a skirt that swept down to the floor. I confess to being a trifle disappointed as her earlier clothing, clearly her nightwear, was far more fetching. Nevertheless the sight of her grin was welcome, indeed. I suppose I must have returned her smile with one of my own. She picked up a small stool, placed it beside my chair and sat upon it daintily.

"So, you're settling in, then, Master Poet?" she asked.

"Just Poet, please," I protested. I was probably grinning back foolishly at the wench, but she was welcome as a summer morning to my eyes.

"You're not drinking your ale," she said, indicating my tankard, which was still three-quarters full. "Is't not to your liking?"

I shook my head. "I like it fine, as I do the hospitality, but I don't..." I struggled with how much of my doubts about this whole affair to voice. I instinctively wanted to trust this open young woman, which was a bad sign right there. Trust is the condition necessary for betrayal, and I'd had far too many pikestaffs up the backside, so to speak, to start trusting anyone now.

"I... I don't even know what this village is called," I finally settled on.

At that she let out a laugh. "Did Master Theiss not say? This be Beyargmunn."

"Beyargmunn?" I repeated the word slowly.

She smiled and nodded. "It means 'The Cliff's Mouth'," she explained, then set to giggling again.

"Cliff?" I said. "I didn't see a cliff."

"You don't see it much in the darkness," she countered. "It's an evil lookin' thing. Apt to make me shudder if I stare at it too long. Most of the village girls don't look at it. They keep their eyes down, lest the sight curse 'em. The men spit in its direction, but their eyes tend not to linger either. Best not to draw the black rock's attention too much, if you know what I mean?"

I didn't, but nodded anyway.

"Either way. You'll see it tomorrow. Can't be missed in the daylight. I spend most o' me time lookin' t'other way. Any approach the gates, I challenge 'em. And I ring the bell should any get belligerent-like."

I smiled, nodded and noted that I had drained my tankard. Another swiftly appeared in its place, filled to the brim.

While we spoke, I noted the aromas from the kitchen that took on a life of their own. They assailed my nostrils the way a lively tune does my ears. Soon the aromatic symphony reached a crescendo. A full roast of mutton was carried out from the kitchen, steaming and dripping and suffusing the air with a savoury yet sweet aroma. A great cut was rendered from the beast, put on a plate alongside some new spuds and some onions. The plate was presented to Sirtago, who picked up a cutting knife and attacked it with gusto, much to the delight of the plump serving girls who seemed to have taken a liking to my companion.

A similar plate found its way to me and I ate cautiously despite the unmistakable growling from my near-empty belly.

Damn me if the mutton weren't the best I'd ever had. The paroxysm of pleasure that my face betrayed brought a laugh out of Laiese. "Is't not a rare meal?" she asked.

I agreed as well as I could around a mouth full of the victuals.

"See?" Master Theiss rumbled from somewhere nearby. "I told you. Mint. That makes all the difference, eh?"

From that point my memory of the evening grows steadily more hazy. It wasn't from anything in the drink, other than drink, I'm chagrined to reveal. The empty tankard was soon chased by a companion who was right full to the top. One by one, they drove my awareness into oblivion. I must have been draining them as fast as Sirtago was wont to. I don't hold my drink like Sirtago can. His capacity to imbibe is legendary, even now as age was causing him to slow down. Me, though, I usually don't indulge like that as I need my wits to be as sharp about me as my dagger. That night though, encouraged by Laiese's wanton giggles, I became insensate.

THE MORNING intruded upon me like a curse. Devil drums pounded between my ears and a party of imps had befouled my open gob. I was laying prone, on what I could not say, but it held my weight off the floor. I opened my eyes, then cursed myself for being so foolish, and screwed them shut again.

I rolled over on my side, my stomach heaving like it was back on the rolling sea when we first crossed the passage to Bradex. I felt myself certain to heave over the side. As my head lolled over the edge of the bed I chanced to open my eyes and see that I already had at some point in the night.

I rolled back into the bed, tried the other side. By chance the sturdy frame did not abut the wall. There was a good cubit's distance from one t'other and I chanced to swing my legs over and let them gingerly meet the floor. The smooth stone was cool under my bare feet. I could see that I wore breeches, though they were stained, and I was still clad in my shirt. My boots, gambeson, and cloak were not in sight.

I stood slowly, my hands braced against the wall. It felt cool but steady. Slowly I shuffled out from behind the wrong side of the bed, my forehead pressed against the cool of the plain wall.

I glanced down and saw my boots beneath a low chair. On the chair were the rest of my accoutrements. Leaning on the chair's arm with one hand, my other quested in a sudden panic for my dagger. It was there, still sheathed. I clutched it, then brought it to my chest, cradling it for comfort.

The sunlight was bullying its way through the windows, attempting to break down the door. I decided to meet it head on.

Outside the door was a covered portico. The boards creaked underneath my feet as I gingerly made my way to the edge. I tried to blink away the sunlight but it stubbornly persisted in lighting the village that spread out before me.

The first thing I noticed was that the structure was not the same one I had passed out in. The great feasting hall had been much bigger and was not surrounded by a rough veranda. I scanned the similar structures laid out before me. I could not even see a building that I recognized as the feasting hall. How I managed to walk such a great distance whilst in my cups I could not fathom. Perhaps I had been carried?

The second thing I noticed was that the small dirt streets... more pathways than anything else... that criss-crossed the town were almost empty. I could hear farm animals in the distance but I could not see where they were. The bleating of sheep and the lowing of cattle floated over the lazy morning air to my ears.

I say that they were almost empty. That was because of the third thing I noticed, which was the dwarf and the giant.

"Well, it's about time somebody got off their ass to welcome us!" the dwarf shouted, his voice high and piping. It made my head hurt in a most particular way. He was dressed in dark furs, breeches and boots. He had a small sword, not much bigger than the dagger I clutched possessively to my chest. His face sported wrinkles and I couldn't tell if it was because of advanced age or some sort of pruning that naturally happens to little men.

"Good Mornin', Sunshine!" the dwarf shouted even louder when I did not reply right away. "Are you the welcoming committee?" His accent was peculiar. Each word seemed to be trying to chisel its way into my brain by way of my ears. Though it felt like the sound wasn't too particular about how it got in. His sarcastic tone and belligerent attitude also managed to get on the wrong side of me.

I closed my eyes, felt myself swaying in the cool morning breeze. "My name is Poet," I said carefully. "And I am an honoured guest of this fine little village."

"Oh," the little man said. "'Honoured' are ye? And what did you do to deserve the honour of such simple country folk?"

"I happen to be their champion," I said, a trifle more haughtily than I'd meant to.

"Champion?" The giant bellowed, his voice impossibly deep and very loud. The giant was dressed in similarly dark furs and breeches, though his attire was a good deal shabbier than his diminutive companion's. He was thin, but impossibly tall,,, taller, even, than Sirtago who usually towered over most men. He had a thick face with prominent cheekbones and sunken eyes. He jaw jutted out like a brick and sported unruly bristles. His hair was cut short as if done with shears and a too-small bowl to guide their snipping.

He stared down at the dwarf with an incredulous expression. "He says he's their champion!"

"I heard what he said," the little man spat towards the other. "I'm small. I'm not deaf!"

"But I thought we were the champions!" The giant's accent was thicker than the dwarf's. It sounded like it came from somewhere deep within his chest cavity.

I clutched at my head, which echoed painfully with the giant's bellowing. "Will the two of you, for the love of all the gods in the pantheon, please SHUT UP!!!" Shouting did not help the pain in my head but the few seconds of silence, that ensued as the outrageous pair stared at me with their gobs hanging open, was almost blissful.

"Hah!" the dwarf cackled. "A fine welcoming committee you're turnin' out to be!"

I spread the fingers of my hand so I could peer through them at the noisome duo. What they had said to me was only now managing to sink in past the pounding agony. "Champions?" I asked. "Were you, by chance, recruited at *The Wandering Goat*?"

"*Wandering Goat*?" the dwarf repeated. "Never heard of it. We've just come from *The House of Wet Grass*."

"*House of Wet Grass*? What kind of an inn is that?" I asked.

"It's not an inn," the dwarf said with a grin.

"It's a brothel," the giant boomed and then sniggered like a boy laughing at a bawdy rhyme. I gave him a closer look and saw that, despite his great size, he was just a boy. His blocky face sported a mossy beard and was covered in spots.

The dwarf could easily have seen over forty summers, maybe even more. What a strange pair, I thought to myself.

"You weren't recruited by a Master Theiss, were you?" I asked.

The dwarf shook his head. "We've never heard of Master Theiss. We were recruited by a man named Dolan, who told us that this village had been supplying nothing but the best fillies to the brothel up at the Southern Pass."

"Is that so?" I asked, starting to feel a distinctly uneasy feeling in my guts that had nothing to do with the amount of ale I drank the night before.

"'Tis indeed. We've just arrived here this morning. We were hoping to get a good look at these country beauties, but so far we haven't seen anyone in the streets except you. And I wouldn't pay a forged copper for any amount of time in your company."

I smiled humorlessly at the little man, rubbed the top of my head slowly. "Charming..." I managed. "Had you considered that the sight of a prancing imp from the gods-know-what-hell and a lumbering, block-faced giant monstrosity roaming the streets of their fair village might encourage the locals to stay indoors where it's safe? They're all likely cowering beneath their beds afraid at any moment that they will be devoured by the two horrors that are roaming their thoroughfares."

"*Charon's Cock*, I hadn't thought of that!" the young giant boomed. "Maybe we should gather some flowers or something?" he asked the dwarf.

The dwarf gave him a wry look. "He's just winding us up."

"I'm really not," I said, though in truth, I was. "Have you two seen yourselves? The half-pint that's been half drunk and the ambulatory menhir? I don't suppose either of you has ever stopped in front of a looking glass and thought: 'Now, there's a handsome fella'. Because if you have, then you can count yourself stupid as well as ugly."

"I'm not an ambuli-tonny-whatsit..." the giant boomed, genuine pique in his tone. "I'm Golath! Golath of Exxenmoor! And this," he gestured to his companion, narrowly missing swatting him in the head. "...is Jemmy!"

"Jemmy?" I said, trying to stifle a laugh. "Where are you from, Jemmy?"

"I'm from all over!" the dwarf barked. "And I don't think I much like your tone. I don't care if you are this village's champion, I've a mind to chop off your head!"

At this I did laugh. "Someone will have to find you a step-stool so you can reach my neck, little man."

I had little worry about provoking the two. The dwarf amused me but even if I angered him to the point where he would be inclined to attack me I had little worry that I couldn't dispatch him right quick. His furs and black clothes may have concealed some armor, but it would likely not be substantial. Leather rather than mail as I could hear no clinking of chain as he moved which he did quite a bit as he became more agitated.

The giant was more of a concern but he seemed to defer to the older man despite his diminutive stature. I reasoned that he would not be an expert fighter. There seemed much more of the farm boy about him than warrior. Whatever training he may have had in combat would likely be incomplete. Even if he was proficient, his movements were slow and clumsy. I was slowing in my age, but I was still quick as a viper.

The dwarf, Jemmy, scowled and opened his mouth as if to utter a retort. I was looking forward to hearing what he would say. The words never found their way out of his pie-hole, which seemed to open wider as his eyes dropped to something behind me.

I turned and saw Laiese rounding the corner balancing a basket on her hip. She stopped suddenly when she saw Jemmy and Golath in the street.

She wore the same skirts as she had the night before, but her bodice was loosened, presumably to facilitate movement in the kitchens. Her ample round breasts were on full display. This was the sight that had struck both the dwarf and the giant dumb.

"Well," Laiese said, her wide grin illuminating the street. "I see you've met our other champions. It's good you're getting to know each other." She climbed the short steps up to the portico, flashing her wonton smile in my direction. "I brought you some breakfast, my silly poet," she said, flashing her eyes at me then swishing past into the structure.

I couldn't help watching her shapely rear as she moved into the darkness of the room in which I had found myself moments before. I could feel a foolish grin twisting my features. As soon as she was out of my sight, I turned back to my fellow champions, my foolish grin replaced with a sardonic smile. "As much of a pleasure as it has been larking with you gentlemen, I beg to take your leave. It seems I have some breakfast to eat." and then I performed the bow from the Southern courts that had so completely failed to impress Laiese the evening prior. It hurt, physically to do it, but when I swept myself back upright the sight of the strange pair's mouths hanging open was well worth it. I turned my back on the both of them and joined Laiese.

When my eyes adjusted to the dim interior I could see Laiese fussing over the spot where I had vomited the night before. She had laid the breakfast basket aside and was vigorously scrubbing the floor. She attacked the stain with a practiced arm.

"No, no," I protested. "Let me clean that. I was its architect, I should..."

"Don't be silly," she said flashing a smile in my direction. "You sit down and eat. I'll have this right in no time."

She had placed the breakfast on a small table. There was a stool near by. I sat upon it. The basket was covered with a cloth. I moved the cloth aside and saw some cold mutton from the night before as well as bread and some fruit. At the sight of the mutton my stomach heaved alarmingly. I replaced the cloth cover and turned my attention back to Laiese.

She had removed her skirt and had folded it carefully on the rumpled bed. She wore a white camisia again but this one was longer. She was on her hands and knees, her rounded rump facing my direction. I could see its pleasing shape beneath the camisia as it rocked and bobbed in time with her arms as they scrubbed.

"What happened last night?" I asked her rounded bottom.

Laiese chuckled softly. "Oh, your friend told heroic stories about your grand adventures."

I nodded. I had heard Sirtago's tales of our exploits before. They intersected with the truth of the events almost not at all, and they almost always diminished my role in the action down to practically nothing.

"You and I," she continued. "We talked for several hours. And you drank. And you became drunk." She turned her head, peering around her buttocks at me with a wonton smile.

"How did I get here?" I asked.

"We walked. Well, in truth, I practically carried you because you were quite out of your senses. Your hands tried to find their way into the most inconvenient of places."

I cleared my throat and dropped my eyes. "I hope that I wasn't..."

She giggled. "You were too far gone to be either cad or gentleman, I'm afraid," she said, placing the brush into the bucket and standing up. She blew an errant curl out of her eye. "More's the pity. I would have been interested to see what you would have done had you better control of your limbs."

I smiled up at her. "We could find out now," I suggested.

She favoured me with an indulgent smile. "'Tis morning now. Besides, there is much to do. Eat your breakfast."

I turned away from her reluctantly as she re-donned her skirt. I ate a few crumbs of the bread and a small sampling of the fruit but avoided the mutton. Laiese dumped the bucket off the portico and then put it and the brush away.

CHAPTER 3: THE FEAST

THE WHOLE village, it seemed, had gathered in the common. Laiese led me by the hand to the village's public area. It was an expanse of short grass cut through with several paths. The common was bordered by several buildings, one of which I thought was the great hall where we feasted the night before. It had a curved roof made of long strips of wood laid one over the other, curving to a centerline like the upended keel of a great ship. Several of the other buildings were squatter and their roofs were covered with a mossy grass.

White geese honked noisily as they waddled among the throngs of villagers who were milling about. I saw chickens clucking about and sheep ate grass placidly, uttering only the occasional bleat. The common was festooned with skulls bearing great antlers. Many of them were stuck on the end of poles, held high above the heads of the people.

A stone dais had been set up in front of a great tree that stood majestically in the center of the square. Its great gnarled branches reached high into the sky and far outwards toward the buildings on either side. I saw several of what I assumed were the village leaders engaged in intense conference. Someone had brought a stump up to the dais for Master Theiss, who sat with his gnarled hands grasping his stick, listening with a grim expression to the words of the conferring men.

I scanned the crowd expecting to catch a glimpse of Sirtago, but he was nowhere in sight. I saw Golath towering over the crowd. He was surrounded by young lasses who seemed to be amused. Golath was laughing as well. I couldn't imagine Golath being the source of the merriment so I had to assume that Jemmy was somewhere near Golath's feet, providing the mirth.

"I don't see Sirtago," I said to Laiese. "What happened to him last night?"

Laiese smiled. "He was carried to bed much like you were," she said. "It took three ladies to carry him out of the hall, so I've been told. He was very insistent that they join him in his bed once they'd gotten them there."

I laughed in spite of my concern. "I imagine his head would have felt like a cracked egg this morning."

"No," Laise said, laughing. "He was up at the first spit of dawn. He ate enough breakfast for three men and then went off on horseback with several of the village lads."

"He – *what*?" I said, incredulous. "Where did he go?"

"Boar hunt," Laise said casually. "He did say he liked a good boar hunt. The forests around the village are full of boar."

"Boar hunt?" I said again. I shook my head. Trust Sirtago to find a way to indulge his passions. It would not surprise me to find out that the villagers played Ungol and had invited him to join the local league.

My attention was suddenly dragged elsewhere by the sight of three women. They were clearly not villagers. They wore dark leather armour and were heavily armed. Two were smaller, and from a distance, looked quite comely. Braided locks cascaded from beneath the women's bandanas. One set of braids was blonde, the other dark. They carried curved swords and shoulder guards. Each had dark, almond eyes.

The third woman towered over them. Not quite as tall as Golath, but maybe alike in height to Sirtago. Her skin was dark as twilight and her limbs were long with rope-like muscles. She wore leather armour trimmed with fur. She carried a great broadsword in a sheath strapped to her back. Her hair was black and tightly curled and prodigious in both thickness and length. She had a broad forehead over large, wide eyes that stood out like hot fire. She was beautiful -- but she looked like she could snap me in half without a thought. She wore long metal wrist guards that rose halfway to her elbows.

I was about to ask Laiese whether these were more champions come to search for the treasure when Sirtago showed up with the other men of the village.

The lead rider sounded a trumpet fashioned from a curved sheep's horn. The men rode towards the crowd. The bystanders parted for them, roaring their approval at their sudden appearance.

There in the middle of it all was Sirtago, a triumphant smile plainly evident even behind his mask. Behind him a boy rode a smaller horse that drew a cart. On the bed of the cart lay the bloodied corpse of a great boar, a long spear lodged in its side. From his triumphant pose and the congratulatory cheers from his fellow hunters it was clear whose spear it was that had felled the great boar. I tried not to roll my eyes but didn't entirely succeed.

The cheering was infectious. Soon the entire gathering had joined in the jubilation. Even Laiese giggled and laughed and clapped enthusiastically, hopping from one foot to the other.

Whatever happened after tonight I knew that Sirtago was going to be insufferable to be around for at least a week.

THE FEAST that night, however, was spectacular.

The boar was cleaned and prepared by the plump kitchen wenches who had all seemed to attach themselves to Sirtago. For his part he seemed glad of their attention, and, indeed, their attention towards him was apparent. I wondered if he had managed to bed any of them (or perhaps all of them) the previous night.

The great beast was turned on a spit over the great glowing coals in the middle of the village square. As Master Theiss had boasted to us before, the flesh was made even more succulent by the liberal basting of mint leaves among other spices. The aroma of the roasting flesh suffused the air and made all mouths water.

By this time my pounding head of the morning was but a memory. Laise grabbed hold of my hand, keeping a grip on it for most of the rest of the day and on into the evening. I wanted to get to grips with the rest of her, kept suggesting we steal away from the throngs and find some private place. She giggled, seemed taken with the idea, but somehow we never managed it. There was always something that we simply had to stay and watch: jugglers, dancers, bear baiters, music. Laise approached everything with a bubbling enthusiasm. It was hard not to get caught up in her joy, no matter that my loin snake's wants were deferred because of it.

Then, of course, the sun set and the feast began. There was no slipping away after that. I resolved to limit my imbibing of the tankards of the village's most excellent ale. I wanted for my head to be clear so that my small head could pursue what it wanted after the feasting was over.

We were sat at a long table and Laise insisted I was by her side. Sirtago was seated close by to my right but was similarly surrounded by his plump kitchen girls. For his part, he seemed to enjoy the attention and the prodigious portions of food and drink that were placed before him.

To my left, I saw Jemmy and Golath. The dwarf favoured me with a grim sneer, but his attention was similarly turned by a small group of fair lasses. When he wasn't shooting dark looks promising vengeance my way, his little hands were wandering, provoking shrieks of outrage from the girls. They scolded the little man, giggling and laughing. All seemed to be enjoying themselves.

One tiny girl had attached herself to the young giant, Golath. She stared up at him with dreamy eyes, which made me suspect she was addled in the head. Golath seemed equal parts pleased and alarmed at the lass's attentions. He was awkward, fidgeted on the bench something terrible, but nothing seemed to faze his doe-eyed attendant.

Further down I could see the other champions: the large, dark woman and the two smaller women sat together. Some of the young men attended them. They were fair youths, callow and beardless, but they seemed not to turn the swordswomen's eyes. The two younger women with the braids regarded everyone with narrow, suspicious eyes. The larger woman sat with a regal poise, her eyes regarding her male suitors with amusement. Her broad lips often drew back from her gleaming teeth.

The tables were wooden and most were bare, but ours was covered with linens. The larger tankards were carved from wood, but there were some glass beakers that held a dark wine. The plates were wood as were the spoons, but the knives were forged from a fine steel. Indeed, it seemed a shame to waste them as cutlery, with a little turn on a wheel, they could have made fine edged weapons.

Along with the wine there was bread, spices and, naturally, plenty of ale. The great steaming boar was the centerpiece of the meal but there were also several plates of fowl, and the mutton from the evening previous went into a stew, which was warm and delicious. There were fruits and nuts, cheese, butter and cream, eggs pickled in brine, eggs wrapped in mutton cooked in a bread casing, pea soup, walnut bread and much else that I could not identify.

The boar's tongue had been cut out earlier. It had been salted and cooked separately in brine mixed with honey and onions. There was garlic and mushrooms, horsebean and candied angelica.

I tried to eat and drink slowly and carefully, but Laise's encouragement was infectious. She laughed and chattered and batted her eyes at me, pressing her ample bosom into my side. She inflamed my ardour while trying to bury it in pickled eggs and drown it in ale and mead.

As the meal progressed, one of the village elders, whom Laise told me was named Fiddick, stood and addressed the assembled. He thanked Master Theiss, Master Dolan, Sisters Brutetta and Margatta from the Holy Seat of the Maryred Agnes, and someone named Kellonas of the Road, for gathering the honoured Champions to the village this night.

"Master Theiss, in particular, is to be congratulated for contracting with not one, but two fine warriors who join us this night. Sirtago, Ka of the Southern Kingdom of Trigassa, for whom we are all indebted for providing us the great boar on which we feast this night!"

At that the assembled let out a roar. The young men of the hunt began shouting Sirtago's name. At this encouragement Sirtago stood, soaking in the adulation.

"...and his loyal and stalwart companion, Poet!" Fiddick finished. The crowd's cheers were somewhat muted for my name. Laise practically pushed me from my seat, I stood, a trifle unsteadily, while meekly acknowledging the half-hearted cheers. I smiled, held up my hands to the crowd before re-taking my seat.

"So where are your rhymes?" a piping voice cried out. I looked to see the dwarf, Jemmy, regarding me with a barely concealed sneer. "Give us a poem, Poet!"

Despite the hate-filled glare I returned to the malicious dwarf, the crowd was encouraged. The cheers grew moderately louder and calls for a poem dragged me back to my feet.

I thought for a moment, then raised my tankard and turned a wry smile on my tormentor, the tiny little prick.

"What beast is't that hoots and screeches
With reed-like voice and shrill battle cry
Hey-ho, to the marsh full of sucking leeches
and toads that will croak and loons that do sigh

"Where is the mighty dwarf Jemmy, our champion??
Why lo there he sits on a gray old marsh rock
Hidden in the shadow of his giant companion,
His legs are as small as the average man's cock!

"His eyes..."

Well, that was as far as I got. The crowd roared with laughter at my little extempore verse. Even young Golath bellowed echoing laughter from deep inside his cavernous chest. But the dwarf found little humour in it. He drew his blade, sprang onto the table and ran heedless of the plates and tankards, cutlery and glass that scattered in the wake of his tiny boots. His high-pitched voice raised itself into an ululating battle cry as he drove his sword towards me, clearly intent on fulfilling his earlier threat to cut my throat.

I reached for my dagger. I would have had it out and thrust into the dwarf's eye before the little homunculus even got close to me. I stood up from my chair in anticipation of making the throw, but Laise hurled herself at my midsection, tumbling us both onto the grass, knocking over our chairs and driving the wind from my lungs.

On my back, I saw Sirtago's great blade swing out and chop down hard. The table shook with the blade's thunderous blow and pieces of broken pottery went flying everywhere.

Laise's prodigious breasts were smothering me. I pushed her off and stood up, hoping beyond hope to see the little man cleaved in two by Sirtago's sword.

Alas, Jemmy was still in one piece. He was held aloft by Golath, his little legs swinging in mid-air, his teeth gritting back a strangled cry of rage.

Sirtago's sword had split the linen and was stuck in the tabletop where Jemmy's body should have been had his giant companion not interfered.

The surrounding crowd had let out a collective gasp at the near miss. Fiddick stared aghast at the tableau, his mouth open in shock. "Laise!" he cried out. "Are you hurt!"

"I'm fine," Laise said as she regained her feet. She was disheveled and tugged at her clothing with an undignified snort. "Well, that were a close 'un, weren't it?" she observed. Then let out a braying laugh.

The crowd laughed as well, though it was brittle and uncertain.

"Put me down, you great ox!" Jemmy demanded. "PUT ME DOWN!"

"You can't kill the other champions!" Golath admonished the little man as he set him back on the ground.

"I'll do as I please!" the dwarf spat, but he sheathed his short sword nevertheless. He shot me a dark glare and I grimaced back.

Sirtago managed to free his sword from the wooden tabletop. "You owe me your life once more, Poet!" he bellowed as he placed his blade back in its leather sheath.

"If you count how many times you put it in danger, I think we're even," I said through an icy smile.

Sirtago knocked back another tankard of ale then bellowed laughter, turning his attention back to his plump coterie.

Though he was nonplussed by the sudden contretemps, Fiddick continued with the introductions as if it were all part of some staged show. "Short in stature, but giant of heart, from the Northern regions we have a champion in Jemmy!" the crowd hooted approvingly. "And his giant companion Golath of Exxenmoor!" The crowd roared their approval and Golath roared back, raising his arms in acknowledgment of the adoring crowd. He stooped and picked up Jemmy, setting him on his shoulders so the crowd could see him, perhaps so the dwarf could share in Golath's view of the crowd.

Fiddick turned towards the warrior women. "From the far, exotic East comes two sister warriors, Nikit and Kaylam. Born into a royal family they were, but a rival warlord usurped the throne and killed their royal parents. These two were smuggled away by loyal court soldiers and taught in the ways of the warrior. One day they will reclaim their rightful throne, but today they have deigned to be our champions, the Sisters of the Sword!"

The two younger women stood, waving their weapons in an ostentatious fashion and striking poses. I had seen better displays from traveling minstrels, but the crowd ate it up along with their boar and ale. "If they're sisters then, the dwarf and giant there are twins," I said to Sirtago. Something about their story struck me as familiar as well. "I'm sure I've read that story in a scroll somewhere."

"Mayhaps you have. A story like that is bound to inspire scribes to write it down," opined Sirtago who had now become a literary critic as well as a champion. Thing is, the scroll I read the story in I'd found in a library in Kandra, and the scroll had been ancient when these two women were still in nappies.

"And finally, from the great city of Baurebec comes Geyero!"

The large dark woman stood with a smooth poise and acknowledged the crowd's approval. I'd heard of Baurebec, but never visited. I wondered if all the citizens had such grace.

THE FEAST was soon cleared away and we were bid to gather around the stone dais. The great tree loomed over the spot, casting moonlit shadows. Lanterns hung from the branches, which gave the platform an unearthly illumination.

Laise pushed me to the front of the dais and she stood by me, holding my hand. I noticed Sirtago being similarly guided... coerced... by his coterie of women who had a job holding him upright. He brandished a tankard from which he occasionally took great draughts.

Golath and Jemmy were similarly led upward. Jemmy by his giggling group of handlers and Golath by his tiny, dreamy eyed Lass. The "sisters" of the sword, and Geyero were accompanied, as well, by their entourage of young men.

A figure wearing a colorful robe strode onto the platform. The assembled crowd hushed in expectant silence. He opened his mouth to speak but was drowned out by a shriek from one of Jemmy's handlers. A whispered scolding put a stop to it. The crowd settled down again.

"And now," the robed man intoned. "Now we tell the tale of the dread and foul sorcerer, Hye Taugn and his doom that overshadows our fair valley!"

The crowd of villagers uttered what seemed like a moan of pain, like a low keening. Then cymbals crashed, breaking the spell. A small band of musicians started playing from somewhere and a group of villagers took to the stage. "Our people settled in this valley eons ago, in the dim and distant past," the robed man intoned. The actors on the staged made a dumb show of herding animals and planting crops. "The land was fertile and rich and we made a settlement. Protected by the rock at our backs and the woods at our front, we thrived in this place and made a beautiful village. The people were happy and content."

Drums were beaten and several of the lamps were shaded. Cymbals crashed again. A figure strode onto the dais that towered over the others. The figure walked on stilts covered in a dark robe. I laughed at the sight of it, which prompted a curt *shhhh* from Laise.

"Then came the dread sorcerer from the East: Hye Taugn! His wicked shadow blotted out the sun and dried up the brooks! His evil magick blighted the crops and caused the animals to sicken and die!"

Here several of the "farm animals" on the dais dropped dead, which elicited a great sigh of grief from the crowd. I had to stifle a laugh at the wretchedness of the performance. I'd seen better theatrics from children's productions.

"The wizard raged," the robed actor continued. "...and demanded tribute from the people of the valley! The people quaked in fear before the black wizard. 'How?' they cried! 'How can we give you tribute when you have blighted our land and caused our animals to sicken and die?' the people cried out."

And indeed, they did. The actors on their knees before the stilted man threw up their hands and wailed in mortal anguish. It was becoming harder to stifle my laughter.

"I will lift the curse!" the actor on stilts intoned to the crowd. "But in exchange I demand half your bounty! You will give to me half your cattle, half your grain! Half your crops! I demand tribute from your populace! A virgin sacrifice! I demand a portion of your newborn children be brought to me to be used as sacrifices to appease the demons that I serve!"

"The people wailed in anguish!" the robed narrator picked up the narrative. "'*No! No!*' they cried, but their wails went unheeded by the wizard's cold heart. He was deaf to the people's lamentation!"

The actors broke out into a paroxysm of grief, their bodies undulating and rolling. Indeed, the assembled crowd was close to joining in. Many members of the crowd were visibly upset to see this history played out.

"But what choice did we have?" the robed man asked rhetorically. "None! We had no choice but to accede to the foul contract!"

Here a low moan came from the crowd.

"Lo, he lifted the curse on the land and then the wizard retreated to the mountain. Within he built a maze of tunnels and filled them with foul creatures and beasts he brought with him from distant lands. Creatures misshapen and unnatural! Beasts of wild temperament with which he subdued the wretched people of the valley."

At this point a young man slid up behind Laise and whispered into her ear. She nodded then squeezed my hand and whispered to me. "Come," was all she said.

Now, I confess that I was only half paying attention to the ridiculous pantomime playing out on the stage. The other half of my attention was engaged in an appreciation of Laiese's prodigious curves and in fantasies of what I wanted to do to her were I to get her alone. So when she led me away I was of the conviction that the little minx had arranged a place for our tryst, which I felt was too long in coming. She led me out of the crowd and around the outer edge of the assembled. I was expecting to be led off to a small, out of the way, hut. Instead, I was led around to the base of the tree. I could see lights on the stage but I was in darkness.

Laise led me to a small stool. "Go on!" she encouraged. I stood on the stool and from there stepped onto the stone dais. I was surprised and more than a little disappointed to find Sirtago standing beside me, weaving unsteadily, his tankard still gripped in a meaty fist.

To my left stood Golath, and to his left, Jemmy the dwarf blinked in the light of the tree lamps that were suddenly uncovered.

We were each pushed to step forward (I assume by our various handlers) and so we moved into the light and I found myself now part of this wretched display.

"Behold!" the robed narrator exhorted the crowd. "The dawn of a new day! Welcome to our champions! Our mighty warriors who will finally rid us of the most foul wizard and free our valley and our people!"

Here the crowd opened up into thunderous applause. They cheered and stamped their feet. They waved and threw flowers at our feet. I was uncertain what to do, but the "sisters" drew their swords and struck what I assume was meant to be heroic poses. Sirtago joined in, brandishing his blade and basking in the crowd's adulation. Golath followed suit and lifted Jemmy onto his shoulders. The dwarf had his little sword unsheathed and held aloft. Geyero, ever amused, acquiesced, hiking her blade high towards the overhanging tree branches.

I sighed and drew my dagger, holding it high and feeling right foolish and – I confess – cheated. My ardour, so remorselessly squelched had begun to transmute into a grim rage and an unaccountable certainty that somehow we were all being played for fools.

INDEED, that certainty overwhelmed my mood for the rest of the night. There were more performances after... music, dancing, merrymaking... but I could not find within myself the heart to participate. Laise was by my side, but she was no more keen to slip away from the crowd than before. I began to realize that she was deliberately attached to me, not out of any genuine desire for my company, but, I began to suspect, out of a duty to see that I did not wander off on my own. As the night wore on I began to feel very much like the proverbial donkey in a futile pursuit of a carrot, tied to a stick.

At least the ale was good.

CHAPTER 4: THE LABYRINTH

THE AIR was still and silent. We... that is -- Beyargmunn's champions -- stood and stared at the massive double doors. The only entrance to the labyrinth...

The wind was cold this far up the rock. Low hanging clouds misted the higher peaks and glowered at our tiny band.

We had been roused early, before the sunrise. I woke in the same bed I had slept in the night before. To my relief, I had not fouled the floors as the night before, but I had not drunk overmuch. I had been in too foul a mood to drink after my suspicions. Laise had walked me to my digs and had bid me goodnight with a chaste kiss. I think she sensed that her beguilement no longer held its effectiveness.

The men of the village conducted the morning's rousing. The whole affair had the air of a solemn ceremony.

We were gathered, each of us, to the great hall and served a modest breakfast. Sirtago had a suitably grim and sullen look beneath his mask. The others were similarly subdued. Only Jemmy caught my eye and that was only to give me a hostile, narrow eyed stare, which I returned. He looked drawn and pale. I could tell his head was hurting the little dwarf something fierce, which delighted me to no end. He turned away. I thought he was going to heave his breakfast but the little fellow managed to keep it down.

The men led us out of the village. Carrying torches, they climbed a path to the black rock with a solemn gait. We followed in grim silence.

We were each given a leather waterskin. I was presented with a blade by one of the young men. I suppose because my only weapon was my dagger, as I was the only one of us so provided. It seems they could not imagine a single knife being an effective weapon. I accepted the blade without argument, though I felt lopsided after attaching it to my belt.

The path led to a set of narrow stone steps. The steps led to a stone platform at whose further edge was a wider set of stairs. Here the young men of the village blanched and dared go no further.

Blind Master Theiss stepped forward, gave each of us some sort of benediction in a language that I did not recognize. After that, he turned and descended the way he had come. The other men followed. Soon we were alone.

The sun had risen now and the early dawn light began burning away the sullen clouds.

Sirtago and I mounted the steps that led up to the entrance. The doors were carved with arcane sigils and hideous figures. Opposite the door two outcroppings of black rock rose like tusks. Between the tusks I could see the village nestled at the bottom of the valley. The sun shone on it and made it sparkle like a jewel. The whole valley lit up in the dawn light. It was beautiful and lush.

Reluctantly, I turned back to the massive doors.

"Well," Jemmy said, his piping voice breaking the silence. "I don't see a bell. Are we going to stand here all day staring at them, or do we go ahead and open the doors? Or do you think we should knock?"

THE DOORS were heavy and rusted shut due to lack of use. It took all of us working together to get one of the massive doors to budge. It moved with a horrendous scraping noise. I noted that the edge of the door scraped the stones below it. Clearly it had been a long time since this portal had been opened. They had obviously settled in their frames somewhat since the last time they were moved.

Dust and rust flakes fell on us as we entered, rotating the door so that the entrance was wide enough for the largest of us to walk in comfortably.

I found this passing strange. If the village gave regular tribute to the wizard, how did that tribute enter? Why were we not using that entrance?

I kept my misgivings to myself.

The villagers had given us torches, and Sirtago, Geyero and Golath each held one aloft as we passed through. I was glad that the door was held open. It would give us a convenient point to retreat to should things go wrong.

IT WAS noticeably colder beyond the doorway. There was an old, musty, damp smell in the air. As my eyes adjusted to the darkness I could see that we stood in a rounded chamber. From the stone floor that spread out around us, the walls sported carved symbols and monstrous sculptures. I looked up and could see a chain ensconced on the wall. I tried to follow it up to see what it attached to but the torchlight could not penetrate the darkness above us. The walls rose high around us but we could not see far. The ceiling, were it actually there, could have been just out of the reach of the light, or it could be as high as the mountain itself. We could not tell.

The floor beneath our feet was littered with broken bits of stone of various sizes. They could have been bits of the ceiling or the walls that had broken away over the years and come to rest on the ground. Geyero's boot kicked at a larger bit of stone. She seemed to be startled by the noise the stone made as it scraped the floor. She looked down to see her boot resting against it and uttered a curse.

A passage led further into the mountain on the opposite wall. Golath approached it, lighting the entrance with his torch. Jemmy peered into the passage, trying to see how far it ran. "*HELLOOOO!*" he shouted in his piping voice. "Anyone at *HOOOOM?* Village champions have come calling!" his voice echoed down the passageway and up the walls of the main chamber to the unseen ceiling.

"Be quiet, you..." Geyero hissed, unable or unwilling to utter the unflattering description of the dwarf.

"Half-witted Homunculus?" I suggested.

Jemmy gave me a sour look.

"You'll alert the wizard!" Geyero scolded. "Or worse!"

"We're bound to run into him anyway sooner or later," the dwarf countered. "If he comes to us, it'll save s a lot of walking."

Sirtago gave the dwarf an unamused scowl. Jemmy shrugged, but said no more.

The walls and ceilings of the passage were festooned with dust, cobwebs and the tattered remains of old tapestries. The floor was similarly littered with broken bits of stone. The passage's ceiling was arched and high enough to allow Golath to walk without having to duck his head. The passage was only wide enough, however, for the group to travel through single file.

"Who goes first?" I asked.

I SHOULD have known better than to ask. "Your eyes are keen," Sirtago said. "You see better in the dark than some men see in the light. You go first."

I raised an eyebrow at my companion. What he said was true, but I wasn't inclined to lead the way. "We should send the dwarf first," I suggested. "He'll trip up anyone who attacks us from in front, giving the rest of us a chance to..."

"I've had enough of your japes, you trumped up dandy!" Jemmy started.

"Quiet!" Sirtago shouted.

And that settled it. I went first.

I held the borrowed sword before me. It looked well made and it reflected the torchlight, helping to extend the light's reach ahead of us. I reasoned that if I couldn't see what was coming it would at least run into the sword. That would alert me well enough in advance to draw my dagger from its sheath and deal with the attacker properly.

Sirtago went behind me, holding his flambeau high into the arched ceiling, lighting the way ahead as well as he could. The sisters came next, then Golath with the other torch, Jemmy and finally Geyero and hers.

The passage was festooned with sculptures. Multi-armed and multi-legged forms were carved into reliefs along the walls. As Sirtago's torch lit the way, bat winged creatures, and women with strange animal heads came looming out of the darkness.

I wanted to stab at each relief as it came into the light, but I forced myself to remain calm. I did not want to appear frightened to everyone crowding behind me, and I certainly did not want to give the dwarf any opportunities to mock my courage. I was gritting my teeth, fighting back the urge to swing my blade at everything in my path. If something actually had leaped in front of me I would certainly have been killed as I would not be able to tell it from another hideous sculpture until it was upon me.

When the passage ended the sudden darkness startled me more than the ghoulish figures. I stopped and Sirtago almost crashed into me.

"What is it?" he hissed.

I forced myself to remain calm." It's a chamber – I think."

I moved forward cautiously, giving Sirtago room to enter with his torch. As he was joined by the other torches, I could see we were in a long stone hall. There were structures around the room that I first took to be some sort of pillars, but they were rounded, like mounds and each mound narrowed at the top to a funnel-like structure, like a small smoke stack. Each was as tall as I was and as round at the base as they were tall.

I counted six that I could see, but there may have been more. The torchlight was not bright enough to illuminate the entire chamber. I could not tell how many there were in the darkness.

Nikit and Kaylam had stopped to examine one of the mounds. They were made of stones, but were not completely sealed up. There were gaps in the surface. The two sword sisters were trying to peer into the gaps. "I think there's something inside," Nikit said.

Geyero brought her torch closer to the mound. "What is it?"

"I think it's a statue."

Sirtago brought his torch closer to the mound next to me. I peered in and saw what looked like a man crouched within the mound. It looked to be made from the same type of stone as the mounds were constructed with, which I found very curious. Even more curious was that the statues were completely ordinary. No beast heads or bat wings, just the figure of an ordinary man.

"Any gemstones?" the dwarf asked.

Sirtago moved the torch around. Nothing glistened like a gemstone would. Only the shadows moved around, which gave the figure the illusion of movement.

One of the sisters let out a sharp breath and backed away from the mound, startled. "It moved!" Kaylam hissed. "I saw it move!"

I shook my head. "It's just the torchlight," I reassured. "It makes the shadows move which..." I stopped talking when I saw the head of the statue I was just examining turn and look straight at me. It glared at me for a frozen moment and my head whirled in shock. Then it opened its mouth and it shrieked.

In the torchlight I could see that the figures within the mounds were all moving. Each head swiveled in our direction, opening to emit the piercing shriek. The chamber was filled with a high-pitched nightmarish sound as all the other statues joined in. The shrieks came up through the smokestacks and echoed all around us.

I covered my ears with my hands but it did little to block out the sound. I saw Sirtago's one good eye wide with shock. He thrust his blade through one of the spaces between the stones of the mound, intent on stabbing one of the shrieking figures to silence, but the point of his blade deflected off the form, as one would expect of a stone statue.

I felt that I would go mad if I were to keep listening to the horrendous din. I moved further into the chamber, searching for a way out.

At the far wall, I saw a large set of wooden doors. I ran for them. They were held closed by a wooden beam-sliding bolt. I pushed the bolt through the brackets. The door gave slightly inwards. I pushed but I was not strong enough to budge it.

I turned to call for help from Sirtago, but Geyero was there. Lending the strength of her ropy muscles to mine. The door slid open. I could barely hear its echoing scrape against the stone floor above the din of the shrieking statues.

The door opened into a dark passageway. It was a good deal wider than the narrow passage that we traversed to get here. In the light from Geyero's torch, I could see the ceiling was a good deal higher. The walls, floor and ceiling were all stone and mercifully undecorated with hideous carvings.

"Sirtago!" I called, trying to make myself heard over the shrieking. Geyero called the others.

The sisters both had their hands over their ears and were looking for a way out. They spied us at the door, waving them towards us frantically.

Sirtago was trying to break into the stone mound with his sword. I suppose he thought if he broke the statue to pieces it might stop its screaming. That was usually Sirtago's strategy in situations like this: hit and keep hitting until it stops.

Fortunately Golath had the presence of mind to grab the Ka's arm. Sirtago glared at the giant with his good eye but Golath gestured towards the door.

The sisters ran through, followed by the dwarf, then Sirtago and Golath. On the other side, Geyero and Sirtago got behind the wooden door and pushed it closed. With the door latched closed the shrieking was no longer assaulting our senses. I could still hear it resounding behind the door but it was thick and heavy enough to block out most of the sound.

There was another sliding bolt on the inside and Sirtago slid it in place, locking it closed and separating us from the horrible screaming stones.

Shaken, I leaned against the wall. The smooth stone felt cool on my back. "Well," I managed after a moment. "If Jemmy's hooting hadn't already done it, I assume that lost us any element of surprise."

Golath nodded in sage agreement. "That was an alarm bell."

"It was hideous," Nikit shuddered. "I can still hear it in my head.

So could I. The shrieks felt like they were rattling around inside my skull like a set of dice in a bowl. I suppressed a shudder and stood away from the wall. "We should keep moving," I suggested. "If something is coming for us it would be better to be on the move."

Sirtago nodded agreement.

The passage was wider and allowed us to move as a loose group rather than single file. I reckoned the original narrow passage was designed to be defensible by a smaller force. Any attackers would be forced to arrive one-by-one. It would make sense that a smaller number of defenders could pick them off one at a time. The shrieking stones were there to warn of intruders when there wasn't any force to hold off invaders.

And now whoever was in the labyrinth knew that invaders had made their way in. We were vulnerable and needed to find a defensive position in case we ran into resistance, which I assumed, we would sooner or later.

The passage widened out slightly before opening up into an even larger chamber. Our torches could not illuminate enough to see the ceiling, which was far above our heads. I could hear a steady dripping all around us and wondered if the ceiling was the natural rock of the mountain.

The floor was stone and littered with broken bits of rock as well as pieces of armor. As we explored we discovered several sets of stairs. One large set went down. The rest were narrower and went up.

"We should go down," Jemmy piped up. "The treasure's more likely to be down."

"What makes you say that?" Geyero asked.

"It just makes sense," the dwarf insisted. "If you want to hide something you bury it, don't ya?"

"We're not just here to find the treasure," I reminded the dwarf. "We've been hired to kill the wizard. The treasure is meant to be our reward for doing that."

Jemmy scowled. "Well, okay, yes. But... were we to find the treasure first, we could always take as much as we could carry, go back to the front door, say: 'Sorry, didn't see the wizard,' then bog off richer men."

"I can carry a lot," Golath put in.

"We're more likely to find the wizard if we ascend one of these staircases," I said.

Jemmy let out a laugh. "And more likely to run into armed guards. The wizard's not just going to let us walk into his bedchamber. Don't be daft!"

"It makes sense that the wizard would have some sort of guard, either natural or unnatural," Sirtago said, looking up one of the staircases. "All of us together would have no choice but to stand and fight. If we separated, one of us might manage to sneak past whatever guard is between us and the wizard."

I shook my head. "Separating is not a good idea. We should stick together."

"I say we go down!" Jemmy spat.

"I say you should be quiet," I said. "And stop farting!" I caught a whiff of a noxious smell.

"It wasn't me!" Jemmy insisted, holding his nose. "Was that you, Golath?"

The giant was holding his nose and shaking his head. Now all of us were reacting to the putrid smell.

I saw something move above our heads, as if someone had lobbed something. I caught only a glimpse of a shape that quickly disappeared into the shadows.

"What was that?" Kaylam said, drawing her curved sword.

All of us had our weapons out and were trying to peer into the upper darkness. The awful smell grew more rank.

I saw something flitter near one of the stairwells. I could hear a slight sound of air moving, like a sigh. The rank smell was overpowering now.

"There it is!" Geyero shouted, pointing with her blade.

The thing looked like a brown fleshy bag hanging in the air. Two spindly stalks grew out of the top. At the end of the wiggly stalks were two glowing orbs.

The thing was gently descending like a gossamer cloth. Then there was another sigh and I saw an orifice open as air was squeezed through it. The smell became stronger. The creature propelled itself through the air by expelling gas.

Nikit let out a disgusted sound. She swung her sword at it but the creature was too high.

I looked to Golath who moved closer to it and poked at it with his sword. The tip of his sword pierced the foul creature's side and more of the gas sighed out, causing the creature's trajectory to spin away.

I swung to try to bisect the thing, but it was spinning away too quickly.

The thing's eyes turned and fixed themselves on me and I felt that it was looking right at me, marking my features, my weapons.

The thing rose up the nearest set of stairs. I leaped onto the stairs and ran up, swinging my sword at the thing.

"Leave it be," Sirtago shouted up at me. "It's harmless."

"It's not harmless to my sense of smell," Jemmy said

"We can't let it get away," I said. "It's seen us. It can tell the wizard where we are... how many we are..." I swung at the thing but it managed to spin out of my reach each time.

The thing let out a final blast of gas and with a *phthuuut* it shot away, leaving me gasping in a noxious cloud.

In frustration I swung my sword at the stone steps. To my surprise the steel shattered against the stone. Broken pieces of fine looking steel scattered down the steps. I stared in disbelief at the broken blade that jutted out from the now useless hilt.

"*Gwut's Cock!*" Sirtago cursed. He picked up one of the shattered pieces from the stair. He held the shard up to his good eye, then tossed it to the ground. "The steel isn't worth the polish they used to tart it up." Sirtago said. "It's a good thing you didn't use that in combat. The only way it could be an effective weapon would be if a piece flew into your enemy's eye."

I shook my head. Why make it seem like a formidable blade? Why go to all the trouble?

My thoughts were cut short when something whizzed by my ear. There was a loud clang as the object bounced off Sirtago's chest plate. Sirtago, startled, looked down at the object at his feet.

It was an arrow.

CHAPTER 5: GOBLIN ATTACK

INSTANTLY I dived off the steps, as the air was suddenly alive with more of them.

I saw one catch Geyero's upper arm. It sank into the flesh but did not punch through. Geyero took one disdainful look at the intrusive point, then swung her sword, neatly bisecting a second arrow before it could lodge next to its fellow.

We dashed away from the stairs. I caught a glimpse of figures descending towards us, no doubt the authors of the hail of arrows that we now fled.

"*Down!*" Sirtago shouted as he made his way to the wide staircase that descended deeper into the labyrinth. We made haste down the stairs. Only Golath had the presence of mind to keep his torch. The others were abandoned in the flight. We followed the giant down the wide staircase.

I had drawn my dagger in the headlong flight. I felt much more confident with it in my hand than anything else, though I keenly missed the presence of its lost companion.

The large staircase ended at a landing. Two smaller sets of stairs descended from it. "Which way do we go?" the giant asked.

Sirtago hesitated for a moment only, then took the left staircase. Golath followed without argument. The rest of us followed behind.

The narrow staircase began winding and we had to go single file. I was getting dizzy from descending in a circle until it emptied into a large chamber with a low ceiling. In Golath's torch light I could see columns interspersed in the darkness, but nothing else.

Sirtago and Golath led the way into the chamber. We followed warily. The light from the torch cast shadows all around us that moved as Golath did. I kept expecting for something to jump out at us from the darkness.

Geyero was bleeding from where the arrow stuck. Her arm was slick with blood down to her wrist guards.

"We have to stop," I said.

Sirtago turned and saw Geyero's wound. He nodded and gestured to Golath to bring his torch towards us.

Geyero sat with her back against a column. I knelt down beside her, gingerly examining the point where the arrow pierced her flesh.

She did not wince at all to my touch. Carefully I grabbed the shaft. "This is going to hurt," I warned.

She shook her head. "I don't feel pain," she said. "Pull it out."

I tugged back on the shaft, slowly, feeling it slide backwards with little resistance. The arrow was short. The arrowhead was merely a point with no barbs. Fortunate for Geyero, but still a painful wound.

She did not cry out as the arrow came out, but fresh blood gouted from the wound.

I opened my water sack and spilled it onto Geyero's arm, trying to make the wound as clean as I could. "Don't waste it," Geyero protested. "You might need it later."

"You'll need to keep a grip on your blade," I countered. "You won't be able to do that if your hand is slick with blood all the time." I emptied the waterskin over her arm and hands.

I pulled out my dagger and cut into the empty bladder. It was made of soft leather and my dagger's edge cut through it without too much of a struggle. I was able to cut a longish strip that I would be able to tie around Geyero's wound. The inside of the bladder was clean, so it would bind the wound and keep her blood from getting poisoned.

Despite Geyero's arm being thick with ropy muscles, I was able to wrap the strip of the bladder twice around and tie it tight. She uttered no cry or even a grunt of pain. "You're being exceedingly brave," I said.

"I told you. I don't feel pain. I never have," she said.

I regarded her skeptically. "No pain? None?"

She shook her head. "Ever since I was little. I don't feel pain at all. I feel pressure. I know when I've been hit, but I can't tell how bad."

"That's a fortunate condition for a warrior," I said.

"Sometimes. But I have to be careful to see my wounds. I sometimes don't know how serious they are. I need to see them and tend to them, otherwise I might bleed to death and never know it."

I regarded her curiously. I grasped her arm just below the bindings. "Do you feel that?"

She smiled. "Of course I do. I can feel touch."

"Can you feel pleasure?" I asked.

She looked up at me with lidded eyes. "Are you offering to pleasure me?"

I smiled. "Mere curiosity," I protested.

"Because I should tell you that I will allow no man to bed me that has not defeated me in single combat."

78

I laughed at that. I couldn't help it. "Do you say that to all men you meet?"

"Only the ones I know I can defeat," she said. "...Or the ones I don't want to."

Before I could ask into which category I fell the air echoed with the sound of a battle horn from somewhere above us.

"We need to move," Sirtago said. "They'll stumble upon us if we linger."

I offered to help Geyero to her feet, but she waved my hand away. We moved further into the dark chamber.

The columns thinned and soon the stone floor gave way to naked rock. A rough path was formed into the rock whether natural or by design I could not tell. The ceiling was covered with stalactites. We had moved into a natural cave system. At spots I thought I could hear water rushing but it came and went depending on where we were.

"I'll wager that treasure's here somewhere," Jemmy was saying as we stumbled along the rough path. "This is where I'd hide a treasure if I had one."

We stumbled through caves both wide and narrow. Sometimes the ceilings were low and even I had to duck my head. Other times the ceiling was so high our meager torchlight could not pierce the darkness.

In one large chamber we found an arrangement of large stones. We sat and rested. I took the opportunity to check Geyero's bandage. It seemed clean. It was stained red but the blood was not leaking through.

"Why can't we have a wizard with us?" Jemmy asked. I noticed he was rubbing his knees and wincing in pain.

"Don't be a stupid little man," Geyero spat. "We're here to kill a wizard. Why would we bring a wizard with us?"

"I don't mean an evil wizard, but just a wizard that could use his magic to heal us when we get injured." He looked at Golath's torch, which was slowly going out. "He could 'magic' us some more light. Or maybe more water."

"That's the most ridiculous thing I've ever heard," Geyero said in disgust. "You're more of a fool than I thought you were."

"I mean, think about it. It would be handy, wouldn't it?"

I laughed and shook my head. "A wizard would bring more trouble than he was worth. You can't trust magicians or sorcerers."

I saw the dwarf rubbing at his knees again. "What's wrong with you?" Geyero asked. "Are you injured?"

"No," the dwarf spat, annoyed. "My knees and ankles are always paining me when it's cold and damp."

Once the dwarf said it I realized that the air *was* damp. Perhaps there was water underneath the rock somewhere.

Before I could say anything an arrow whizzed through the air, narrowly missing the dwarf as he leaped from the rock. We had lingered too long.

The air was alive with missiles. Golath leaped up just as his torchlight went out.

I had my dagger out and whirled to try and find an enemy. There were orange lights coming towards us. Torches held aloft by short figures. Their skin reflected white in the light of their torches. Their faces looked like bleached bones and their limbs were emaciated like cadavers. They wore some armor, but not much. Their eyes glowed white in the torchlight.

An arrow whizzed by my head and a small figure ran towards me. I sidestepped the creature but struck with my dagger. I felt the point pierce flesh and was satisfied to hear the creature cry out in pain. It fell to the rocks and writhed like a snake.

Out of the corner of my eye I saw Sirtago swing his blade. Several of the small figures were cut down. Golath roared as he attacked. His blade did not connect but his size and fierce booming voice served to drive the attackers back.

Even Jemmy ran to engage one of the attackers. Despite his diminished size and his pained knees and ankles, the dwarf had fight in him. I could not help but admire his ferocity as his short sword felled two before their fellows retreated.

My dagger found the soft parts of another attacker.

One of the retreating attackers had dropped his still lit torch. I retrieved it and held it aloft. Sirtago blinked in the torchlight. "What manner of creatures were those?"

"They were men," Geyero said. She was crouched over one of the corpses of the attackers.

I held the torch close and I could see that she was right. What I had taken to be bleached bone and emaciated limbs was only white paint over black."

"*Gwut's hairy ass!*" Sirtago breathed.

The man beneath the paint was small. Not as small as Jemmy, but a good foot shorter in stature than either of the sisters. He wore mostly leather armor with a few pieces of plate here and there. He had a metal wrist guard that was festooned with spikes.

Underneath the paint his skin was dark. His hair was black and drawn back into a tight braid.

Two other corpses lay in the vicinity and each carried similar armor and body paint.

"I've never seen such people," Jemmy said.

"I have," Geyero said. "My home, Baurebec, is a port city. These people worked the ships there. Tiny brown men who climbed the ropes all day. They were said to be natives of a far chain of islands."

"What are they doing here so far from home?" Jemmy asked.

"Right now, trying to kill us," Sirtago said. "We have to keep moving,"

Golath held the lighted torch high and we moved deeper into the tunnels.

THE WAY narrowed and for a while we had to move in single file. I worried that the passage would narrow further. If it did then only half of us stood a chance of making it through. We would have to turn back and that put us at risk of running into our attackers.

Fortunately the passage led to a larger chamber.

The caves were cold but this chamber was decidedly frigid.

It was also divided by a ravine.

Golath stood at the edge of the ravine and held the torch out. It only lighted the way so far. Below us was blackness, but the cold air was definitely coming up from the ravine. The torchlight just picked out the rock on the opposite side of the ravine. But it was too far to jump.

A little ways up we found a rope bridge.

It was rickety, but otherwise sturdy. It was clearly made for lighter bodies, though.

"The lightest of us should go first," I said.

"I suppose that means me," Jemmy snarled. "You can't wait to get rid of me, can you, you poxy-bottomed cox-comb!"

"You go first because you're lightest, you brainless runt!" I said. "You have the best chance of getting across and not having the bridge snap under your weight."

Jemmy scowled at me, nevertheless. "Fine," the dwarf spat. "I'll go first, then."

Jemmy hesitated for a moment before gingerly stepping a foot onto the first of the bridge's slats. The thing creaked and swayed a bit but the dwarf's weight was negligible. Slat by slat he walked, keeping one hand firmly on the hand rope. Soon he was over. His foot found the last slat and he stepped upon the rock on the opposite side.

As he brought his rear foot to join the other on the rock he tried to adjust his grip on the hand rope.

He missed his grip and lost his balance. His squat form slipped over the edge.

I let out a gasp. I thought the little man was done for, but his hand grabbed onto the lower rope on which the slats were tied.

We froze in shock, watching the dwarf hang precariously below the final slat.

"*Help!*" the dwarf called in a strangled cry.

Nikit and Kaylam should have been next, then me, but I could not be certain that either of them had the lightness of step to make the passage without dislodging the hapless halfling, or the strength to lift him were they to manage it.

I, on the other hand, knew that I could traverse the bridge. I had learned enough fighting styles in my travels to know that I could make my way over the slats, using as much muscle control as I could to not cause the bridge to sway and the dwarf to lose his grip.

Once on the other side I dropped to my belly. I hooked one foot around the opposite rope and reached for Jemmy's hand.

"I'm gonna fall!" Jemmy said, panicked. "I'm gonna fall!"

"You're not going to fall," I said through gritted teeth. "Grab my hand."

"I can't" the dwarf said, panic causing his throat to tighten.

"Yes, you can." I insisted. I reached and gripped his thick little wrist. "Let go of the rope and grab my forearm. I'll pull you up."

Jemmy shook his head. "I don't trust you!"

"I don't trust you, either, you sad excuse for half a man, but right now you have no choice... not unless you want to go down into the blackness. Now let go of the rope!"

The dwarf let go. He was a little heavier than I expected him to be, but nowhere near as heavy as a full-grown man. I could have held Sirtago were it him that needed to be rescued, I had little doubt that I could lift the imp.

His hand grabbed at my forearm. His hand was slick with sweat but he managed to find a grip and I pulled, levering his weight up and forward onto the cliff edge. Once his trunk was on the rock he managed to wriggle himself the rest of the way to safety, scrabbling with his other hand. Once I was certain he would not fall I unhooked my foot from the opposite rope and got to my hands and knees.

"There, you see?" I said to him. "You weigh hardly anything at all. I've dropped heavier loads than you into the privy."

I reached for the hand rope to pull myself the rest of the way up when Jemmy suddenly snarled. "I've had enough of your japes!" he growled. He flipped his body over, lifted one stunted leg and kicked me full in the chest.

My hand missed the rope. My other hand slapped the edge but it was still slick with the dwarf's palm sweat. My grip slipped.

Before I could blink I had toppled over the side.

CHAPTER 6: BENEATH THE LABYRINTH

HOW LONG I fell I do not know.

Long enough to anticipate coming to a bad and messy end on the rocks below. Long enough curse the half-witted dwarf, to curse Sirtago for getting me into this situation in the first place, and to curse Laise for teasing me along when I should have seen the danger right in front of my eyes and left that damned valley when I had the chance.

Long enough to admit that last one was my own fault. I did see the danger, but my desire to bed the silly trollop led me into it nonetheless.

It was a surprise, but not an unwelcome one, when I hit the surface of the water and was plunged deep into the icy depths.

As the cold water slowed my rapid descent and brackish fluid shot up my nose and into my lungs, a part of my mind reassured myself that I *did* hear running water in the distant cave system.

Not that any of that would matter now if I didn't take advantage of it and swim for my life.

I kicked against the freezing water. My head broke the surface. I sputtered and coughed out what I had in my lungs and nose. It was pitch black. I blinked my eyes, trying to make out anything in my immediate vicinity, but I could see nothing. I opened my ears and listened. I could hear the water moving. I stilled my movements so that I would not be distracted by the sound of my own splashing.

I could hear something moving on the surface of the water. I could feel the water moving against me, causing me to bob up and down like a cork.

The sound became more distinct. The waves grew more violent.

Something... something big... was moving in the water!

Moving towards me.

My arms and legs beat the surface. I had learned to swim as a youth in Trigassa and had, on various escapades, many an opportunity to hone those skills. I employed them now, instinctively moving through the water in the direction that took me away from whatever it was that was moving towards me.

Again, I do not know how long I desperately swam away from whatever beast of the depths was following me, obviously intent on devouring me. Long enough to imagine all manner of horrid sea-dwelling creatures I had encountered throughout my life – more than I cared to. I certainly did not want to come to a bad end because of one.

My hand banged against stone. I scrabbled at whatever purchase I could find, desperate to drag myself out of the water.

I grasped at an outcropping and kicked up my legs. Soon I was scrambling up a tall rock.

I heard something splash behind me. Something slapped the rock to my left. I had the impression of something long, sinuous and wet slithering back into the icy water. I paused only for a moment to catch a few breaths. My legs were shaking under me, I did not want to risk them seizing up in the cold. I scrambled up the rock and kept going as long as it was taking me away from the surface of the water.

The stone eventually flattened out. I lay, fully prone, cognizant only of my labored breathing, the shivering of my arms and legs.

I managed to sit up. I tried to peer into the darkness and saw a slight glow coming from somewhere ahead. Some light reflected off the wet rocks. I followed, carefully, trying to find the source.

Soon I could see well enough to discern than I was in a rounded tunnel. The light reflected off small pools of water that dotted the ground. Ahead the tunnel was illuminated like a ring of bluish, green light, though I could not see where it was coming from.

As I moved further into the tunnel I began to see spots of illumination on the rock above, scattered about like stars. Except these lights were moving. They crawled about the surface, slowly picking their way among the nooks and crannies. Insects, worms or moving plants, I could not tell. Any opportunity to examine their nature was cut short by the sound of voices.

The sound was echoing and faint. As I moved farther I could hear it coming from a smaller tunnel that shot off from the main one.

I had to crawl on my hands and knees but as I did the voices became more distinct, speaking a language that I recognized. It was a northern dialect, but they were definitely speaking Sanvorish, which was a language spoken along the trade routes.

As I traversed the tunnel I could see light again, but this time it was torchlight. Someone was carrying a brand. More than one someone by the look of it.

The tunnel became wider and more spacious, but I remained on my hands and knees and tried to stick to the shadows, moving as silently as I could until I could ascertain just what manner of people were bringing the light into the dark caves.

I saw a torch moving towards me held by a scrawny looking man wearing worn clothes. He was youngish and bearded but he had a desperate sort of look to him.

He came to the entrance of the tunnel where I was hiding and thrust his torch forward. "This is it!" the young man shouted back to his companions.

They would discover me eventually. I decided that the best course of action was to take control of the situation.

I leaped from the shadow in which I was hiding. I grabbed the man from behind, sliding one arm around his chest and with my other hand I pressed my dagger against his throat. "Don't move," I hissed. I felt the man stiffen in my grip. "Don't cry out," I warned.

Just then the man's companions arrived, both carrying torches. Both looked just as scrawny and worn as the one I held at knifepoint. The older one had an eye patch and wore a kerchief over his head. He blanched when he saw his companion with a knife to his throat and I thought perhaps they might be kin to each other.

He held up a hand. "What do you want?" he demanded, his voice echoing off the cave walls.

'I want to know if I'm addressing friends or foes."

He gave me a hard look. "If you hurt my boy, then we will be foes, make no mistake about that."

The man wore a blade on his belt. The sheath that held it looked like it had seen better days. The stitching was coming undone and I could see a blade resting within. The metal did not look like it was well burnished.

The other man approached. He was a younger man. Closer in age to the man I held in front of me. He wore a blade as well and I could see him biting his lips, weighing his chances of drawing it and rescuing his friend or brother or cousin.

"Don't think about it, friend," I said to him. His eyes went wide as they met mine. "You may think yourself fast with a blade, but you don't want to gamble with this one's life, now do you?"

The younger man's eyes began welling with tears, which gave me pause. This was a family trying to survive, not brigands or bandits.

"Don't do anything rash," I whispered to the young man. I lowered the knife from his throat and took a step back. The boy stood resolute, or perhaps still too afraid to move. The older man gestured and the boy walked shakily forward to join him.

I held up my blade and my other hand to show it was empty. "Let's not do anything hasty, then, eh? I've made a gesture of goodwill. Let's try not to make foes of each other now. At least not any more than we already are."

"Who are you?" the older man asked. "You're not a goblin."

"Goblin?" I asked.

"Goblins. Trolls. The mountain is lousy with them. Haven't you seen them?"

I let out a rueful laugh. "I have," I said. "I killed a handful of them just this morning."

"You killed a goblin?" the young man whose throat I threatened asked incredulously.

I shook my head. "They're not goblins. They're just men like you and I. They paint themselves to frighten their enemies, but they're not any less human."

This information caused some consternation among the three. "How do we know you speak the truth?" the older man asked. "What business have you in these caves?"

"I'm hunting for the wizard and his treasure." I said.

"Treasure?" The younger man asked. "What treasure?"

I furrowed my brow. "Have you not heard the stories of the great treasure hidden in the mountain? Everyone, it seems has heard the stories of the wizard Hye Taugn and his horde of treasures from far lands."

The older man shook his head. "I've not heard of any treasure. I've been trying to find a way through these caverns for years and I've never seen any treasure."

"Then why are you trying to find your way through the caverns?"

"The treasure is on the other side. There's a rich valley on the other side of the mountain."

"Beyargmunn?" I asked.

"You've seen it?" the older man asked, an intense light in his one good eye. "You've seen the valley?"

"Seen it? I slept in it last night. I ate roast boar and drank ale there."

The look on his face was like a dog at a dinner table, waiting in hope for some morsel to drop. "You live in the valley?"

I shook my head. "I don't live there. I was a guest. I am, among others, a hired champion. I've been tasked with killing the wizard and my reward was to be the famed treasure."

The older man laughed. "You've made a bad bargain," he said. "There is no treasure in the mountain. The only treasure is the valley on the other side."

Well, this had me stymied. If there was no treasure then what were we doing risking our lives to kill a wizard who posed no threat to us?

"Where are you three from?" I asked.

"We're from Abelton. It's a small village on the shores of the lake. It's a ways below the caves."

I nodded my head. "Alright then. I take it you have no crops or sheep?"

The man shook his head. "There's no game in these hills. There's no vegetation to speak of. We fish for our food, but there's precious little of that in the lake anymore."

I let out a grunt. "Can you not trade with other villages?"

The man let out a harsh laugh. "There are two other villages and they are as poor as we. We've had to repel raiders from both of them twice in the last year. There's nothing north except rocky cliffs and ice. If we could get to the valley we might strike a deal with those who live there."

"You made it through the caves," the younger man said. "Tell us how you did it. What route did you take?"

I laughed humorlessly. "I fell. Or, rather... I was pushed. I would have died had I not hit the surface of an underground lake, but there was something in that dark water that was not well disposed towards me being there."

The older man grunted and nodded. "We try to steer clear of the black lake," he said, grimly. "We've lost too many men to the creature that lurks under the surface. You were lucky to have survived."

I shrugged. "I'm harder to kill than I look."

"Will you help us?" the younger man, the one who I'd threatened with a knife only seconds before, asked. "Help us find a way through the mountain?

I honestly wasn't certain that I could help them. Nevertheless, finding my way back through the mountain is what I had to do. Or, at least, find a way to rejoin my companions. And kill the dwarf.

If these villagers had been trying to find a way through for as long as they say they had, then they might help me to find my way back to a part of the labyrinth that I recognized. After that they were welcome to follow me as long as they could keep up.

The man with the eye patch was Cirdan. His son, the one whose neck I held a knife to, was Conner. The older boy was Conner's cousin, Elam.

They led me through a network of interconnected caves that they had mapped out over the years. The cave led to a narrow chamber and at the end of the chamber was a set of wooden doors. I helped to lift the bolt and open the doors.

Through the doors was a stone staircase. The stairs were wide enough for two but they were steep. Cirdan held his torch aloft and I could see that the stairs switched direction as they rose. "We've only made it to the top of the staircase once," he said. "It takes hours to climb. It opens out into a larger chamber with several exits. After that we're not certain which direction to follow. Perhaps you'll recognize the way?"

I shrugged. "Mayhaps."

CIRDAN did not exaggerate. The stairs did take hours to climb. As I said, I had no idea how long I fell, but I was aware of every step I made to get back from whence I had fallen. Especially after the first hour. Every step was agony. The large muscles in my legs felt like they were aflame.

The men of Abelton, however, did not flag or slow. They climbed without complaint. I was certainly not going to admit that I was any less than their equal. Far from it.

I gritted my teeth and climbed on.

After almost a second hour had gone by we arrived at the larger chamber. Here the villagers deigned to rest their legs. I did as well, though at that point everything hurt not only because of the climb but also of the effort it took not to cry out in agony with every step taken.

The chamber was big and dark and several columns held up the ceiling. I chose one and sat at its base, leaning against it, my legs stretched out before me. I swore I could see my thigh muscles throbbing through my breeches.

I took in the measure of the chamber as I rested, or at least as much as I could in the gathering darkness. It was much the same as the chambers we had passed through shortly after we entered. There were several entrances. Two had wooden doors with bolts. The others merely led into blackness. I could hear wind whistling from the open passages, but little else.

Suddenly Elam made a disgusting sound. Laughing, he pushed his cousin. "You're such a swine," he said.

Conner made a disgusted face. "It weren't me!" he laughed.

"Come to, boys," Cirdan growled. "That's enough!"

The boys settled down and I smelled the odor that had caused the ruckus. Ignoring the pain in my legs I leaped up, snatching my dagger out of its sheath.

I heard a hiss of air and the smell became more rank. I saw a movement in the shadows. Sure enough it was another of the fleshly creatures, its eye stalks pointing in our direction. It may have been the very same one that had eluded me earlier.

"What is it?" Cirdan demanded, leaping to his feet.

"A spy for Hye Taugn," I said, following the gasbag with my eyes. "Its eyes are the wizard's if we don't stop it." I moved swiftly in the floating creature's direction. It let out another hiss of air but before it could move away I slashed at it with my dagger. The blade parted the fleshy skin but the thing spun away as it had done before. It flew into one of the darkened tunnels.

I chased after into the dark. I assumed that Cirdan and the boys would follow. One of them had a torch and I needed light to catch the vile thing before it reported what it had seen to its foul master

The passage was narrow, barely wide enough for one man to pass through. The stone seemed unadorned, though I could not see for certain, Had it been carved, I'm certain I would have been caught on an edge, or dashed my brains out on a low-hanging curlicue. I ran my hand along the wall to steady myself, but felt only plain stone.

The rank smell was all around me, getting stronger the farther I moved within. With a great ragged hole in its side. It made little sense that the creature could hold enough gas to allow it to keep going, but, again, it was unnatural... a product of magic, perhaps... and followed rules that mortal men could not ken.

More worrisome was that there was no light behind me. Had Cirdan and his boys been so paralyzed by fear that they were loath to follow me into the dark passage? Or perhaps their sense of self-preservation took over and they ran back down the stairs, preferring to make a retreat than to assist me. That seemed more likely a happenstance.

The passage ended in another chamber. How vast it was I could not see. I was in complete darkness.

I could still smell the vile gasbag though, and I could hear air moving... whistling almost, as if passing through wetted lips.

Using only my ears, I followed the sound until I was right on top of it. I reached down and felt the loathsome creature. It was collapsed on the floor.

The thing's odor was almost unbearable. It was coated with a slimy ooze... what passed for the thing's blood, I assumed... I felt its eyestalks. They were stirring. I grabbed hold of them. I did not know if it could see in the dark but I wasn't going to leave that to chance. With two quick strokes I severed the stalks, tossing the eyes aside.

The thing let out a scream then, a high-pitched shriek that was like the sound that the stone sentries had made, though not quite as loud.

It startled me, nonetheless. I stabbed at the deflated bag again and again until the shrieking stopped.

I was exhausted. The stench from the thing's ruined corpse was overwhelming. I couldn't make it to my feet so I crawled in the dark, not knowing in what direction I was moving, not caring. The only thing I wanted to do was move far enough away from the putrid smell.

I bumped into a pillar. I crawled around it, then leaned against it. I got my legs around it and let them stretch out. My chest heaved. I tried to breath in through my mouth and out through my nose but that did not help much.

So the men of Abelton had abandoned me to my fate. I was unreasonably angry about that. "*Fish fuckers...*" I managed to gasp through the fiery pain in my lower extremities.

I tried to console myself that I would probably have done the same thing in their position. Except, that didn't really square with my actions the many times I had been in their position. Even if I did begin our relationship by threatening the life of the man's son. Only he didn't know that I would not have actually cut the lad's throat.

Nevertheless, it stung. I can't lie.

"*Fish fuckers...*"

I don't know how long I sat against that pillar, ruminating. Too long, obviously, because I was still there when the painted men showed up with torches.

CHAPTER 7: HYE TAUGN

THEY WERE the same short, dark skinned folk who had attacked us earlier. I could barely stand up, but I managed to make it to my feet, holding out my one dagger in as threatening a manner as I could manage.

They were wary, circling me and the pillar that I was still leaning on for support. Their markings made them look like fearsome goblins or trolls, especially in the flickering torchlight. The illumination also reflected off the metal of the swords, axes and knives they carried.

How many of their fellow creatures I killed I could not remember, but I wagered that these dozen or so had the numbers burned into their thoughts. They closed in. I waved my dagger at them menacingly, but I think they sensed that the game was up.

They surrounded me. I felt arms coming in from everywhere, wrapping around my arms and legs. I heard my dagger clatter to the stone floor. I cursed the creatures then, and I struggled to get free, but it was for naught. They had me firmly. I was carried from the chamber.

Their torches illuminated the ceilings of the passages through which I was carried. In the torchlight, I could see multi-legged insects scuttling around in the sudden brightness. I saw worms blindly undulating their way across the ceiling stones. Even spiders as big as my head occupied the corners.

I wondered if they had been there all the time while our fellowship of champions had moved throughout the labyrinth. Had we only failed to notice them simply because we did not bother to cast our eyes upwards? I shuddered at the thought.

Along the way my band of bearers made several turns left and right. I was completely lost at this point. I had no idea how deep within the maze I had been carried.

After a particularly long passage that felt like it was sloping downwards, my bearers entered a very large chamber. From my position on my back I could see the low ceiling give way, sloping higher until it was lost in the darkness above me. The chamber was roughly circular. Torches and lanterns ringed the walls and I could see growths climbing up them, like tree roots.

My bearers slowed and came to a stop. I could see them looking at something and, despite their ghastly painted faces I thought I could see fear in their eyes.

Before I could apprehend what was happening my bearers turned me sideways and then unceremoniously relieved themselves of my burden.

They dropped me into some kind of pit. Before a scream could erupt from my lips, I unceremoniously hit the ground and the air was pushed from my lungs.

I had landed on a leafy, rooted tangle. I turned around and tried to get my arms and legs underneath me but the tangled undergrowth seemed to move whenever I did. I saw insects crawling and flittering among the tangled mass. I saw caterpillars and small rodents, snakes and lizards, scuttling around the sinewy growth.

The roots were coated with moss that made grabbing hold of them tricky, even if they were to stay still. Between the slippery growth and the undulating movement, I could only roll around. It felt like I was being tossed by the heaving waves of the ocean.

"You come in to my house," a voice boomed above me. It echoed around the chamber as if amplified by some sort of trumpet. It had an odd, hissing sibilance that I found unsettling. "...*unbidden... unwanted... unwelcome*."

I tried to turn my head to pinpoint the direction from which the voice originated, but it just seemed to come from everywhere.

"You attacked a harmless spore. You killed several of my house guards..."

"They attacked us!" I protested. "We were defending ourselves..."

"YOU ARE NOT WANTED HERE!" the voice boomed.

There was only one being to whom the voice could conceivably belong. "Am I addressing Hye Taugn, the dread wizard of the Labyrinth?"

The voice was silent for a moment. "You know who I am. What of it?"

"Allow me to introduce myself," I said, vainly trying to climb to my feet. "I am Poet, from the Southern Kingdom of Trigassa, though I have traveled far in my..."

"Your identity is of no interest to me," Hye Taughn replied, curtly. "You are an interloper... an infection in my realm and you must be eradicated."

"I was sent here to kill you," I said. "...by the citizens of Beyargmunn."

At the mention of that name the voice rumbled a wordless growl. As the voice rumbled so, too, did the tangled growth underneath me undulate more violently.

"UNGRATEFUL WRETCHES!" Hye Taughn roared.

I suddenly had the awful sense that I was not only in the presence of the Wizard of the Labyrinth, but I was in the foul sorcerer's clutches.

"How can you expect them to be grateful for the blight you brought to their land?" I said, trying to climb to the edge of the pit where it looked to me like roots and other growths climbed the walls. If they climbed to the lip of the pit then there was a chance that I could climb out.

"BLIGHT!??" the wizard roared. "What blight? I brought life to a lifeless valley!"

Well that was a different story from the one that I had been given. "They said you blighted the crops and sickened the animals and demanded a tribute of half their bounty to lift the curse."

"LIES!" Hye Taugn bellowed. The nest or roots quavered underneath me and I almost lost my footing. "Their lands were barren when I arrived in this valley! They themselves had stripped it bare. I offered to bring it all back to life. All I asked was enough food to feed the ones that I had brought with me."

"Beasts. Fearsome unnatural creatures, they said. Ones that you used to keep them in line."

The tangly growth shook again. "Outrageous! OUTRAGEOUS!" the wizard said, naked fury choking his voice. "You've seen my guards. They're men, like you. They are loyal and brave. All I asked was for the villagers to welcome them, to let them live among them. But they were suspicious and distrustful. They would not accept the men in their village, nor their wives or their children. They attacked them in the night. My people had to flee to the labyrinth for their own protection. And so I required food to keep them alive."

"Half of what they grow?" I asked.

"No! NO! It was so little at first. But even without being able to live in the sunlight, they have grown and flourished here. There are more of them now than there were two hundred years ago."

"Two hundred years?" I said, incredulous. "You're two hundred years old?"

"I was over a thousand years old when I arrived here," the wizard said, his voice and his roots calming. "I had made many enemies in my time. I needed a place to retire to where I wasn't always looking over my shoulder. This place suited my needs. The natural caves were easily adapted into chambers and passages. The people carved the stone and decorated the walls with sculptures of the animals from their far lands. They built this chamber for me as my body became one with the earth."

"How?" I asked. "How can your body be one with the earth?"

The wizard did not reply, but a great tangle of roots began to undulate in the center of the chamber. They writhed and moved aside as if something were pushing them away from underneath. Slowly a figure pushed its way through the tangle of roots. A ghastly white head with a long tangle of stringy hair sat atop scrawny pale shoulders. Two arms, cadaverously thin, broke through the tangle and pulled the rest of the wizard up.

There wasn't much left of him below the chest. The rest of his body seemed to either be intertwined with the roots and branches or it just didn't exist anymore. All that was left of him was a tangle of roots, shoots, moss and dirt.

The wizard's face was like that of a corpse, pale and shriveled. His eyes were still intact, but the orbs were dry and covered with dirt. The tangled roots rose. His body loomed above me.

Whether he could see my shocked expression I could not tell. He did not face me directly. I got the impression that he was aware of his surroundings through some kind of unnatural sense.

"You think me diminished, I know. My servants and guards feel the same way – that I am somehow only the shell of the man that I once was. They do not understand how I am so much more now than this remnant of a shell could ever have been. I can feel the water as it moves beneath the stone. I can feel the sunlight through the growths above. I am greater now than I ever was, even at the height of my mastery of the magik arts."

"You are... terrifying to behold," I admitted.

"Your tiny mind cannot conceive a fraction of my existence," he spat. "You and your companions have run up against a force that cannot be killed by mere blades or clubs. You were foolish to think that you could kill something as transcendent as I am."

"Well, I was against it from the beginning, if I'm being perfectly candid," I said. "My companion was convinced against my better judgment. Speaking of my companions... do you know if they yet live?"

Aye," the wizard said. "They live. My people overwhelmed their numbers, but you..." he pointed a bony finger in my direction. "...you proved problematic."

"Yes, well, one of my companions decided to send me down to the lake to swim with your monster," I said.

The wizard let out a wry chuckle that sounded to my ears like sodden branches rubbing together. It sent a chill down my spine.

"So, you encountered the Lurker?" he said. "I'm surprised. Few men escape Kanal's embrace."

I shrugged. "She seemed not to want to share her bath. I obliged her by taking my leave as swiftly as I was able."

The wizard laughed again. "You are an amusing creature, and quite resourceful."

"Not resourceful enough, I fear." I said. "After all, I too, was captured in the end. And now I am here, at your mercy. I am unarmed and barely able to keep my feet."

"Weapons... yes..." the wizard said with what sounded like a sigh. The roots moved the wizard's body higher and over to the edge of the pit. The wizard reached out for something over the lip. When the roots retreated the wizard held my dagger in his bony hands.

I steeled myself for the inevitable death, a nasty end at the magician's hands. I suppose it was always destined to be like this. I was only annoyed that I would end up being disemboweled by my own weapon. It had been a faithful companion through many years of my travels and it irked me that it would, at the last, be turned against me.

"This is a rare blade," Hye Taugn said, delicately fingering the weapon. "These were the specialty of a blacksmith whose acquaintance I made in Surunna, which I believe to be a neighboring city of Trigassa."

I nodded cautiously. "It is," I confirmed. "I have been there."

The wizard nodded. "The blacksmith made two daggers from a single piece of steel. Each was meant to be twinned with another."

"I did have the twin," I confessed "Sadly, I lost it in a misadventure in Kandra."

"So you did have two? Twin daggers? I would dearly have loved to have seen them."

I let out a rueful laugh. "I would love to have shown them to you. I would give anything to have the twin back. They were as alike to each other as any two things could be."

"It is rare for the twins to have traveled together. The blacksmith started his trade more than nine hundred years ago. He made only a small number of twins. For someone to have one of these daggers is a rare thing today. For someone to have had two... that is rarer still. Where did you find them?"

"They were gifted to me," I said. "By the Empress Vivisana." As I said her name I felt a wave of sadness and longing overcome me. The Empress, Sirtago's mother, was the closest thing I ever had to a mother. It had been a long time since I had laid eyes on her. I felt a sudden, overwhelming feeling of loss.

"She must have held you in high esteem," the wizard said. "Surviving twins were rare enough several lifetimes ago. For someone to have possessed twins as recently as one lifetime ago... well, they are a rare prize... rarer than anything I have seen in many hundreds of years."

I could not speak just then. Emotion overwhelmed me. My throat would not allow words to pass. I stared at the ghastly apparition in silence.

"Here," Hye Taugn said suddenly, and handed me the dagger, hilt first. I stared at it in disbelief for a long moment, then gingerly retrieved it from his bony hand.

The roots shifted again. Hye Taugn's wasted form lifted up high into the darkness of the cavern's ceiling. For many moments I watched as the long root tendrils twisted about, undulating to and fro.

Then the tendrils began to fall. Hye Taugn descended from the darkness back into the light of the torches and lamps. He clutched an item in his hand. He held it out so I could see it. It was a dagger in a sheath. It was much the same as mine in length and width and, I assumed in weight. There were clear differences, but a casual glance would not have revealed them unless one was as familiar as I was with the blades.

"The blacksmith himself gifted me with a pair of these near the end of his life. Payment for services rendered. They were not as valuable then as they are now. I lost the twin in a petty gambling match a few years after the blacksmith's death. Had I known then what their value would have been now, I would not have been so careless with it." The wizard heaved a great sigh and the tendrils and roots moved with it, even the ones beneath my feet. "Such is the way of the world. The things that matter... the things that endure... we treat like mere trinkets. It is only after they are lost and gone that we realize the great value that they had for us."

He held the dagger out to me. I stared uncomprehending.

"Take it," he said. "Cherish it. It is a treasure beyond value to have two such rare things, even if they are not actual twins. Go on!"

He thrust it towards me and I took it, marveling at the workmanship of the metal and the leatherwork. To think that this... and mine... were almost nine hundred years old. My mind reeled trying to fathom it.

I looked up at the ghastly wizard, his root coiled umbilical. "Am I to be spared?"

The wizard let out another chilling laugh. "You were never for the chop, if that's what you were thinking. I've killed many men in my time... too many... and good ones. I am no longer in the habit of taking lives unless I absolutely must."

I nodded in gratitude. "I have taken lives this day – and the previous – that I regret taking. Stouthearted men defend your household. I rue the circumstances that led to their deaths at my hand and those of my companions. Are they to be spared as well?"

"No harm will come to your companions, not from my hand nor from those of my people. I have seen to that."

I nodded. "I am grateful for your mercy."

"It is not mercy, but weariness that stays my hand," the wizard said. "I have lived too long. My time has been drawing to a close for longer than most mortal men have been alive. I have held on for the sake of my people. When I pass from this world all the magik will pass with me. All the life that I have had I have given to the land. I have caused the crops to grow. I have grown the flowers that attract the beasts from the smallest insect to deer and the boars. When I am gone, all that, too will vanish."

"All of it?"

"Oh, not right away. Perhaps some proper tending will cause it to linger a while yet, but all will fade in time."

The wizard grew quiet then. The twisted roots holding him up slowly lowered him until I was face to face with his sightless, and yet, all-seeing eyes.

"I will ask a boon of you," he said, his voice raspy now and almost a whisper.

"Ask," I said. "I will fulfill it, if it is within my power to do so."

After a long moment of silence in which I almost believed he was gone, he rasped: "Take care of my people. See that they come to no harm. The people of the village will not brook their presence. They never have. I fear for their safety. If the villagers will not help them here then take them away. Take them somewhere where they will not come to harm."

FOR A LONG time we sat still. His eyes never closed, but his root entangled body stopped writhing and twisting. There was a feeling of eerie stillness.

I sat for an hour or more, watching his lifeless form before I stood. The roots and tendrils underneath my feet were still now. It was easier to move. I walked to the wall of the pit and I climbed out.

His guards were nowhere to be seen. An unnatural silence had settled on the labyrinth. As I walked, clutching my daggers, all I could hear was the sound of my footfalls echoing off the stone walls.

There were several passages leading out of the great chamber, but only one that sloped upwards. The others either led down or remained level. To be sure, any passage, even the one that I had traversed earlier, was bound to get me hopelessly lost, but I could not stay here among the dying vegetation. I took the upward sloping passage.

The passage looked different from on my feet as opposed to on my back, I could see narrow passages leading off. I ignored them though, and continued upwards.

Before long I heard voices coming from somewhere ahead. The passage opened up into a long chamber. The room was full of the wizard's people. They sat on the floor, silently weeping.

"*GWUT'S HAIRY ASS!*" I heard Sirtago's voice at the back of the chamber. He was seated at a long wooden table with the rest of my fellow "champions". "We thought you were dead!"

"As did I, several times over!" I replied, sauntering over.

Sirtago got to his feet and surprised me by taking me into an embrace. This almost took the wind from my lungs and caused the daggers I'd been clutching to slip from my grasp and clatter to the stones of the floor. I returned his affection, though not quite so enthusiastically.

He saw the daggers at his feet, stooped to pick them up for me, an uncharacteristically unselfish gesture, which surprised me once again. As Sirtago bent to pick them up I saw Jemmy at the table drinking from a flagon alongside Golath and the others. My mood turned black at the sight of the small man.

"You found another one?" Sirtago asked, handing me the two daggers.

"You didn't kill the dwarf?" I countered.

Sirtago regarded me quizzically. "Was I supposed to?"

"He pushed me off the ledge. Didn't you see?"

"He pushed you?"

"He kicked me in the chest"

Sirtago shook his head. "From where we stood, it just looked like you'd missed your grip and fell." He turned to look at the dwarf and let out a snort. "The little imp swore up and down he'd tried to grab hold of you as you fell. I thought it the bravest thing, for he would certainly have been dragged down along with you if he had." Sirtago glowered at the dwarf. I was certain I could see the imp blanch.

"The little shit," Sirtago said. "I'll cut him in two right now if you want."

I shook my head "No," I said. "I'll enjoy watching him squirm for a bit."

CHAPTER 8: THE DEAL

APPARENTLY my fellow champions had all been captured after they had made it over the bridge. Hye Taugn's people had overwhelmed their numbers and taken their weapons.

"But there were six of you," I said. "Mighty warriors all, and you were overwhelmed by an unruly mob of men half your size?"

Sirtago shrugged. "Well, it turns out our fellow champions oversold their abilities."

"Really?" I said without surprise.

"The dwarf's knees gave out and the giant claimed his head was beset by a dreadful pain. Truthfully, giant though he is, he couldn't mount an attack to save his life. I'd wager he was little more than a farm boy not too long ago. The sisters were equally unskilled. All they had was a few practiced moves, but no real combat knowledge. Their story about being trained by the palace guard was a complete fabrication. *They aren't even sisters!*"

"I'm shocked," I said, though in truth I wasn't. The not-sisters sported bruises, black eyes, and their once braided hair was in a frightful state of dishevelment. The tracks of tears stained their dirty cheeks. They looked like they were well ready to go home, wherever that actually was.

"Only Geyero fought with any ability," Sirtago went on. "She kept on, receiving cut after cut, until she was almost ready to pass out from loss of blood. Even then it took almost a dozen of our attackers to finally subdue her."

I hoped she hadn't told them about only allowing men to bed her who could defeat her in combat. That would be a lot of obligation.

Me, they took for dead. I could have walked out of the labyrinth and they would have all been none the wiser, had I not insisted on going back in.

"That's what loyalty gets you," Sirtago snorted a laugh.

I told the others about the wizard's dying request. No one seemed keen on fulfilling it. I had not expected them to. I reasoned that as I was the only one to hear the request, it would fall to me to fulfill it.

I fully intended to do just that, but Geyero stepped forward, bandaged and a trifle unsteady. "I will fulfill that promise," she said. "I know roughly the country from whence they come. It is near Baurebec."

I shook my head and was about to protest (for form's sake, at least), but she stopped me. "I have not seen my homeland for many years and I never expected to return. Perhaps this task is the impetus I needed. I will stay with them, and help them to make the passage back to their homelands."

AS FOR the treasure... well, the men of Abelton proved correct. There was no hoard of treasure. Hye Taugn had brought a few tokens... memories of his thousand years as a feared sorcerer... to his labyrinthine home. His people showed us the room in which he kept them. They were mere trinkets, covered in thick layers of dust. They had no obvious value, though, like the dagger he had gifted me, I was certain that each item had a provenance that, with Hye Taugn's passing, was likely lost to time.

I saw Jemmy and Golath circling a small sculpture of a bull. They were arguing about the value of the few gemstones that were inlaid along the bull's horns.

When he saw me approach, Jemmy tried to back away, but he found himself literally in a corner of the trophy room. The bull on one side and two solid oak chests on the other blocked his escape.

I slid my dagger from its sheath and felt a great joy upon seeing the abject fear in the little imp's eyes. "What are you going to do?" he asked in a quavering voice.

"What do you think I'm going to do?" I asked with a smile.

"Now, wait, just a minute," the dwarf stammered. "Sure, I was angry, but I didn't mean for you to fall..."

Golath stepped between us. "You leave him alone!"

I ignored the giant and ducked down so I was face to face with the little man. "What did you think was going to happen when you kicked me in the chest?"

That made Golath start. He turned to look at his diminutive companion. "Did you push him off the ledge?"

Jemmy's eyes flicked up to Golath's. "He was insulting me! He compared me to shit!"

"That was a trifle unfair..." I admitted. "...to shit. Shit, at least, is useful. It helps crops grow, as opposed to you, you little pygmy, who is of no use to anyone!"

Jemmy's eyes shifted back to mine. He shook his head and tried to disappear into the corner in which he was trapped. "I didn't mean to hurt anyone! Please, don't kill me," he grabbed on to one of Golath's legs, but the giant shook him off.

"Did you push him off the ledge?" Golath asked again, leaning down, looming over the dwarf.

Jemmy stared up at his only friend in the world. "I didn't mean to hurt him! I didn't mean to..."

"I told you, you can't kill the other champions," Golath spat at the dwarf. Then he stood up and walked away, leaving his friend to his fate.

"Golath!" Jemmy called, his face utterly crestfallen. "Where are you going? Golath! He's going to kill me!"

The pathetic imp turned back to me as I stepped closer, my dagger held casually in my hand.

"Please..." he said, shaking his head. Tears limned his lower lids and all the color drained from his face. "Please don't kill me! I didn't mean to... I'm sorry... I'm sorry... I'm sorry..."

"Yes," I said, leaning down until I was nose-to-nose with him. "You are sorry. You're the sorriest creature I think I have ever seen. Yes, I taunted you. I insulted you. I made you look a fool, though to be honest it wasn't hard, as you do not seem averse to making yourself look like a fool. Perhaps I have not been kind, and though I threatened it, I certainly did not try to kill you."

The little man was openly weeping now. The joy at seeing his fear soured within me. "What kind of warrior are you?" I asked.

"I'm not a warrior!" he said, blubbering, snot running out of his nose. "I was a court jester!"

"A what?"

"I was a fool for a nobleman. I used to make him laugh. But I made fun of the wrong man... one of his advisers didn't take well to being the butt of my japes, so he got me sacked. When I found Golath, he was starving. We stole food from a village. A villager startled us and we ran off, but we'd got the whole place worked up. They thought that we were brigands. So we stole some weapons and some armor and presented ourselves as warriors who could rid the village of their enemies. Which we did, because the brigands were just us."

I laughed. I couldn't help myself. "How many times did you pull that trick?"

Jemmy dropped his eyes and shrugged. "We lost count. It got us a fair bit of coin and the gratitude of several villages... and their maidens."

I heaved a sigh and stood up. I sheathed my dagger.

"You're not going to kill me?" the dwarf asked.

I shook my head. "My one wish for you is that you live a very, very long life."

The dwarf scowled up at me. "*Awww...* that's all I need."

I turned and walked away, leaving the dwarf truly alone.

GEYARO had begun the work of organizing the exodus of Hye Taugn's people. There were hundreds of them... men, women and children... and most of them were half-starved.

"Hye Taugn did make an agreement with the people of Beyargmunn," Geyero told us, after she'd got the story from a few of the elders. "The wizard wanted his people to live in the valley, but the villagers wouldn't abide them. So he came to an agreement for a portion of their crops. But as the population grew within the labyrinth, there was resistance among the villagers to increase Hye Taugn's portion."

I let out a rueful laugh. "So that is why they have been seeking champions to rid them of the wizard. They spread stories of a treasure to attract those brave enough to dare the labyrinth."

HYE TAUGN'S people showed us the way back to the village. I was a little surprised that it was not the main gate in which we entered, but a small passageway that came out below. The tunnel ended in a wooden door that the people opened. On the other side was a cart laden with a meager pile of provisions. Mostly it was root vegetables, a few bags of grain and some fruits that looked like they were on the turn. There were some cuts of meat, but they looked like they were taken from the scrawniest of beasts. Hye Taugn's people pulled the wagon into the tunnel while Sirtago and I, a tired Nikit and Kaylam, and Golath and Jemmy, who were not talking much now – either to us or to each other – walked out into the sunshine of a new day.

We were back in Beyargmunn proper within a few moments. I could not fathom why we couldn't have just used that entrance to the labyrinth. Perhaps the village leaders did not want to risk us seeing how meager their "tribute" to Hye Taugn actually was. That would have undermined the lies they'd told us with their entertainments. It was also a less impressive setting for the solemn ceremony they'd cooked up for us. It would have been a damn sight easier to open those wooden doors than it had been to lever open the main gate.

The village was quiet in the early morning. I saw a few people about their business, but no one paid us any mind. The common was peaceful. Chickens, geese, sheep and goats went about their business clucking, honking and bleating happily. We saw a handful of women entering the great long hall carrying baskets. "I need an ale," Sirtago said. "And some breakfast." He wandered towards the longhouse.

Golath wandered towards the great tree in the center of the square. The stone dais had been taken away. The giant sat upon the grass, his back resting against the thick trunk.

Perhaps it was my imagination, but I felt that somehow the tree did not look as alive as it had two days previously. The leaves, it seemed, were not quite as deeply green as they had been before. Had Hye Taugn's magic been keeping it lush? Was it destined to fade now that he was gone?

Jemmy wandered aimlessly around the common. I could not see Nikit or Kaylam. I assumed they had found a quiet place to sleep off their first taste of adventure.

Then I spied Laise, carrying a basket and walking towards one of the smaller buildings that ringed the Common. I hurried to catch up with her. Before I could she was out of the sunshine and into the structure's darkness. I entered after her, had to pause while my eyes adjusted to the sudden darkness.

As my eyes grew accustomed, I saw her standing with another figure... a man. He was sitting at a table. The basket she had brought was set down before him. Her head was bent towards him when she caught sight of me. "Master Poet? You're alive?" Laise said. She stood up straight and took two conspicuous steps away from the man. I recognized him then as one of the village elders, Fiddick, the one who had served as master of ceremonies at the feast.

"I am alive," I said. "Which is more than I can say for Hye Taugn."

The two of them stared at me, dumbfounded. "You killed the wizard, then?" Laise asked.

"Was that not what you wanted?" I asked. "You sent me and my companions...your champions... into the labyrinth to kill the wizard, yet you seem surprised when I tell you that he is dead."

She blinked. "I... I... I didn't expect you would return so soon," she said hesitantly. She glanced at Fiddick.

"Go fetch Master Theiss," Fiddick said quietly. "...then go back to the watch tower. I'll be there presently," Laise looked uncertain, but she nodded and ran off, holding her skirts.

I watched her go, then turned back to Fiddick. The man stood up and approached me with a disingenuous smile. "The wizard is dead, you say? This is happy news! Happy news indeed!"

"Who are you?" I asked. "Are you the head man of this village? The... mayor?"

Fiddick shook his head, amused. "I'm the watch. I man the watchtower," he said.

"You are the watch?" I said. "But I thought Laise..."

"Laise is my wife," he said.

I was dumbfounded at this and must have looked it. "Your wife?"

Fiddick laughed. His bearing changed, then, as if dropping a pretense "Yes. What did you think? Did you think she was really taken with you?"

I did not answer, but my expression must have betrayed me.

"All the women and men of the village know what they must do to keep our champions happy. They tease, to be sure, but they know how not to let it go too far."

"But what about...?"

"Your companion, Sirtago's three kitchen maids? Two of those three are married. And the one who isn't doesn't like men. She prefers the company of ladies."

Just then Master Theiss bundled his way through the door, led by the boy, Yolus. "I have heard that the Champions have returned," Master Theiss said.

"Indeed, Master Theiss," Fiddick said. "Poet is here with us now. He brings us welcome news. The wizard is dead."

"Dead?" Master Theiss repeated. "Are you certain?"

"He died before my eyes," I said. "I watched the life leave his body."

An expression of profound joy came over the old blind man. Tears began to stream from his milk-white eyes. "After all these years," he said. "We are rid of the troublesome menace."

I felt an anger building inside me. These villagers had nothing to fear from the wizard or his people. They never did. They were never living in fear. I had begun to suspect that they simply did not want to live with the obligations that the wizard's presence implied.

"There is the matter of Hye Taugn's people," I said.

"What?" Master Theiss said, distracted from his tears. "What matter...?"

"His people. They're leaving, you see?"

Master Theiss blinked. "Well, that's... that's wonderful."

"But until they do leave they will need to be cared for... properly..." I said.

"Well... naturally..." Master Theiss said, though he did not mean the words he uttered.

"Of course," Fiddick assured. "They will be taken care of." Fiddick, I noted, was better at dissembling than Master Theiss was.

"You see," I said. "Geyero... you remember your champion, Geyero?"

"Of course,"

"Geyero will be overseeing their passage back to their homelands. Until she is able to organize their exodus, you will, of course, share the great bounty that you enjoy here, will you not? The same hospitality that you showed all of us champions, should be extended to Hye Taugn's people, would you not agree?"

I saw Fiddick blanch at my words, though I give him credit for not losing the false smile he pointed in my direction. "Of course, we agree. Champion Geyero will be able to expect our full cooperation in this matter."

"That's good," I said, returning his disingenuous smile with my own, feral one. "Because Sirtago and I will be coming back this way and we will be be keen to see Geyero's progress with her task. We would be most displeased... most displeased... were we to find that she had not enjoyed the fullness of support that she so richly deserves. Believe me, it isn't easy to cut an entire village's worth of throats, but we've done it before. And we're perfectly capable of doing it again."

Fiddick's expression never changed, but I could see by his eyes that he understood exactly what I was saying to him. Master Theiss did not even try to hide his shocked expression.

I turned as if to go, but then stopped and turned back to the hapless pair. "By the way," I said, raising my finger to them. "It turns out that the horde of treasure that you spoke so convincingly about, Master Theiss, does not actually exist."

Master Theiss started, the color suddenly draining from his face. "Indeed...?" he stammered. "I'm... I'm shocked..."

"I thought you would be," I said, wishing fervently that the old liar could see the smile upon my lips.

Fiddick forced a smile that he did not genuinely feel. "We appreciate that this is a devastating development for you... for all of us. We certainly do not want to see you go unrewarded for the monumental and profound service that you have done for us... for all of us... this day. Would one-hundred Kroner be reward enough for...?"

"Five hundred," I said. "Gold coins."

Fiddick sucked in a breath. "Five... hundred?"

"For each of us," I said. "Including Geyero."

The color and the smiles drained from both their faces.

I shrugged. "It's a small price to pay to be allowed to continue living in this wondrously rich valley. Even more rich now that it is free of the burden of Hye Taugn's presence. Wouldn't you agree?"

They said nothing, only stared at me with open mouthed incredulity.

I lifted the cloth on the basket that Laise had brought in. Bread, cheese, fruits and cold meats. A fine breakfast. I laid the cloth back and tucked the basket under my arm.

"One more thing," I said as I made my way towards the door. "On the other side of the rock are a number of small villages. The people of those villages have long regarded this valley with envious eyes. I've met those people. I've seen those eyes. They are attached to bellies that are very hungry. Now that the wizard is dead, there is nothing stopping them from finding their way through the labyrinth and into this fine, rich valley. If I were you, I would try to cultivate good relations with your neighbors on this side of the rock. Make good friends with those that have strong arms and strong swords. They might be more amenable to coming to your aid if they feel something for you... other than that you covet their coin."

I ATE some of the bread and a bit of the fruit. I found Jemmy sullenly sitting alone. He looked up at me warily. I passed the basket over and suggested that he might want to find a friend and offer to share it. I walked away, hoping he would do the right thing, but honestly, not caring if he did.

I SAT in the sunshine on a stump I found lying on its side. I assumed it was Master Theiss' stump, the one he made use of the night before the feast, so I was quite content to let it hold my rump off the ground.

I was admiring both my daggers, the old one and its new companion. They were much alike, though not exactly twins. Still, I reckoned I could fight effectively with them, nonetheless.

I saw Sirtago coming from the feasting hall. I could tell by his gait that he was unsatisfied. I smiled and looked down at the daggers which were twins and yet not twins.

They were much like Sirtago and I. Born from different mothers and fathers, raised in different circumstances, brought together by fate. We were now as alike as any two brothers could be.

IT HAD not taken Sirtago long to comprehend the villager's true attitudes towards their champions, now that we had rid them of their burdensome wizard. He was quite ready to move on by the time they made good on my suggestion of a reward for accomplishing that task.

A bag full of five hundred gold coins would keep us in ale for a very long time. It is, however, very heavy and not something we were keen on lugging with us as we left the village of Beyargmunn.

"So what do we do?" I asked, hefting my bag of coins, appraising its weight.

Sirtago adjusted his mask, then stared up at the snowy mountains that loomed over the valley. "I say we steal a couple of their nags, ride back up the mountainside to *The Wandering Goat*, order two rooms, two wenches, and the largest mutton roast they have. We'll drink ourselves insensate, then decide where we go after that."

"My dear friend," I said. "There are times when I believe that you are the wisest man in the world."

The Daughter of Lilith

Michael Ehart

West of the Euphrates River, in the seventh year of the reign of Shalmaneser I of Assur, 1267 B.C.

"LOOK at this." Ninshi knelt over the corpse where it lay in the dirt of the torn-up camp. She pointed with her sword at the wounds in the man's torso.

Miri wrinkled her nose. "How long have they been dead?"

Ninshi shrugged. "A day. Two maybe. The sun has ripened them considerably."

Miri nodded agreement. "Considerably." She bent closer. "Looks like claw marks." She moved to another tattered figure. "Hmm... I would guess bandits, from the ragged appearance and many, many weapons. They didn't seem to do them much good."

Ninshi rose and dusted herself off. "None of our concern, I think. Still, if we hadn't backtracked a day after leaving the caravan, we wouldn't have found them. The nearest city is Sumugan. I doubt we can make it there before tomorrow, but it would be best, I think, if we were to put some distance between whatever did this and us."

Ninshi sounded unconcerned, but Miri could see that there was something that bothered her, something that she wasn't ready to share with her.

Five summers ago, Ninshi on a whim had bought Miri from a slave trader, intending to free her. Instead she had adopted her, and Miri, who was now perhaps thirteen summers, had travelled with her ever since. Already she was taller than her mother, though thinner. Her mother was small but muscled from her steady training with sword and spear. Miri already showed signs of a longer, leaner look. Her memories of her birth family were starting to grow vague, but she remembered her birth mother as tall and willowy, and her father even taller.

Ninshi mounted her horse and set off at a brisk pace, and Miri followed, frowning.

NINSHI froze. Miri dropped the rabbit leg she had been gnawing at and stood, stringing her bow in one smooth motion. Another swift action had an arrow from her nearby quiver nocked and drawn.

Miri looked in the direction her mother was staring. She could see nothing in the darkness past the firelight except the vague movement of the trees in the light wind.

Ninshi moved slightly to the right, still staring. Her right hand held the spear they had practiced with earlier in the evening. Miri had not seen her take it up.

"You have followed us for several days. Since we left Ikizepe, in fact. Who are you and what do you need of us?" Ninshi's voice was harsh, but strong.

"You know me, sister." The voice came from the shadows, sibilant and low.

"*Lilu!*" Ninshi spat. "Have you come to die then?"

"No. I wish only to speak to you, to deliver a message. Will you bid me enter?"

"I can hear you quite well from where you stand."

The lilu emitted something very much like a sigh. "I must first tell you a story. I think you know it already, but there are a few things that may be new to your ears. Let me sit next to your fire and I will obey the laws of guesting, and offer you no harm, nor the one you travel with."

"Why would I want to do that?" Ninshi's voice was harsh, but steady.

Once again, the lilu gave something close to a sigh. "If not by the rules of guesting, then, by truce. I truly mean you no harm. I know what you can do, and believe my words, I have the greatest respect for your ability to do me harm."

Ninshi nodded, and the darkness shredded and became an ape-like figure, sickly white, with a small head and an extra set of arms. It was roughly formed, as if molded by a child out of clay. It moved to the fire, and sat, forming, and folding itself into a shape better suited for sitting. It was silent for a moment as its shape changed, then spoke.

"It is said that our mistress was First Man's wife, but when her womb produced no offspring, he cast her aside. She knows no death, having never drawn Enki's wrath, but wanders the desert, friendless and alone. Able to bear no children herself, she snatches the still-born daughters of the desert tribes, breathing life into them. These she raises as her daughters. We live a very long time, many lifetimes of men, doing her bidding as she commands. Because we have tasted death before drawing our first breath, our new forms have no set shape and we have no names. We are the Lilu.

"Over the years, the barren women of many tribes have worshiped my mistress as a goddess, which she may be. One of the priestesses called upon her to send her daughter to avenge a wrong done to her. I am that daughter, who you defeated in battle. You nearly killed me, you know. While we fought, both of us were wounded, and our blood exchanged."

The lilu's face shifted, then, forming to the shape of Ninshi's, but not quite. "I gave the message to my mistress. She was displeased, of course, but in the end she agreed. She will no longer send her daughters to plague the maidens of Ikizepe."

"But...we are linked by blood. I can see some of your thoughts and feel the great pain and the horror of what you bear, the beast, the Great Manthycore whom you serve with murder and death. I cannot help, I cannot silence what I hear, and I cannot return to my sisters. You are my sister now, until one of us ends, however long that may be."

Miri looked at Ninshi in amazement. She was just sitting, her face set as she listened.

Ninshi stood. She moved her hand to her sword but did not draw it. "I don't need another to watch after, and I don't need a servant. I most especially don't need some monster of the night following me and making my life even more difficult. Those bandits we found today. An example of your work. Leave me, us alone. You may go in peace, but if I see you again, I will kill you. Find someone else to haunt."

"They followed the caravan and then they followed you. They hunted you. I killed them for you."

"I don't need a protector, either."

"I am neither protector, servant nor ward," the lilu said. "I am now your sister, in blood and intention. This child you watch over is now my blood as well, though neither of us are bound by birth to her. I told you that I hear your thought. I know that you serve the Beast that Devours Men, the Manthycore. I know that you serve unwillingly and seek your freedom from your long curse. I know that you have lived these many lives of men, murdering to feed that beast. I have heard songs of you, sung by men by campfire as I lay in the dark, hungry, and yearning. And I know that you love this adopted child and would do anything to protect her."

Miri saw Ninshi glance at her, an expression she had never seen on her mother's drawn face. It was an odd combination of rage and something else. Miri could see that Ninshi was very angry, but could not read her face any clearer, even after years together.

"Can you tell me then, monster, how I may free myself? Because if you can't, there is nothing I need of you."

The lilu shifted a little. "I know many things, have heard many things. I have walked this earth even longer than you have. But I have no answer. Your freedom from this curse is beyond anything I can do, or anything I can tell you."

"Then go!" Ninshi took a half step towards the lilu, stopped herself.

"I will. But I cannot leave you altogether. My mistress said that I must commit an act of love to be free from you, or to walk with you until the end of one or both. Only then can I be my own being, to do as I please. This I have never been but think I would like to try. I will be waiting for your call, for when you need me, I will come, and only then." The lilu shifted form, her arms became a second pair of legs, and she loped off into the night, leaving only a sickly-sweet scent behind.

"Let us break camp. The moon is full and the road plain. If we ride all night, we can be in Sumugan by dawn."

"SUMUGAN is an obscure god of the plain," Ninshi said as they walked through the sagging gates of the city. The mud brick gateposts had eroded away, and the great bronze hinges were green and pitted with age. "He was married to some fertility goddess or other, I think. I haven't been here for many years but seem to recall that there is a temple to him somewhere in the city, which makes sense as it was named for him. Still there can't be many worshippers of the old demon, or whatever he is anymore. If it is not abandoned or taken over by another cult, it most likely has fallen down by now."

"Or converted to the cult of the Mother of Jermaish," Miri said slyly.

"Wretched child." Ninshi glared and Miri giggled. The cult worshipped the mother of King Jermaish, "Strangler of Lions, Son of Goddess and King, Ruler of Ikizepe." The goddess, of course, was Ninshi, who had traveled with Jermaish when he was young and helped him regain his throne. Jermaish, who was a lummox, but a shrewd one, played upon rumors that his companion was his mother and converted a little used shrine in his city as a temple to her. Any mention of this made Ninshi furious, as did the occasional follower, who could be identified by the broken-tooth talisman that each wore in imitation of the one around Ninshi's neck.

It was Ikizepe where they had encountered the lilu. Ninshi had defeated it but came very close to dying of the wounds she received in the fight.

The city looked very run down. The road it was on was little travelled. In the past it had been of greater importance, one of the Hundred Cities of the Plain, but now was dirty, decaying and near abandoned. They passed a small market, where the stalls displayed wilted produce, fly covered meat, and poorly made garments.

"Let us find a bath and some supplies and go back to the caravansary and see if we can find a caravan travelling in the direction we are going." Their horses were waiting there, and their travelling gear.

Miri nodded. She studied her mother's face. It was drawn, and her color was poor. She had been wounded several times the last few months and even though her talisman had great restorative powers, the wounds had had taken their toll. Miri believed that her mother could do anything. But Ninshi looked very tired. Miri decided to find an excuse to rest for a few days, maybe in the next town.

Miri spotted a sign with the faded painting of a jug pouring water into cupped hands. "The baths!" she exclaimed and took several steps towards them. There was a commotion behind her, the sound of feet and grunts. She whirled around and groped for the knife at her girdle.

Five or six men surrounded Ninshi. She staggered. At least two men struck her with cudgels, hard. Miri leapt forward, pushing aside the people who were between them. She ran at the nearest assailant, but they already were carrying Ninshi's limp form deeper into the market. Miri shouted and swung at the rearmost man with her knife. It snagged in his robe and he backhanded her, as if she were a bothersome fly. Miri fell, and by the time she got to her feet, they were gone.

NINSHI'S awareness grew slowly, starting with the pain from her wrist. The room swam into focus. It was made of stone. Her wrist was shackled to something holding her weight. Ninshi stumbled to her feet, swaying against the chains that hung from the ceiling of the room. They were patinaed, and in places had what was likely dried blood crusting their square links.

Her vision cleared. The room was large, with a low dais at one end. The figure of a man sat on an ornate backless chair, his chin on his fist, watching. "There is something I don't understand about you."

He stood, moved toward her. "You smell like someone I once knew, long ago." He was tall, bulky. His robes swirled around him, as if they were animated by something other than his movement. "I remember that scent. You, or someone like you was here, oh, ninety years ago or so. That presence woke me from my long slumbers. But the memory of that scent is much, much older." His features were odd, like the statues of the old gods that were worshipped by her family, so long ago.

He sniffed again, shook his head. "There is an odor of death on you. But something else, too." He leaned forward, extended a finger to her face.

It almost reached her. As his hand stretched near, the tip disappeared. He yelped and yanked his hand back. A small trickle of sand fell to the floor, making a tiny dune. He stared at his hand. The forefinger was missing to the second joint. No blood flowed, just a tiny trickle of sand.

He stared at her, his gray eyes piercing. "What are you?" He stuck his finger in his mouth, withdrew it made whole again. He paced around her, muttering to himself, sniffing at the air around her. "*Atta kimaki mupad munus, nigini?*"

"Not *nigini. Igibala.*" Her voice was weak, rasping. They must have hit her intending to kill. Only her talisman had saved her, just as it was preventing any sorcery from affecting or touching her. The demon, or whatever he was, must have held his physical form through sorcery, so when he approached, the sorcery dissolved, along with whatever part of his body held together by sorcery that got too close.

He frowned and poked a finger at her once more. Once again, he snatched back half of the extremity, leaving a small pile of sand on the floor. He walked slowly back to the dais and sat back down, resting his chin on his hand.

"*Igibala.* The Betrayer. Much to ponder here, I think. You are old, or very learned. The old language like this is only spoken by priests, and there are very few who know more than incantations and such. All who spoke the *eme-sal* of Uruk are now dead. And I can't seem to touch you."

Ninshi's head throbbed where she had been struck, and her right wrist was cut and chaffed from where she had hung by one arm in the shackle. "Where is my companion?"

"Unimportant, *Betrayer.* Betrayer of what? Am I supposed to know you? Are you some lesser power I have never heard of, walking the earth, and causing mischief? I used to keep up on things, but it just seems to be too much trouble anymore. Here's a thought!"

He got up and strode to Ninshi, being careful not to get too close. He studied her for a moment, then chuckled. "The broken tooth around your neck!" He rocked back and sucked his teeth. "That is what I smell. It is the tooth of one of my cousins, I think, though I can't for the life of me remember which one. So, *Betrayer.* You are just a woman after all, and not a very comely one at that. I shall have my servants remove it and put it somewhere safe. I think that I shall have them put you to the question while they are at it, see how you came to have this dangerous little bauble and who you really are. Not that it matters." He clapped his hands. A door behind her creaked open, and five men rushed in, bowing and trembling.

"Cut that tooth from around her neck and place it in my quarters. Question her and find out who she is, who sent her and how she came to carry that talisman. Then kill her." He left the room.

THE PAIN was overwhelming. "Who are you?" the round-faced man would ask. "Who sent you? Where did you obtain that talisman?" When she didn't answer, he would grab another finger, pushing it back and wrenching at it until the bone cracked. They were at four, and her right hand was starting to swell in the shackle, puffy and red, with fingers pointing in directions they weren't designed for.

He stepped back and tugged at his beard. "I think we shall have to try other methods. Strip her." He licked his plump lips in anticipation. The two men who had held her arms and the one with his arm around her neck pulled her torn shift down to her waist. The plump man gasped.

"Look! No wonder we were having a little trouble getting answers from you. You've been questioned before." His finger traced one of the scars that crossed her torso.

"There are scars back here too, some pretty nasty looking ones." The voice was young, probably the beardless one that had cut the talisman from her and hustled off, returning to hold her as they broke her fingers.

The plump one made a face. "Well, boys, we'll have to do her anyway. It is unlikely that she will tell us anything, but orders is orders. And she might be a goer." The men laughed. He undid his robe, revealing spindly legs under a stained nether cloth.

He stopped, looked startled, then gurgled and fell over. A short arrow jutted from his neck.

Someone behind her screamed, and there were sounds of scuffling. The fresh-faced boy backed past her; his hands raised. A white figure flashed at him, and blood sprayed from his neck as a talon ripped across. Another stabbed rapidly at his chest, four or five times. He slumped into a heap against the dais.

There was silence for a moment. The lilu turned and looked at Ninshi, no expression readable on its featureless face. Miri stepped around her and grabbed her, still holding a bloody knife, hugged her tightly.

"Step back, child, and free me. I am mostly whole."

"Oh Ninshi! Your hand!" Tears ran down her cheeks as she fumbled with the shackle. She poked at the latch with her knife, causing Ninshi to wince as it moved.

"Let me, daughter of man." The lilu stepped to one side of her and formed her hands into something like tools. A few seconds work, and the shackle fell apart, the two halves clattering on the floor. Ninshi pulled the chain from where it was looped over a beam with her uninjured hand and it crashed down in a pile of bronze.

Miri knelt to wipe her knife on the robe of the man she had killed with the arrow. She stood straight as she could, all thirteen summers of her. "My name is Miri. Lilu, I name you sister and friend."

"Sister, then, but we have little time. We will talk when we are out of here. Help me put this robe on her."

Ninshi grunted. "I am right here, you know. And I am not putting that pig's robe on. Give me your belt, and we will pull the remains of my shift together." Miri gingerly helped Ninshi get dressed. With her left hand, Ninshi picked up the spear that dead boy had carried. It was short and ill balanced, but it had a head of bronze and would serve.

"Did they harm you, child? When they took me?" Ninshi's voice was a little stronger.

"No!" Miri wailed. "They ignored me."

"And you? Why are you here?"

"I was called."

Ninshi shook her head. "I did not call."

"I called her," Miri said. "And like you, she came."

She picked up her bow where she had dropped it and opened the door to the room. It was dark, the full moon gazing wearily over the wall of the courtyard. The room was set against the wall of the temple, and there was little activity.

They hustled across the courtyard. The temple seemed abandoned. Weeds wilted in a fountain, and there were piles of sand along the south wall.

"You have slain my servants, I see." The voice came from the darkness ahead, soft and menacing.

Ninshi stumbled back, raised her spear. Sumugan stepped forward, large and menacing in the moonlight.

The lilu flashed forward, a pale streak against the black of Sumugan's cloak. His arm licked out, and the lilu was knocked back and landed at the edge of the fountain with terrible thump and lay motionless.

Miri drew her bow, hands shaking with fear. She let fly an arrow. It hit squarely in the center of Sumugan's body. A second arrow, and a third. Sumugan seemed not to notice, and moved slowly toward Ninshi, focused on her.

Ninshi ran to the side. She thrust with her spear. It was torn from her hands and fell clattering to the paving stones. She scrambled for it, fell.

Sumugan regarded her as she scrambled up. "My dear, how much more dangerous you seemed with the broken tooth around your neck. I have it safely hidden in a dark corner of my temple, where none but my servants go."

Ninshi stood, grasping the spear.

He shook his head. As he did, he seemed to grow larger, more menacing. "Without it you are just a woman. Of dwindling interest to me, and soon forgotten after I kill you."

Miri watched in horror as the dark figure enveloped Ninshi.

Sumugan cried out. His form seemed to contract, and swirl. "I am betrayed!" he cried and collapsed into a pile of sand.

Ninshi stood in the middle of a cloud of settling sand, spear still held at ready.

"How is this?" she marveled. She felt her neck. Still bare.

Behind Miri, the lilu stirred. It slowly raised to its feet and stumbled toward Ninshi. "Are you uninjured, sister?"

Nisi turned to face the lilu. "Not your sister," she snapped.

"Perhaps your talisman has been worn for so long that it is no longer needed to protect you."

"Perhaps. Still let us search the temple. It is small. I would like my talisman back, for I cannot summon the Manthycore without it, and if I go long enough, the torment becomes great. I would also like my sword back."

Miri looked at the lilu. It was reforming into the shape Miri had first see it in, the ape-like shape it had worn before. "I will give you a name." She was surprised at how steady her voice was.

The lilu stopped, inclined its head.

"I name you *Aialu*. Rescuer."

The lilu nodded. "It is good."

Ninshi pointed with her spear across the courtyard. "Let's start with that building. It looks large enough to be important."

The large twin doors were slightly ajar. Aialu altered its form slightly, slipped inside, pushed them further open.

Inside the great room was dark, illuminated only by small lamps that burned in niches in the wall, by a group of candles around an altar at the far end, and by the inconstant moon who peered down through gaps in the roof. A breeze danced though the open doors, stirring dry leaves and drifts of sand on the floor.

They started for the far end, but before they took a handful of steps, the breeze exploded into a fierce gale, extinguishing candles, and lamps, and blinding them with the sand from the floor. Small bits of debris pelted them, and they were driven back by the sudden storm, retreating behind the pillar-posts of the broken door. They stood for a moment choking and coughing, spitting sand and dirt.

"Not a coincidence." Ninshi's voice was harsher than usual, filled with pain and fatigue. She adjusted her tunic and slapped at the dust. "I think we shall try another way." She looked around.

There were four buildings surrounding the courtyard. The temple they had just come from, the smaller stone building Ninshi had been held in, and two smaller buildings flanking the gate out of the temple compound. Ninshi gestured with her spear, "That one first."

Miri watched Ninshi hobble across the courtyard with a growing sense of alarm. Her mother's stride was irregular, and after just a few steps she started using the spear shaft to lean on. Miri glanced at the lilu. The creature was hanging back, its features impossible to read, but Miri thought she could sense the lilu's unease. This was a bad situation, and Ninshi seemed in no way strong enough to fight again, if they were to face the sand demon.

Both small buildings were largely empty, the first with scraps of broken pottery and trash, most likely the refuse of the few temple attendants that they had killed. The other had a few pieces of old wooden furniture, none of it whole. Ninshi collapsed on a semi-whole bench. Miri rushed to her side, but Ninshi waved her away. "I must rest. I fear that the loss of the talisman will mean that I do not heal entirely, even though it seems that it is restoring me somewhat."

She thought for a moment, then sighed. "We will make our way back to the gates of the city, and then to the caravansary. I would like to rest there, but I do not trust the distance of Sumugan's influence or power, or the zealotry of his followers who may remain."

Ninshi pulled herself up. Miri took one arm, and after a second the lilu Aialu took the other. Ninshi glared, first at Miri and then the lilu, but nodded and they started off.

Through the gates of the temple compound they found the night city deserted except for the occasional stray dog. There was no sign of a watch.

The streets were narrow, with buildings overhanging the passageways. There were piles of refuse, dumped from the windows. Though some of the streets were paved with worn brick, it was only in the center that it could be seen. The edges were grown up with night soil-fed low growth, and the decaying scraps of offal thrown out by the inhabitants of the rough brick houses added a pungent accompaniment to their slow progress. There was little light except the pale moon that illuminated their path, and the occasional candle or oil lamp that flickered behind ragged shutters.

Twice they had to backtrack, their way blocked by mud brick structures that had collapsed across the streets. For a time, a pack of dogs followed them, yellow eyes gleaming in the uncertain moonlight. After a few turns, one of them suddenly barked, and the pack went baying off after some unseen prey, smaller and easier.

Finally, the street opened out into the main plaza of the small city. The market was gone, packed up for the night, a few bare tables and some small scraps of waste growled over by even more dogs was all that remained. A vague figure by the bathhouse hummed and grunted as he pissed against the wall. He turned, tugging at his breeches, and spotted them as they slowly made their way across the plaza. He stared drunkenly at the lilu for a long moment, then yelped and half ran, half stumbled into the darkness between buildings.

The gates of the city were ajar, decayed enough perhaps that they could not be drawn closed. Two guards sat on each side of the opening, their spears propped against the gates, their chins on their chests. Miri, Ninshi and Aialu quietly shuffled though the opening, the guards undisturbed in their slumber.

Outside the gates there were a few wooden structures. They made their way between them to the low dark shape of the caravansary. It was flanked on one side by the wall of the city, here a little sounder, and by the corral made of salvaged mud brick and scraps of wood. A small boy, tasked with watching the livestock, peered at them through a gap in the bricks, but said nothing. Miri could see the low shapes of sleeping camels, and several horses as they passed.

The door was shut. Miri slapped her hand flat on the panel, making a booming sound. There was no response. She banged again louder, and kept it up for several minutes, but no one answered. "I don't think we can knock down this door, and the rest of the building is pretty sturdy," Miri said, rubbing her hand.

Ninshi turned to the lilu. "Can you get in?"

The lilu nodded. "I think so." Her hands molded into hook-like appendages, and she scrambled up the side of the wooden structure. Miri could hear her scrabbling at the roof, and the quiet sounds of the lilu tapping and prying. There was a small sound of breaking wood, and then a thump inside the door. Miri could hear the bar being lifted, and the door opened, the lilu standing by the inert form of the caravansary keeper in a heap on the floor. "I did not kill him, as he was little threat. I hope that is satisfactory."

It was dark inside, the only light from a small fire that flickered in the grate. The roof was low, and the moon peeked in where the lilu had torn a hole in the roof. All was quiet. At best this caravansary seemed to have little trade: if there were other guests as suggested by the camels in the corral, they were sleeping elsewhere or in hiding.

"Yes, yes," Ninshi mumbled, and made her way into the corner where Miri and she had stowed their packs and other gear. It seemed undisturbed, and in a few moments Miri and the lilu gathered it up while Ninshi leaned against the wall.

"Food," Ninshi said. Miri was able to find a few loaves of hard bread and a pot of lentils, and a half-eaten chicken. She stowed these in the bags, the lentils wrapped carefully with towels she found near the cooking grate.

Once again by the corral, they pushed through its gate. The terrified boy cowered in a corner as they made their way to the horses, and Miri quickly saddled them and loaded their meager gear on them. The lilu had to help Ninshi mount her horse, but once on she seemed steady. They rode out of the corral, the lilu beside them. An owl hoo-hooted softly, and somewhere in the distance a dog barked as they passed through the gate and into the darkness.

The false dawn before sunrise, called the wolf's tail by the dwellers in the desert, spread its faint red light across the night sky, chasing the shy stars away with its dim flickering. Ninshi stopped her horse and pointed at the lee of a small cliff, where there remained the cold traces of previous campfires. "This will do, I think," and then tumbled off her horse into the dust and lay still. Miri slid off her horse's back and onto the dusty ground and ran to Ninshi. She was breathing, and Miri gave a cry of relief. With the help of Aialu, Miri made her as comfortable as possible, then arranged the camp while the lilu gathered wood for the fire. The brush here was oily, and

Miri's flint was old, so starting the fire was difficult, but at last the spark caught, and she was able to partially warm the pot of lentils against the unsteady flames. Her belly full, Miri gave Ninshi a final check, then bundled up next to her, and silently cried herself to sleep.

She awoke in the early evening. At first, Miri didn't know where she was. She sat up, her face stiff from dried tears, and brushed her matted hair out of her face. Beside her, Ninshi still slept, her breathing regular. The lilu was nowhere to be found. Mir got up, brushed the dust of her leggings, and took up her water skin, splashing some on her face and swishing a little around her mouth. She spat, and behind her Ninshi grunted. "Pass me that, child."

Miri handed her the skin, and Ninshi took a deep draught. Her color was better, and some of the deep lines that worried Miri so much last night had faded. "There are lentils," Miri said, and bent to poke the embers of the fire. There was more of the greasy wood stacked beside the coals, and it took only a few minutes to make the fire grow into something at least marginally respectable. While the lentils heated, Miri peered at her mother. Ninshi was slowly stretching, trying each bruised muscle against the other, one at a time, and slowly moving the fingers of her injured hand, wiggling each finger and wincing. The fingers had straitened during the day as she slept, but the hand was still dark with bruises where her fingers had been twisted back and broken.

"Where is the creature?" Ninshi asked as she accepted the warmed lentils handed to her in a smaller clay pot they carried for washing. She held it in her injured hand and used her other to dip the lentils and push them into her mouth greedily. Miri had never seen her mother eat like that. Usually she was measured, but now Ninshi seemed ravenous, and only interested in the lentils.

Miri shook her head. "Gone when I awoke. She brought this wood while I slept and must have tended the fire. Do you think she'll be back?"

Ninshi shrugged and wiped the last of the lentils from the brown pot. "No way to tell. She is a creature of the old world, when men were only one of the peoples who walked the earth. Before I faced her in Ikizepe, I had only heard of her kind in old songs and camp tales. What she told us may very well be true, or partially, or have no truth at all. Or it even may be that it is her truth, from a vanished world, that has no small or no relation to the truth as we know it."

Ninshi thoughtfully wiped her hand on her soiled tunic, grimacing. "I have lived for a long time, perhaps a thousand years, perhaps more. There is so much that I have forgotten. I don't remember my family. I can only remember scraps of the language I spoke as a child. The city where I was born is no more, not even the ruins of old walls to be seen, lost to the dusts of the years."

She scratched at a smear of dried blood on her scarred cheek. "I may have known something about the lilu at one time, or maybe I knew only what I can now recall. The world is still a strange place, full of mysteries veiled to all daughters of Zarpandit. I am very old, but I am still just a woman. Will she come back? If it suits her to, yes. Is she our ally? For now, she may be, I think. But remember, less than two moons ago she tried to kill me, and had she succeeded, she probably would have killed you as well."

Ninshi stood. "I will wash some of this off in the stream, and then must rest again. Either the loss of the talisman of the Manthycore has caused me to draw on my own strength for healing, or my wounds are more than I thought. Either way, I must sleep. Wake me if the lilu returns."

Miri sat through the night, adding wood to the fire as it burned down and listening to the sounds of small animals and birds, and other noises of the night. Sometimes she got up and wheeled her arms or walked around the camp. Every few hours she checked on Ninshi. She was not used to her mother sleeping this much. Normally Ninshi slept two or three hours a night, and an hour as they rested in the heat of the day. For her to sleep this long and this hard seemed unsettling, and Miri could not keep from watching her mother as she slept.

Less than a year ago, Ninshi had been badly wounded by a bandit's arrow, and then two moons ago had fought the lilu and was wounded again and poisoned by the lilu's blood. And now this. Miri knew that the talisman had remarkable powers of healing for those who wore it and served the Manthycore, but Ninshi had suffered three terrible wounds in a very short time, wounds that probably would have killed anyone else. And now she did not have the talisman.

Eventually the long night ended, with no appearance by the lilu. Their supplies were nearly exhausted, only a few figs and some dried meat, and the little bit of hard bread she had scavenged from the caravansary. Miri shook her mother awake. "I will see if I can find something," she said. "During the night I think I heard a rabbit, or perhaps a hedgehog. I will hunt upstream and see what I can find."

Ninshi nodded, sat up and stretched. "I am feeling much stronger this morning, child. I will bathe while you try your luck."

Miri was back in a short time, carrying two brown hares. She dressed and skinned them like her mother had shown her and soon they were spitted, roasting over the fire.

As they ate, Ninshi said little. She appeared to be deep in thought. Finally, she sighed, and tossed a bone into the fire. "We must have weapons," she said. "We seem to have left our spears at the caravansary. This spear can barely be called that. I could almost make better by sharpening a stick. And they seem to have stolen my boots and well as ruining my tunic."

Miri thought for a moment. "There is the bandit camp, two days away. There were weapons there."

Ninshi nodded. "I thought of that, but what I saw was of poor quality, and most likely someone has come across them already. It would be two days there and two days back, for most likely nothing." She looked Miri in the eye. "Child, you will soon follow the moon. You look to be thirteen winters or so and are nearly a woman. This means that I will take your council. We must decide what we will do. As far as I can scry, we have a choice. We can prepare ourselves, go back and recover the talisman and perhaps my sword. At this point I don't see how, but something might present itself. I just don't know enough about this city, its people or political structure to even know where to begin planning."

"Didn't you say you were here before?"

"Yes, but many years ago, and then only for a day or two. It is no longer an important place, even if it ever was, on a little-used road between more memorable places. I fear that my presence, or rather the presence of the talisman, may have awoken the demon we faced. Many of them still dwell on this earth, some of them active but most in a sort of sleepy state, dreaming of past glories and forgotten places."

Miri fidgeted, opened her mouth to speak, thought better.

Ninshi slapped her thigh. "I said you were to speak, child. Spit it out!"

Miri gulped. "We could... that is, we are only a week from Ikizepe. King Jermaish is strong, and he has soldiers. Perhaps he could help?" She watched Ninshi's reaction carefully, not wanting to anger her mother. Instead, Ninshi only frowned, and was quiet for a moment, clearly thinking about it.

"No," she said finally. "The great oaf would come if I asked, I am sure of this. But Jermaish has his own problems, a city to rule and neighbors, some of whom are unfriendly. And wives, many, many wives. Besides, his whole army is no more than a few handfuls of soldiers and city guards, and a few chariots. Not enough to take a city, even if he were willing. Let us do this; we will rest until I am whole and wait for the lilu for a few days. We passed an abandoned farmhouse the other night. While I sleep, I will task you with searching for anything there that might help."

Miri found the farmhouse to be little more than three mud brick walls with a few boards leaning against them. There were signs that it had been used as a livestock shelter, probably both before and after human habitation. She kicked at a pile of what looked to be ancient household trash but found only old bones and broken pottery. There were also the remains of what may have been a barn, but now was pile of little more than firewood and a few bricks.

After an hour of shifting boards and piling trash, she went and sat in the meagre shade the falling-down walls of the farmhouse provided and inventoried her finds. There was an almost complete axe handle, a small oil lamp made of clay, its reservoir filled with an oily residue, and half a whetstone. She pulled her water skin around and took a pull, swished it around her mouth, and spat.

Something caught her eye on the floor where her spit-out water landed. She leaned over and wiped the mud and dust away to expose a small bronze figure in the shape of a vastly pregnant woman with six large breasts. Miri scratched her nose, where a bead of sweat had formed. She had seen figures like this in taverns and in the occasional household where they had stayed. She had never seen one made of bronze though. Usually they were made of clay, and never made this well.

She rubbed at the figure's belly. Some of the patina chipped away, revealing the dull bronze that lay underneath. How had this come here? It was too grand for a household god; bronze was too expensive. Had the farmer stolen it, or had it dropped from some later visitor's pocket or pack while sheltering for the night?

"Well, little Ninhursag, or Inanna or whoever you are. You will come with me. We shall see if Ninshi knows who you are." She tucked the little statue into her pack, along with the small stone lamp and the whetstone. After a few moment's thought, she discarded the axe handle. Too old and brittle.

She stood and brushed the dust from her clothes, then froze. Just on the other side of the wall was a fallow deer, nibbling at a bush. Miri dropped her pack and strung her bow in two fluid motions, nocked an arrow, and drew the string. The deer blinked at her and bounded away.

Miri's arrow caught the dappled deer just behind the shoulder. It took a half dozen staggering steps, and then fell, got up and fell again, lay still.

Miri slung her bow, drew her knife, and walked to the deer. *At least we'll have meat*, she thought.

Five days passed. Ninshi grew stronger and her scars faded. She no longer had the broken-tooth talisman, which made her heal at a tremendous pace, but it seemed that there was a residual effect. Wounds closed, joints straightened and by the fifth day she was whole again, where a normal person would have been weeks in the healing--and perhaps never have healed at all. Miri found a straight branch, which Ninshi fashioned into a spear shaft, to replace the shoddy one she had taken from Sumugan's man. The bronze spearhead she sharpened nightly, changing its shape, and honing it to a fine edge.

On the fourth day they resumed training, using the replaced haft of the spear and another straight branch Miri had found. Ninshi was a little slow at first, something that Miri thought impossible. She was still incredibly quick and centuries of practice with sword, spear and bow had made her both skilled and crafty, but Miri sometimes saw openings as they clashed back and forth, though she was never fast enough to take advantage of them.

Ninshi pushed herself harder than Miri had ever seen before, sweating and grunting, sometimes with her, sometimes alone. By the sixth day she was back to her old speed, blindingly fast, nearly impossible to touch.

The fallow deer was down to a few scraps of meat, which they had smoked, and the bones. Days before, Ninshi staked out its skin and spread the deer's brains and some water on the inside to tan it. The hide was now in a high state of stink, stiff as a board, but looked to be starting to cure.

"In the morning I will hunt for us. Perhaps I can find a hare or some other animal. The fallow deer seemed to be the only one here." Miri examined her arrows. There were seven. She needed more but wanted to buy them if she could. Ninshi had taught her how to make arrows, but it was one of the few skills Ninshi herself was poor in, and she wasn't able to teach Miri much more than the basic tasks of fletching.

Ninshi stopped sharpening her spear and stood up. "I thought you gone, six days from here already."

The lilu moved into the light cast by the low fire, its sickly white color reflecting the yellow flames as it scuttled sideways on four legs. It started to shift, and Miri looked away. The lilu's changing made Miri feel vaguely nauseated, like the world was suddenly wrong. When she could see from the corner of her eye that the change was complete, she looked back. The lilu had resumed a near human shape, though the edges and details were uncertain and ill-formed.

Ninshi sat back down on the rock and resumed sharpening the bronze head of her spear. "What news, then?"

The lilu settled into herself, then spoke. "I have been to the city, listening and looking, searching round the temple and its surroundings. It looks to have been abandoned for many years. There seems to have been some excitement in the last few years, with a group of thugs moving in and claiming to be acolytes of the god Sumugan, but with the gossip I was able to overhear from the market and near the city fountains, most do not think they are anything but road trash and drunkards."

Ninshi nodded. "How is it that you were able to gather so much information?"

The lilu made something like a shrug. "Mostly, I lurked."

Ninshi raised an eyebrow. "You lurked?"

The lilu nodded. "I am very good at lurking."

Miri snorted, covered her mouth. Aialu and her mother looked at her, her mother expressionless, the lilu even more so.

After a moment, Aialu continued. "No one has worshipped at the temple of Sumugan for many years. There was an order of priests, but the last one seems to have died three or four generations ago. Strangely, there is no shrine to Ishtar, but there are small ones to Enlil, Utu and even one to Nergal. They all are seldom visited, as the city-dwellers seem to prefer household gods and gods of the hearth or fertility."

"And what did you learn about us? Are we pursued?"

"Not from the city. From what I could gather, the city elders think that it was a simple robbery, that your body was dumped, and that the thugs from the temple went to the caravansary and roughed up the keeper to steal your things. They don't seem to do much to police them. I think the thought was that you were a stranger, and so of no importance. There is also a gentle dread of the temple itself; not really a deep fear, but more of an uneasiness, like perhaps something evil happened there long ago. But no one remembers exactly what."

"The temple grounds themselves are small." The lilu formed one hand into a point and drew in the dirt. "There are the four buildings we saw, temple, guardhouses or such, and the throne room where we found you. There is a building behind that, and another behind the temple. The wall is broken in a few places. I didn't go in. I could feel the malevolence within and didn't want to awaken it again."

The lilu hesitated, shifted. "There is something more. On the road, you commanded me to no longer follow you. I of course ignored that but dropped back far enough that you could no longer perceive me. In doing so, I discovered something else."

"What?"

"There is a large group of men, dressed in the fashion of the soldiers of the temple of Ishtar in Nineveh, though how they got here is a mystery. They were clearly following you and seem to be part of a larger body of men. I led them off along the great river road. Tell me why, sister, they would pursue you this far and with so many?"

"I burned their temple and killed their high priestess. Twice."

Miri stared in amazement as the lilu burbled in laughter. It was so unlikely from such a creature, that in a moment she was caught up, and started laughing herself. Ninshi stared at them, patiently waiting for them to finish. But as each fit of giggling started to wind down, Miri would glace at Ninshi or the lilu, or the lilu would look at Miri, and they would start again.

Finally, Miri was able to catch her breath. Ninshi hadn't moved.

After a moment, Ninshi glared at the lilu. "And I am not your sister."

Which of course set them off laughing again.

NINSHI shook Miri awake. Miri sat up, opened her mouth to complain. Her mother shook her head. "Gather your weapons and gear. I will get the horses. The soldiers have found us."

Miri hurriedly brushed sleep out of her eyes. The night was moonless, but the pale stars were out. She quickly gathered her pack and her bow and turned to find Ninshi with the horses on leads standing behind her. They clambered up on the horse's backs.

Less than a bow shot away, men with torches approached the camp. There may have been a dozen, maybe more, and as Ninshi and Miri wheeled their horses, one of them spotted their dark forms against the sky, shouted something, and the men charged forward.

"Follow me," Ninshi said and rode away from the men. Miri followed. It was too dark and the way too uncertain to gallop, but the horses seemed to sense Miri's alarm, and made their way quickly. An arrow buzzed past Miri's head, and another lodged in the pack that swung by her side. They were soon far enough away that their pursuers could no longer see them in the faint starlight.

"This way," Ninshi whispered, and they turned at a sharp angle from the direction they had been riding.

The torches became pinpoints of light in the distance, then one by one disappeared. The night was cold, and Miri had left her blanket in her hurry. She shivered but knew better than to complain. After an hour of riding, Ninshi signaled a stop, and Miri gratefully dismounted. She removed the arrow from her pack. It was hard to tell without light, but it looked to be black, or a very dark color. It felt balanced, and was fletched well, with what seemed to be black feathers. She dropped it into her quiver then rummaged through her pack to get her spare shirt. She pulled it over the tunic she had fallen asleep in and was immediately warmer.

After a quick trip around a nearby bush to empty her bladder, Miri returned to find Ninshi standing on a rock, listening intently. Ninshi shook her head and clambered down. "They are on our trail again. Fix your pack. Let the horses rest for a space, but then we must flee."

Miri squatted, and stuffed the little she had saved from the camp back into her pack. "What happened to Aialu?"

Ninshi gathered a few handfuls of grass and fed it to her horse. "It was the lilu who first saw them. She was out hunting whatever it is she eats, spotted them searching the abandoned farmhouse near the road."

"Rats and hares, I think, and other small creatures. I know she doesn't eat cooked meat." Miri finished with her pack, slung it over the horse. She hopped twice as the horse shied, but managed to clamber on its back. "Where will we meet her?"

Ninshi swung up onto the back of her horse. "She will find us. She tried to lead them astray again, but I don't think she succeeded. Or maybe there are more of the soldiers chasing her in another direction, I don't know."

The torches were visible again in the distance, moving their way.

"We will ride this way, I think, towards the city. If we can lose them, we will circle back to the camp and see if they have left anything behind."

By dawn, the horses were exhausted, and so was Miri. Three times they had evaded their pursuers, and each time the soldiers picked up their trace after only a short time.

They were back at the road, the early morning light revealing a few farmers with their carts of produce on their way to the city. Other than that, the road had little traffic.

Sometime in the night, Ninshi's horse had stepped in a hole, and was limping. She slid off the horse's back and lifted the mare's front leg to examine it. She bent it a few times, then dropped it and stood. "Not broken but can't be ridden for a while." She stripped her blanket from the gray mare's back, gathered her pack, and took the reins of Miri's horse from her hand. The gray mare, left off her lead, wandered over to the side of the road, pulling the tough weeds and grass that lined the road.

"Sleep awhile, child. I will lead your horse and keep you from falling." She set off down the road. Miri nodded in and out of slumber as they walked.

For a time, it seemed that they had somehow evaded her pursuers. The morning was warm, with a pleasant light breeze. Miri laid her head on the horse's neck.

She woke to the horse's stop. They were behind a large cart. Ahead, in the distance she could see more soldiers, dressed in the black of the soldiers of the Temple.

"Down!" Ninshi snapped, and Miri tumbled off the horse onto the dusty road. She grabbed her pack. Ninshi spoke briefly with a farmer, then tied the horse to the back of the cart. Ninshi and Miri scrambled into the nearby brush, bent over. They waited until the cart had gone a bowshot down the road, then Ninshi signaled Miri, and they snuck across the road to the olive orchard on other side. If the soldiers stopped the farmer, he would tell them that they had gone the other way.

They ran through the trees, through the shadows that dappled between the trees, cast by the bright morning sun. Small olives hung from the trees, half size, hard and green.

At the edge of the orchard there was small track that lead from a wooden shack and the river. Brown water moved sluggishly down its course, on its way, perhaps to the great Euphrates and then to the sea. On the other side were more trees and a low bank. Ninshi grabbed Miri's hand, squinted down the lane both ways, and then pulled her across the road and down into the river.

They waded across, never more than armpit deep. Miri held her bow over her head and carried both packs and her blanket. They splashed awkwardly onto the bank and scrambled into the trees. A few steps into the gloom and they could no longer see the road.

Ninshi turned and leaned against a hawthorn tree. "That should break the trail, I think. They must have dogs, though I didn't see any. I don't know how they could have found us in the dark like that."

She handed Miri her pack. "Eat, and then we must move once more. The more I think about them finding us again and again, the less easy I am. I am starting to suspect some witchery."

The hawthorns gave way to scrub oak, then another long-fallow field. Ninshi often had mentioned that much of the world here between the great rivers was in decay, with trade diminished, crops less bountiful and cities in semi-ruin where once they had prospered. After a time, in another grove of scrub-oak in the lee of a hill, they found a small shack, the remains of a charcoal- burner's camp. Miri kicked a corner clear of debris and thumped down. She half emptied her pack and rolled it to form a pillow, laid down and slept.

Miri woke abruptly. She sat up, listened hard. Ninshi stood in the door, her small figure blocking the sun's last rays. "They are near."

Miri started to re-stuff her pack.

"Wait." Ninshi's voice was hoarse, with a questioning tone. "What is that, child?"

Miri held up the small idol she found in the old farmhouse, day's ago. "I think it is Inanna."

Ninshi took it from her. She scratched at the patina, turned it in her hands, licked at the bronze. She sighed. "Child, do you know another name for Inanna?"

Miri shook her head.

"Inanna has had many names, taken many forms. Some call her Ninhursag, though that I think she was her servant. She is Ninanak, and Hannahanna, but she is most worshipped as Ishtar."

The room was suddenly colder. "I do not think that Ishtar herself pursues, but it may be that some clever priestess has found some way to have her idol spy on us. Perhaps all idols and figures of her. The talisman prevented such before, but I am without it and so it may be that it is small sorceries that find us, again and again."

"Throw it in the river," Miri wailed. "Oh mother, I had no idea!"

Ninshi gestured for her to gather her things. When Miri was ready, they stepped out into the early evening. In the west, the last glimmerings of light clawed at the horizon, unwilling to leave. Ninshi stood for a moment, weighing the small bronze idol in her hand. "I think that knowing this gives us an advantage. We will lose them again, and then circle back to the camp as planned. I have an idea, but we will need the lilu for it to work."

THEY WERE cautiously making their way to their camp, and were only a few yards away, when the lilu rose from a shrub to its full six-limbed height. "I am sorry," she said as she shifted into a more human form. "I was only able to lead a small number of the soldiers away. They seemed determined to follow you."

The campsite was little disturbed. The belongings left behind had been lightly ransacked, but nothing seemed to be missing. The lilu scuttled over to some bushes, and returned holding two spears, a sword, and a half-dozen black arrows. "I took these from the soldiers who pursued me. They were little threat to me in the dark."

Miri lathered the arrow and thrust them into her quiver. They were exquisitely made, black, of some sort of wood that was oily to the touch. The heads were square, with whorls and incantations or blessings etched into the patinaed bronze. They were spiral fletched with black feathers.

Ninshi nodded. "They were determined. I think they have some sort of incantation or ritual that has allowed them to follow us using this." She produced the small bronze idol, and the lilu took it from her, sniffed it.

The lilu handed it back. "There is no scent of sorcery on it. It is old though. It is redolent with the years and the many hands that have touched it."

Ninshi nodded. "And yet, I think this is how they have managed to find us. Every time we evaded them, it took only an hour or two for them to find us. I would guess we have only a short time before we must move again."

Aialu cocked her head to the side. "Why do you still have it then?"

"I want the soldiers of the temple of Ishtar to help us get the talisman back."

The lilu made a small snorting sound. "This sounds like something from the old tales, I think. How will you do this?"

"The soldiers follow the idol. If we take it to the city, they will follow. At the gates, we can cause some incident, and see what happens. At the least they will be a distraction for the city and perhaps with luck, for the sand demon as well."

THE SOLDIERS soon appeared, and Ninshi and her followers led them carefully forward to the city walls, staying mostly just out of sight. The lilu was able to get a good count from when they first attacked the camp. "Forty-nine--and two priestesses. The soldiers, save one, afoot, the priestesses on onagers. There were three more, who chased me until they died."

They trotted to the city wall on the other side of the caravansary. There were a few lean-to structures against the wall, and grey-green brush had grown up against the crumbing mudbrick. The lilu shifted again, hands turned to spikes, a third hand grasping the idol, and scurried up the wall and over the side.

Miri and Ninshi sat in the shade of a babul tree growing alongside the city walls and waited for the lilu. They could see the gates quite well from here. Occasional farm wagons and solitary farmers made their way out of the city, traveling back to their farms for the evening, their business in the city completed for the day. The sun was nearly down, but it was still uncomfortably warm, with little breeze to relieve the heat.

Miri waved a fly away, kicked at the fragment of a mud brick, fallen from the wall. There was writing stamped into the brick, and some numbers. She picked it up, turned it over.

"The old kings would sometimes do that," Ninshi said. "Put their name on every brick, so that all would know that they had built something, and no later king could claim it." Ninshi took the brick from Miri. "Whoever had this wall built is long forgotten now, his city wall falling down." She tossed the brick aside.

"Why do you think this city is so... ragged?" Miri asked.

Ninshi frowned. "I do not know. It seems sometimes that everything in the world is diminished. Less than four lifetimes ago, this city was like any other city of the plains, with a busy trade and a growing population. Some say that the great empires of the past kept trade going. Some say that men nowadays do not have the faith in the gods they once had. And others, that the gods have lost interest. As you have seen, the world is in turmoil and little prospers. You saw with your own eyes a city destroyed. I have seen enough through the years to know that kingdoms rise, and kingdoms fall, but in the past, it always seemed that what replaced those things that came before was bigger, stronger, and more prosperous. Now, where there once was hope, there is just this." She gestured with her left hand and spit. "Just dust and despair, rotting wood and tired people."

"And yet, the world is still beautiful, and people find love," Miri answered quietly.

The lilu scrambled back over the wall, half a roasted duck in one hand. "I threw the idol into the temple," she said and held up the duck. "This was unattended." They divided it between them, and Miri was wiping duck grease from her chin when the soldiers appeared in the distance, marching toward the gate in the fading light.

"Let them see us enter," Ninshi said, standing. "Aialu, climb back over, and meet us past the center square, in the alley near the bath shop." The lilu scrambled away, back up the wall.

Miri picked up her bow and quiver, now with a dozen black-shafted arrows filling it nicely. She was excited, but not so much that she missed the fact that Ninshi had called the lilu by name. As far as she had seen, Ninshi never did anything by accident. What this signified she didn't know, and there wasn't time to think of it now.

They walked through the gates, making a show of how tired they were, glancing back at the approaching soldiers. The guards at the gates were crouched in a circle playing knucklebones. The sound of the soldiers approach sent them scurrying into place, one on one side, two on the other side of the old and broken gates, a fourth dashing back inside, perhaps to gather more guards.

Ninshi trotted across the square, Miri behind her. They crouched in the alley by the bath house, unnoticed in the excitement. They watched the soldiers, armed with spear and bow, approach the gate.

"Stop!" One of the guards shouted and shook his spear at the soldiers. The soldier on the horse signaled them to halt, just outside the gate. "What business have you here?"

The captain looked down his nose, tall on his horse. "We are on business of the Goddess Ishtar. We search for an enemy who has come this way."

The square was rapidly emptying of people. The guard who had run off at the soldiers' approach dashed back, followed by two other guards and a heavy-set bald man, robed in red, who waddled self-importantly behind them.

"Here now, what is this?" the city official asked in a trembling voice.

The captain rode forward, glared down at the sweating official with distain. "We know that those we pursue entered this gate only moments ago. We will enter and search for them. Stand aside."

Ninshi turned to Miri. "We can't have them agreeing to let them in. We need more chaos. Can you put an arrow into one of the temple soldiers from here?"

Miri strung her bow. She selected the best of her old arrows, squinted at the crowd at the gate, knocked and drew slowly, let fly.

For a moment it looked like it would fly true, but the angle was bad, and the arrow caromed off one of the gates and into the pavement stones of the gateway, bounced and skittered across the road, thumping gently into the hoof of the captain's horse.

The captain looked down at the arrow in the road. For a moment all were still, staring in amazement.

The captain looked up, smiled slightly. "Kill them. Find the woman and her brat."

The soldiers surged forward with a shout. The city guards turned and ran. Most were speared in the back, but some got as far as the square, and scattered.

"Run," Ninshi said as they raced into the alley.

They made two turns into the twisty streets, moving toward the temple as best remembered. They dashed across a main street, then into a smaller way that smelled of blood and fish. "Butcher. Wait for a moment."

A light breeze wafted the odors of old garbage, human waste and rotten wood thought the air. Miri wrinkled her nose in disgust. Cities stank, but this one seemed to be in even more disarray, with all the attendant odors of despair, poverty and lack of sanitation amplified by the dreary nature of its decay. Like her mother, she had no love for these small cities, but this one generated an especial loathing, made of equal parts anger and disgust.

After just a few seconds the lilu swung down from the roof of the building behind them. "Most of the soldiers have made straight for the temple, but two hands of men are prowling through the city, searching for other ways out, and one hand is at the gate."

"The priestesses?"

"On their way to the temple as well."

Ninshi nodded. "Then all we must do is avoid any strays until the soldiers of the temple of Ishtar have met with Sumugan. I think I would like to see this."

They snuck through the darkened streets, avoiding the light, and only crossing into the next street after careful watching. Their progress was slow. Miri was relieved to see Ninshi move with her familiar grace. She hadn't seen her like that for weeks. The lilu appeared and disappeared, moving in and out of the shadows, sometimes scaling a wall to travel on the roofs of the looming buildings that in some places covered the streets.

They came to the temple square, and the lilu went ahead, silently vanishing into the gloom. The square was dimly lit by the pale half-moon and a few stars scattered desultorily across the visible sky. The square was abandoned, its edges filled with trash, the doorways of few buildings facing it black squares or boarded up. The temple gates were ajar, and as far as Miri could tell, unguarded.

There was light shining through them, the sound of wind howling as if a storm raged within, and a low ululating cry like a wounded animal. It went on and on, a female voice, chanting in a low moan.

Ninshi signaled to the lilu, and they spread across the square, approaching the gates from three sides, Ninshi in the middle. She carefully peered into the temple compound, then straightened, waved Miri and Aialu to join her.

They walked through the gate and stopped. In the middle of the courtyard stood one of the priestesses, arms raised and chanting, her purple robes ragged at the bottom, her hair blown straight back. Blood streaked her cheek. Wind and sand whipped past her as she chanted. Dead soldiers littered the ground, and a dead horse, the officer who rode it half underneath. Two soldiers still stood, huddled in the corner of the courtyard, holding the torches that provided the light. The other priestess was nowhere to be seen.

"This way," the lilu gestured, and they crept along the wall, unnoticed to the building where Ninshi had been tortured. Miri stooped and pried the guttering torch from the hand of a soldier, his face ripped open, and his clothes torn by the wind that the priestess now fought. The full force of the wind from the temple seemed to be diminished here, but it must have been fierce, indeed. They slipped into the building through the cracked double doors. Ninshi and the lilu pushed them closed while Miri twirled the torch, causing it to flare up and burn more steadily.

She raised it above her head. The light revealed the chains still on the floor, and dimly lit the dais and throne beyond. The corpses of the men who had snatched Ninshi were gone, dark stains on the floor where they fell.

As they moved toward the throne, they could see that there were two doors at the back behind the throne. They were both closed. One door hung from its hinges, the other barred on this side. Ninshi looked at the lilu. "I don't know. I could only see this from the outside atop the wall."

Ninshi lifted the bar, and cautiously opened the door. Miri raised the torch and they peered through the doorway. They could see nothing, so Ninshi went through, spear at the ready. Miri followed, torch in one hand, her strung bow in the other.

Their nostrils were suddenly assaulted by the strong stench of decaying meat and blood. In the corner of the small room, the bodies of the thugs who had waylaid and tortured Ninshi lay piled against the wall. A cloud of flies swirled over the bodies. Small insects scuttled away as they approached. A few bags of what looked to be spoiled grain, and some broken boxes were the only other things in the room.

"I guess it's the other one," said the lilu behind them.

They backed out of the room and went through the broken door. There they found a dark hallway, littered with what looked to be the debris of decades. A rat skittered away from the light of the torch. It was lighter here, the moon peering through cracks in the roof. At the end of the hallway was another door, which opened into a larger room. This appeared to be some sort of combination living quarters and treasure room, though there was little of value to be spotted in the piles of rubbish that choked the corners.

Ninshi's sword rested by a heap of ragged sleep silks and pillows in the center of the room. A large lamp was next to it on the floor, and a drinking bowl. Ninshi tossed aside her spear and lifted the sword, hefted it, and pulled it from its faded gray scabbard, looked at its heavy-tipped form, turning it in her hands as she inspected it. She sighed. "This has been my companion for a great many years. I would have been sorry to have lost it after all this time."

They kicked through the pile of bedding on the floor and rummaged thought the trash that lined the walls and was piled in the corners, but the broken-tooth necklace wasn't there. Other than a few pieces of silver tossed in a corner, there was little other of value.

"This way." The lilu lead them trough a door on the side. Unnoticed, she had reshaped herself into what nearly looked human, only with an extra pair of arms ending in blade-like claws. Outside, Aialu's pale, sickly white skin seemed to glow.

They found themselves in an alley, the back of the temple looming over them, with a large structure butting up against it. To one side there was the temple compound wall. Miri spotted a door, moved toward it.

"Wait," Ninshi said. "Your torch." Ninshi used it to light the twisted wool wick of the lamp, then tossed the torch back into the room they had just left. The dry wood and debris caught readily. She handed it to the lilu. "You seem to have hands enough to spare," she said dryly.

They could hear the priestess chanting, and the wind howling in the temple courtyard. A booming voice said something, and another voice answered. Neither seemed like it came from a human throat. "What are they saying?" Miri asked.

Ninshi and the lilu both listened for a moment, then Ninshi shrugged. "Unclear at this distance, but it seems to be Sumugan arguing with someone. It may be the priestess, but the voice seems very powerful. Perhaps something arguing *through* her."

The lilu nodded. "It seems to be *eme-gir*, the language of Gilgamesh, from long ago, or something like it. But as you say, too far away."

"Through the door, then." They entered a large hallway, with an open arch at the temple end, and two doors twenty arms apart. The nearest door opened into what looked like a workshop, with benches and tools lining the wall, and more piles of unidentifiable debris heaped along the edges.

On a wooden workbench was the broken-tooth talisman. It was no longer on its leather cord. Tools lay around it, a bronze hammer, a small shaping stone, clay pots and instruments of craftmanship and labor. Around the talisman, the surface of the bench was dented and splintered, as if someone had tried to use the hammer to break the item. Ninshi picked up the tooth, examined it.

"Is it whole?" Miri asked.

Ninshi nodded. "I think it took the strength of something much more powerful than a ragged follower of this forgotten sand demon to break it, an age of the earth ago. Something with the

140

strength of a god, or something very near it." She looked around, pushed aside tools, dug under piles of the unidentifiable broken objects that littered the room. "Ha!" She lifted a small pouch, discarded in a corner. She dropped the tooth into it, pulled the leather strings shut, and tied it around her neck. "I have something to say to Sumugan."

"He seems a little busy right now," Miri said.

"Best time for a conversation." Ninshi started for the door.

"I was afraid you might have decided to run," the lilu said. "I am not disappointed."

They passed through the arch into the back of the temple. All the debris they had seen when last there was either gone or blown to the front. In the doorway facing out was the figure of Sumugan, clad in a black robe, waving his arms as he argued with the voice coming from the priestess. As they approached the shouting became clearer.

Ninshi put out an arm and they stopped, six arms away from Sumugan. Ninshi cocked her head, listened. The lilu started snorting, a harsh chocking sound, and Miri looked at her with alarm. The clay lamp was trembling in the Aialu's grasp, flickering as the lilu's body heaved in spasms. She almost dropped the lamp, grabbed at it, spilled a little oil but recovered.

Miri looked at her in amazement. The lilu was laughing! She spun around to Ninshi, who stood, sword in hand with a very odd look on her face. Ninshi looked a Miri, then Aialu.

"I am hearing right then?" Ninshi asked the lilu.

"Indeed. We seem to have caused the reunion of very old adversaries."

Miri shook her head. "What are they saying? What are *you* saying?"

"This seems to be a domestic quarrel," the lilu said. "They are going at it like fishwives in the market, fighting over who gets the stall near the road."

"I don't know," Ninshi said thoughtfully. "It is more like when some husband comes home full of beer, smelling of the harlots by the dock. You are right, he is speaking *eme-gir,* but in the manner of an enraged husband. But she speaks *eme-sal,* which means high speech. She is not Ishtar though. She is one of her handmaids, sent to find us, but instead it seems she found her wayward husband, and is giving him every sort of hell."

The lilu looked at Ninshi in amazement. "You planned this?"

Ninshi shook her head. "No. I had hoped only for a distraction." She stepped forward to the figure of Sumugan, without warning or sound stabbed him through his robes.

The bellowing wind died to nothing as he collapsed into a pile of sand. Ninshi kicked it aside, strode rapidly toward the stunned priestess, who suddenly found herself standing in the middle of a courtyard, surrounded by dead men. A spiraling cloud of smoke whirled above her head and disappeared into the darkness. She blinked at Ninshi as she stalked toward her, opened her mouth, gave a hoarse croak, and fell in a heap and was still.

Ninshi turned to the two men who huddled in the corner. They scrambled up, eyes white and large, and half stumbled, half ran out of the courtyard into the night.

"Gather arrows and anything that looks useful," she said. "We need to be out of the reach of Sumugan as soon as possible. I took him from the rear, by surprise, and while he was distracted. Next time will be far more difficult, I fear."

Miri grabbed a few more of the excellent black arrows from the quivers of the dead soldiers. She found a few copper coins, and the dead horse's saddle bags had bread and dried meat. Behind them, the throne room and connected buildings were cheerfully blazing, casting a bright light into the courtyard. She also found the small bronze figure of Ishtar, kicked into a corner and forgotten in the battle between the goddess and her erstwhile paramour.

They trotted to the gate of the temple compound. Almost there, they heard a voice behind them. "I thought myself forever shut of that harridan," Sumugan said. "They just don't make forever like they used too, eh?"

A small dust-devil whirled into life in front of them, formed itself into Sumugan. The lilu charged at him and was slapped aside. Ninshi stalked to the tall smirking figure and slashed at him. He danced back, and the wind around him blasted dust into Ninshi's face.

Ninshi stepped forward again, slashing back and forth, never catching him or getting close enough that the talisman could harm him, but pushing him back, blinded by the sand but able to follow by the sound of the dust devil that surrounded him.

Miri put two quick arrows into him. As before, he seemed not to notice.

Something came over Miri, perhaps a combination of fear for her mother, fatigue, and anger at the sand demon who plagued them. She dropped her bow and pulled out her knife, ran to him, screaming out her fear into a screeching war cry. She was grabbed from behind by the lilu. "He will kill you," she hissed.

"I will kill him!" Miri screamed, and struggled in the lilu's grasp. Aialu twisted the knife from Miri's hand, and it clattered to the ground.

Through the gate, Miri could see Ninshi, steadily backing Sumugan away, her face and hands bloodied by the cuts from bits of debris flung up by the wind. She stalked forward, one hand over her eyes, and slashed back and forth, driving the sand demon away from his temple. She was starting to slow, but the figure of Sumugan was growing less certain.

Miri shrugged free of Aialu's grasp, ran through the gate, the lilu behind her. A few steps and she was close enough. She reached into her pouch and grabbed the little idol, and raised her arm back, threw hard it at Sumugan's head.

It passed through the sand demon's head and clanged against the wall behind him, doing no damage. But Sumugan looked down for just that moment, and Ninshi's sword slashed across his middle. Once again, he collapsed into a pile of sand.

Ninshi wiped the sand from her eyes, spat. "Run," she croaked, and they set off across the square, into the alleys and passageways of the city.

For a time, the burning temple lit their way, but soon they were lost in the dark, twisted back streets. Once they came upon one of the groups of soldiers that were searching the city, but the men were going away from them. A few minutes of quiet waiting behind a low wall and they were clear.

After what seemed an eternity of stumbling and climbing over unseen barriers in the dark, they came to the market near the gates. There were soldiers waiting there, too, but they were staring at the growing conflagration of the temple, and by now other buildings, aflame in the center of the city, lighting the sky. They crept past before they were noticed and were out of the city.

The three of them walked down the road to the caravansary. They made no effort this time to wake the keeper, and the terrified boy who watched the livestock just trembled in the corner. But there were no horses to steal, only a tired old mare that refused to stand when they prodded her. There were three camels. Ninshi considered the camels for a moment, then shook her head. "Saddles are in the caravansary. No time to find them." They went back out the gate, the lilu loping beside them, once more on all fours.

They walked and ran for several hours, until the moon set, and it was too dark to continue. Ninshi led them off the road, up a hill, and they made cold camp under a grove of wild olive trees.

Miri was almost immediately asleep, rolled in her cloak with her pack as her pillow.

When she woke, it was near dawn. Birds caroled from branches above her, and the earthy scent of the wild olive trees was thick around them. She sat up, rubbed her eyes. Ninshi was awake, standing, facing in the direction of the road, the lilu beside her. Ninshi turned, lifted a finger to her lips. Miri got up, stood beside them, looked in the direction of their gaze.

The road lay only a short distance from the small hill they were on. Twenty or so soldiers of the temple of Ishtar were tramping their way, oblivious to the watchers above them. With them, riding an onager, was the figure of one of the priestesses, supported on each side by a soldier. She seemed unsteady on the donkey's back, and every few steps one of the soldiers pushed her back upright, where she sat for a few more steps of the onager, then started to lean the other way, and was pushed back again by the soldier on that side.

They eventually made their way down the road and disappeared.

"I think we should go that way," Miri said pointing away from the direction in which the soldiers had vanished.

The lilu turned to them. "I will be leaving you here," it said.

"Why?" Miri asked, surprised.

"I was called, and I answered. I am still not free, but I can now at least try to find my own destiny, for the first time in many long years." The lilu held out Miri's knife. "You dropped this last night. I was not going to give it to you until I was certain that you wouldn't stab me with it."

Miri stared at Aialu, blinking back the sudden tears. "I would never..."

"I know child, I know."

Aialu turned to Ninshi. "It was an honor to fight you, and an honor to fight by your side. If we meet again, it will be far from here and years away. Go in peace, Mistress of Tears."

Ninshi nodded, and the lilu loped away through the trees and was gone.

"Break camp. This will not be the only soldiers sent to find us, I think. We will buy or steal horses at the next caravansary."

"Will we see her again?" Miri asked, as she gathered her things.

"The lilu? Unlikely, I think."

"It was good, I think, that you had her in your time of need. A sister is a good thing."

"Not my sister." Ninshi grunted, but there was no heat in her words.

The Work We Have In Hand

G. W. Thomas

"The gods do not let us chose what deeds we will accomplish. Instead, we must suffer the work we have in hand." -- Vectorides

i

EMMERANT, wizard, conjurer and wealthy purveyor of information and other necromantic secrets, surveyed the collected rabble and wondered for the twentieth time why he had left the comfort of his highest tower--and the only thing that brought any joy into his long life, his collection of mystical gazing crystals—to be summoned by some new magister with promises of grand and stupendous power. He saw several of his customers and competitors, including the tall Narabezan Zu Man Dee with his ebony skin and

147

facial tattoos; Rheximal of the Sunken lands, sage and advisor to kings; the sleek and artificial Sheelma, the courtesan-turned-witch, her long legs sheathed to great effect in semite silk. There were a few other minor practitioners, the humble Boret-Tar with perpetually rank breath, and ZanderrednaZ the Hadisan of low order, plus witch doctors, hedge wizards and even a few midwives. All had the same red stone in their hands, some openly, others secreted away but close at hand. Each had received the same mysterious invitation. "Meet in the Temple of Sestiqil this dusk." The sun had long set over the abandoned shrine of pitted red tofa and weather-stained marble. Little used by priests, more often now by lotharios bent on stealing some virgin's gift, the gloomy walls were sturdy enough to keep out the wind but not the spiders, which danced about in the corners and over the doorframe.

"By Blaal's swinging bag!" cursed Rheximal. "Do we have to wait all night? Emmerant, is this some joke of yours?"

"When did you ever know me to jest – about anything— Sinklander?" Emmerant punctuated his distain, first for the man and secondly for inane questions, with a look he used on poor customers who didn't pay their bills. In fact, Emmerant was just as unhappy to be wasting an evening in a dusty shrine as the other.

Rheximal never answered that pinching retort. All the red stones began to glow in unison, to throb with mystical energy. Emmerant's brow darkened. He had applied a dozen spells and tests to the jewel, without any result that spoke of it being magical. This dark thought ended with him placing the stone into a special pouch he used for the collecting of manticore bolts and unicorn barbs.

There was a general shuffling now, as each wizard and witch examined the burning stone in his or her hand. Emmerant leaned over and watched the stone in the palm of a hedge wizard he knew casually but not by name. It was only when Rheximal looked up that they noticed a figure standing in the doorway.

"Who?"

The shadow moved forward, to reveal the face of a simple country bumpkin, a man with ale stains on the front of his suit of badly patched clothes, though the look in his eyes was not that of a peasant.

"Turgin?" howled the Sinklander and a few others. "What do you have to do with this?"

Though Rheximal did not say more – for all present knew the whole story and many had witnessed it themselves— of Turgin's

148

expulsion from their ranks for gross incompetence was known to them all.

"I have called you all here—" began Turgin in a powerful voice.

"Bah!" cried Rheximal, throwing his stone at the newcomer. "You waste my time, fakir!" What the wizard intended as his next move none ever knew for Turgin's hand came up, exposing another red stone, this one set in his palm like a tick bored into its victim, burning with a wicked and chilling light. Alien words sparked from Turgin's lips in a sudden and harsh burst, forming a syntax none in the room knew, diction from a language two hundred centuries old.

The Sinklander hurled himself at the newcomer, his hand forming the extremely painful but not-often fatal Glyph of Sundered Breathing. The red burst of light covered Rheximal's face but no face remained a second later. What arrived at Turgin's feet was no longer a man. It was merely ash. Turgin took a second to place his buskined foot in the little gray pile and kick. The mighty Rheximal of the Sunken Lands filled the cracks in the stones of the temple's floor.

The other wizards and adepts did several things—some tried to throw their stones from their hands, and failed; others attempted to attack Turgin with their own brands of sorcery—and also failed.

After a few seconds of flopping about like gaffed halibut, they all dropped their hands to their sides and began chanting the same unearthly phrase Turgin spoke. *"Skelq scoruscorum sheek shek Nyoglatha —"* One of the weaker hedge wizards screamed, his body and possessions lit brightly for a second from his burning palm, then turned to the same gray ash as Rheximal.

"Come!" said Turgin, who had been shunned by his brother and sisters, speaking in a new voice, one that was as terrible and uncompromising as it was flat and emotionless. "Come, let us begin."

With this last command all the remaining sorcerers gathered about him and their voices rose in unison—

Not quite all, for Emmerant had not been holding his stone when the others succumbed to Turgin's power. Instead of attacking, Emmerant pulled his cloak about himself and became part of the wall. Not quite invisible, he exploited the chaos and shadows to hide while terror took place around him.

He waited. The singers went on endlessly, chanting in the weird language he did not recognize—he who spoke fourteen languages and cants and read over twenty! *I have never heard nor read these foul words*, he told himself as he waited.

And suddenly it stopped. The collective body of sages dropped their hands, which had been held palms up in a circle, and turned and looked at Emmerant all as one.

Speaker of fourteen languages, including the cannibal tongue of Gaki, he simply said, "Shit!" before he ran.

ii

ABERDIN VOL slid the dagger between the fat man's third and fourth rib with a gentle smile, such as a kindly uncle might give his favorite nephew.

"Sorry, Faku, not today."

The big man fell over with a grunt, dropping his own stiletto to the dirty city street.

Vol cleaned the dagger on the dead man's sleeve then sheathed the weapon. He paused long enough to straighten his hat, comb down either side of his long moustache before stepping back into the deeper shadows. No point in making it too easy for Jorn Stepok's men. This was the third assassin who had tried to collect the bounty on Vol's head in the last two days. This couldn't go on.

An idea, a grim idea, came to the man who others called The Falcon of Grimswood because of his curved nose and his gray feather-colored hair. Handsome, good at riding both women and horses, he found himself alone and in the middle of trouble for the hundredth time since he had come to Stormcock, the City of Birds. Where else could a falcon go? he would jest. He didn't feel like joking now. Stepok wanted him dead and eventually one of these snipers would succeed. He had to do something. When he left the street he took away with him a grisly prize wrapped in a sack made from Faku's shirt.

He'd need a disguise. The long hair and the moustache would have to go, but what was that to him? First, he'd have to go to a secret room he kept in the Street of Blood-letters, also known as Leech Street. Good, the blood leaking from his new prize would not be suspicious in that charnel house row.

He quickly skipped over the Street of Purchased Pleasures and the adjacent Avenue of Unwanted Babies and came up to the stair to his hidden roost when he heard steel being drawn from its housing.

"I thought you might come this way, Falcon." It was Jumal, a half-caste Narahbezan who had shared more than a few tankards with him in *The Bleeding Nun*.

"Jumal, what is this nonsense?" Aberdin asked, seeing the other weighing his sword and loosening his wrist.

"Come, come, my friend. The bounty is six hundred florens. Even I can not resist."

"But friendship—"

"Six hundred," was all he offered with a shrug.

"Alright, just let me put this down—" With a feinting move to put the bag down, Aberdin instead hurled the heavy, wet mess into Jumal's face. The Narah-bezan cursed as the gruesome package connected with his nose. By the time he had wiped the blood and gore from his eyes, Vol had his own blade free.

"Last chance," Aberdin offered.

"I think not," Jumal returned, now angry with his former friend.

Their swords came together in a sharp clatter. These were not heavy broadswords thrown about by savage Gelts but thin rapiers, long and lethal, each a flashing, crafty silver missile. Despite the finesse, this was no contest of cultured gentlemen either. Skill was simply another way to go about killing someone.

Jumal pressed his attack, managing to score the first hit, a red gash on Aberdin's right cheek.

"First blood," acknowledged Vol. "I surrender. Take me to Jorn Stepok." He dropped his sword point only a little.

"Forget it. The bounty is very specific. Stepok wants only one—small part of you."

"Not that small, I assure you," returned the other. "To the death, then."

"You never should have touched his daughter."

"Believe me, I did much more than *touch* her. At her request, of course."

Jumal stopped talking and plunged into another attack. Vol blocked every cut with swift steel until he got close enough to send his boot soundly into Jumal's crotch. The Narah-bezan buckled, leaving himself open for a coup-de-grace. It never came. Aberdin slammed the hilt of his sword into the other man's skull, knocking him to the ground, and into the darkness of unconscious waters.

Vol sheathed his sword quickly, pulling Jumal's unconscious body into a pile of bloody rags thrown into the gutter by the leeches of the jurisdiction. Not one to take an insult too freely, Aberdin fished in a pouch and came out with a bottle of dark squirming bodies. Leeches, the real kind, kept as part of a disguise, for when he wanted to walk the streets unnoticed. He opened the small pot and began to apply the black, hungry denizens to his sometimes friend. The cream of the jest--for the blood loss would keep Jumal from trying to collect again for several days—was Aberdin applied them only to his lower, manly organs. Small part, indeed!

Gaining his secret cubicle within the house on the Street of Blood-letters, Aberdin took off the wig of long gray-blond tresses, exposing a completely bald head, then peeled the waxed mustachios from his lip. Here was the real Falcon that no one saw! It was only a matter of seconds to apply a tincture of yellow to his face, a small pigtail wig to the back of his head, a fake scar opposite to the real one he would soon have from Jumal's blade, false teeth and lastly, an outfit of Ijuan manufacture, to make him look like a vendor of charms and other geegaws. A ready assortment of these was at hand. The Falcon was gone and Su-jan was born. He placed a few other choice items into pockets and in his boot. The lovely sword he left standing in one corner, like a lost child, replacing it with a wrist blade.

He stepped back out onto the street, his new wound covered with a paste bandage and he was nothing more than a customer returning to work. He did stop for a second to see how Jumal was doing in his pile of refuse. Sound asleep, good.

Making his way slowly--so the bag he carried would not drip too often, and to allay suspicion--Aberdin left Leech Street and headed south for many blocks until he came to a tall house with a massive oaken door. Above the door was a set of stage antlers. Huge steel bolts spoke of security for the owner. The little fake Ijuan stepped up to the vast planks and knocked quickly, professionally. A little window in the portal clacked open. A hoarse voice said, "What business?"

"I come to collect the bounty," Aberdin said with just the right amount of accent. Only a slight intonation, for most actors over-do the foreign element and come off false immediately.

"What bounty?"

"The Falcon."

A bolt shot back, then two others. Finally the door opened, showing a pot-bellied Taavsite in black velvet. Stepok and his men had lived in Stormcock for fifteen years but to the day they still carried their rustic natures with them. It was custom to pay a gold coin into the hand of the doorman but this was different – the bounty of Jorn Stepok's most sought after enemy.

"Let me see!" demanded the doorman.

"No, no, no," said Aberdin, clutching the bag to his chest, his body stooped as with age. The doorman, a warrior of experience though now growing soft in luxury, grabbed the bag from Aberdin's suddenly frail fingers. He tore open the loose cloth bag. The head rolled out and onto the stone doorstep.

"Fuck, we wanted his cock, not his head, you stupid slant!"

As he cursed, the man backed up to avoid the bloody mess, made bloodier by Aberdin's knife. The skull was missing most of its skin and was quite unrecognizable.

"Want my money!" barked the false Ijuan, stepping inside.

"Fuck you, you'll get nothing—" The doorman stepped in to meet him, to shove him out the open door. Aberdin's hands were no longer weak or empty. His dagger came up with one expert thrust into the man's throat, silencing him as well as killing him.

Aberdin waited a second to see if anyone observed him either in the street or in the house. No one. He closed the door but didn't lock it. Quickly shucking his disguise, he pulled off the doorman's attire, making sure to preserve as much of the blood on the chest as possible. Another wig with beard, this one flaxen haired not unlike the dead Taavstite's. He rolled up his Ijuan equipment into his vendor's caddy and set it aside in case he should have time to leave with it. The naked dead man he shoved in behind a tapestry of the Battle of Halkin Half-Blood over the Narahbezans, a famous Taavisite conquest.

Aberdin made his way carefully down the hall, hiding the blood on his shirt. Timing was important for the right effect. He made it to the doorway of the main hall where Jorn Stepok sat on a throne much like a king's. The arrogance of these warrior-merchants! Vol could hear Jorn yelling, "Who's at the fucking door, Clar?"

The fake Clar took a second to see who else was sitting about the room. Three others, Jorn's two sons, Frigik and Yurik, and another, an older man, quite fat and tied to a chair. Both hands bound separately and far apart. He bore several wounds, no doubt, inflicted by one of the heirs apparent.

"Clar! You clapped up horse's arse, where are you?"

The perfect moment, for Jorn got up from his seat and started for the doorway. Aberdin threw himself into the room, making sure the copious blood on his shirt was evident. He collapsed face down, as dead appearing as possible. He waited. He felt a hand pulling him round. The dagger flashed up and into a throat. As he rose, he saw it was not Jorn but his oldest son who clutched his neck before sinking into a pool of blood.

"Falcon!" roared the Taavisite, stepping back to draw his four-foot long sword from its scabbard, strapped to the side of his throne-like seat.

Aberdin made no reply to this, instead threw his dagger at the other son, who dodged the missile and drew his own sword. The dagger landed harmlessly into the wood of the chair of the bound fat man. Their enemy weaponless, the two men pounced to vent their anger on his sorry corpse.

The son's sword flew past Aberdin as he rolled away. The father's weapon wasn't far behind and the newcomer had to block the blade to one side with a brass stand that held candles. Aberdin was able to step to his left and shove the base of the stand into junior's face before blocking another stroke from papa. The move was brilliant but doomed for both men stepped back then launched themselves at Aberdin. Only one of the men froze as stiff as a statue, allowing Aberdin to concentrate on the father. That the son was immobile he could not explain but neither did he have time to examine the man, busy dodging and blocking with his poorer weapon. Finally he heard Jorn exclaim, "Yurik, why do you stand there?"

Yurik made no reply. Another voice spoke behind him, the wizard who was no longer tied to the chair but standing with both hands free and a dagger in one of them.

"I have frozen him, Jorn. Stop now or I will set him ablaze."

"Damn you, wizard, I should have killed you when—"

"Now, Jorn. Stop while you still have one son."

The Taavsite swore to his northern gods then dropped the sword with disgust.

"Magic, bah!"

Aberdin dropped the heavy end of his candle stand, though he kept it close in case he needed it again.

"Took you long enough," he said to the fat man.

"You damn near took a finger off with that toss," complained the other.

"Don't be a baby. What do we do with them?"

"There is no need to do anything. Jorn Stepok will be no further trouble."

Aberdin kicked at his candlestick like a pouting child. "But he has a price on my head."

"That will stop, right, Jorn?"

"Damn you, he is the Falcon. He robbed my daughter –"

"Nonsense," humphed the wizard. "It's a well-known fact your daughter has been loose with her favors. The Falcon here wasn't even her second. Let alone her tenth!"

"How could you know? Wizards are liars and cheats."

"I am the farseer. Believe me. I have seen. I know."

Jorn cursed some more. "He killed Frigik."

"What is the weirgild for your son?'

The old man paused, cursed, and finally came up with: "A thousand."

"Really? Do you take me for a fool?" asked the fat man.

"Alright, seven hundred."

"That's better, Let us not bicker like fish-wives. What is the bounty you set on our dear Aberdin Vol?"

"Six hundred," provided Aberdin.

"That's a difference of a hundred gold florins. You don't have to pay the six and you get a hundred." The large wizard looked at the other man. "Pay it, Aberdin."

"I'd rather kill them both," the Falcon said picking up Jorn's weapon.

"Nonsense, you'd rather sleep at night. If you pay the hundred I will let it be known that the weirgild is paid, the bounty is off and everyone is friends again. Deal?"

Aberdin thought it over then agreed. "I will have to get the money. Shouldn't be more than an hour."

"Good," said the wizard, taking the chair he had been tied to and sitting. "I have a little score to settle with Jorn and his boy, Yurik—I mean they found me on their property certainly, tired and unconscious, but that hardly gives them the right to torture me and all."

Jorn's face blanched. He turned to run but found himself as immobile as his son.

Aberdin headed for the door. He stopped. "You sure there's going to be anyone here to give that hundred to when I get back?"

"Certainly. We aren't barbarians, are we?"

Aberdin nodded, despite the fact that he had no idea what the answer meant. He left.

Emmerant pulled himself up off the couch, eyed the frozen Jorn. "You're probably thinking he'll never come back. That is a chance I am willing to take. If he doesn't come back I will pay you the money. I have plans for Aberdin Vol." He pulled up his sleeves. "Now, about this matter between us…"

Aberdin Vol slunk from the house with the big oak doors, not sure if he heard screaming inside or not.

iii

"I WANT TO thank you, Emmerant," said Aberdin Vol as he drained his mug.

"You are welcome," acknowledged the wizard from his own seat in the *Pregnant Virgin* Inn. He did not drink ale but wine in a tiny cup, little bigger than a thimble. The concentrated liquid inside was deep purple and three gold coins a shot.

"Now that Jorn and I are no longer at odds I find myself with a little breathing space," said the Falcon.

"Don't get too comfortable."

"I won't. I'm sure if the opportunity arises, Jorn will put an arrow in my back."

"I did not mean that. Surely you are right. Stepok doesn't forgive or forget. But he will not concern you for a little while at least. I've made sure of that."

"I thank you again." Aberdin looked about for a bar wench to refill his cup. He was now dressed once again in his graylocks and beard. He hoped the bar maid might fill more than his cup alone.

"What I mean," said Emmerant, who stared into a purple ring on one finger, "is that I have work for you. For both of us, really."

Aberdin laughed. "No need for charity, my good wizard. I can find plenty of work on my own."

"I do not mean mere employment – for gold."

"What other kind is there?"

"Service to your country – your Fellow Man." The wizard stopped there, letting it hang.

Aberdin howled at the suggestion, banging his empty mug on the rough board table. "Fellow Man! Those bastards are the fools I bilk and steal from. They want no service from me unless it's slitting my own throat."

"Let me ask you this—" interrupted the wizard, laying a hand on the other man's restless mug. "—how many wizards are sitting in this room?"

Vol stopped mid-laugh and looked around, mostly for the barmaid. "None, just one, you."

"And most nights?"

"A few – maybe three or four. This is Stormcock after all."

"Yes, my point exactly. Now, watch as the evening progresses. How many will you see?" The wizard said no more, seemed to withdraw into his own mind.

Aberdin laughed again then stopped. He noticed the far corner where often he saw Korquit the magister make coins jump for the amusement of the locals. The fellow had proven useful for Aberdin could assume his identity with only a few costume items. The magic trick was simple enough. Aberdin had done it and many others for his knowledge of magic was considerable though he tended towards locks and dodges.

"What is your point, fat one?"

"Fat one, is it?"

"Well, when you sit there with your lips twitching and your eyes closed—"

"I'm thinking. You might try it."

"Ha ha, what are you on about? So what if a few wizards haven't shown up? It might be some kind of ceremonial conjunction or other."

"I assure you not. There is no important celestial conjunction for another twelve years. They—the wizards and witches—simply aren't here. And if you go out into the street, you'll see they aren't there either."

"And you know where they are?"

"Yes."

"And you're going to tell me?"

"No."

"This service to humanity thing would be easier if you'd gave me a clue."

"If I told you, you'd do something heroic and stupid and end up another pawn for that which threatens us all."

"And what is that?"

"I'm not exactly sure. I've witnessed what it is capable of. Tonight I will use my scrying glass to find out more. Then, and only then, will I formulate a plan."

157

"This has something to do with Jorn, doesn't it?"

"Not exactly. I was fleeing this—menace—almost became trapped like the other wizards. I happened to stumble onto Jorn's estate, weak, half-crazed but alive. One of his men found me and brought me to his master."

"Who thought he'd have some fun torturing you."

"The Taavsites are not fond of magic."

"Bunch of straw-headed barbarians—"

"Yes, yes, let's not waste time on them. We have dealt with Jorn for now. Let's concentrate on this other problem."

"Which is--?"

"I'm not sure yet. But I need a strong arm in this matter. You will be that arm, Aberdin Vol."

"Why me? As if I even wanted the stupid job!"

"Because you are resourceful. You can get into places I cannot without being noticed. You can think. You can use a blade, or I suspect maybe even a little magic. Yes?"

"Just on the ladies." With this Aberdin shifted his attention away from the fat wizard and smiled at the short, dark-haired girl with the ale pitcher who had finally showed up. Vol spoke with her separately for a few minutes before returning to the table.

"I have to go."

"The young lady—"

"Yes, but tell you what—I'll come see you tomorrow. Do your crystal ball thing and we'll talk some more. Gotta go."

"Tomorrow, my tower, by noon. Don't be late."

Aberdin left the wizard with a wave and the dark-haired wench under one arm, partly because she was young and willing, but also for another reason. He wanted to test this wizard's theory later that night.

iv

MIDNIGHT. Stormcock, unlike most cities, was still alive and lit with activity and smoking fires. The bird song that characteristically fills the City of Birds with a constant cacophony of trills and piping was softer, broken only by the occasional sad, sweet voice of a nightingale. Into cool and quiet streets came Aberdin Vol, disguised as the lowly Korquit the magister, performer of humble tricks. He headed for *The Bleeding Nun*, favored hangout of wizards and practioners of the magical arts. The place was empty except for a few posers who knew about as much about magic as the king did about politics.

The Pregnant Virgin was the same, as was *The Honest Butcher*. Patrons of other professions, but magicians--none.

His next stop required a change of clothing. Where he was going he did not want to resemble any form of wizard. Instead he took on the appearance of a leech, carrying a jar of black slugs and a case full of sharp pointed things. For where he went was the outskirts of Jorn Stepok's estate, resting a half-mile outside the city walls. He arrived well after moonrise, so he had some light to navigate the rough road. He saw no one so the disguise proved unnecessary. All the blond-haired Taavsite workers were snuggled up with their mannish-looking blond wives, snoring away. He only wished he had more light so he could look for signs of Emmerant's desperate passing. He said he had ended up half-conscious on Jorn's estate. So where had he come from?

There! A fence had been knocked down. Certainly the wizard's prodigious bottom could have done that. He stepped closer and looked off in the distance. Nothing out that way except the necropolis. Now, there was a place he did not care to venture into. Ghouls and worse, no doubt. Then again he might go—do something 'heroic and stupid' after all. His curiosity wasn't satisfied. He watched a while longer. A dull reddish light flared up and died in the distant ruins of the city of the dead. Was it real or a trick of the eye? It did not repeat itself. No point in stumbling around in the dark, barking his shins on old masonry. Still—

Aberdin Vol did one of the smartest things he had ever done. He turned around and headed home. It appeared Emmerant had told the truth, some very small part of it. Perhaps something terrible was happening here in Stormcock. Two questions battled inside Vol's head as he made for his roost in the Street of Blood-letters. Why get involved? And how could he make a nice pile of coins out of this all?

v

IT WAS WELL after the eleventh hour of the morning when Aberdin Vol spied Emmerant's tower loft high on a hill overlooking the River Valhallan. The road was little more than a goat path as he drew closer to the tall structure. Aberdin's horse, a stolen nag he had found in a small stable outside one of the poorer inns--he had every intention of returning it by dinnertime--stumbled on stones the size of robin's eggs. The rider dismounted, leading the animal the rest of the way to the large oak portal at the bottom of the tower.

Aberdin banged on the door with the pommel of his dagger. He had to admit to himself he was a little disappointed. If Emmerant was such a great wizard why did he not have a dragon parked on his doorstep or at least an ogre? This was all too mundane. Anybody could—

Then the door formed gigantic lips and said, "What do you want?"

Aberdin stepped back only an inch, but step back he did.

"It is I, Aberdin Vol, expected guest."

"So says you. Only Aberdin Vol could answer this question correctly, 'What is the twenty-seventh sign in the Partushian heterogoogy?'"

"I wouldn't know that. What is this crap?"

"That is the correct answer. Vol would not know. Enter—*stupid*."

Vol paused only a second to contemplate whether he wanted to sheath his dagger in the door's frame but thought better of it. The mouth widened into an open doorway and he moved inside, looking up for any teeth that might top that awesome jaw. Once inside he saw he stood on an ordinary doorstep with a table, a vase of dried flowers and a chair. Behind him was the back of an oak door and before him about a thousand stairs leading up.

He sighed and began climbing.

When he reached the top he found another door, this one inset with a piece of metal and no door handle. He touched the metal plate. It tingled. He placed his hand flat against the cool metal and heard a click a second later. The door swept inward without so much as a breath from him.

"Come in, " called a voice from somewhere above him.

"I have a hard time imagining you walking up all those stairs, Emmerant."

"Of course not. You didn't use the lift?"

"The lift?"

"You just sit in the chair and it whisks you up. You didn't really walk all that way?"

"I'm not talking to you if I can't see you. Where are you?" demanded the breathless Aberdin.

"Up here. It's just three steps. If you can manage it?"

Biting his tongue, Vol slogged up the remaining steps to find a spacious circular room. In the center of it was Emmerant sitting in a high-backed comfortable chair. In front of him was a small table, almost more of a stool, upon which rested a large crystal. Looking up, Aberdin noticed for the first time that the surrounding walls were filled with niches. In these were a thousand different gazing crystals.

"Go ahead," said the seer. "Everybody says it."

"You must spend as lot of time dusting."

"What?" The fat wizard turned from his glass and looked at his visitor. "That's not what they say."

"It's not?"

"No, they say stupid things like, 'What a lot of crystals you have.' or 'Why do you need so many? Isn't one enough?'"

"I hardly think either of those things. What I was really thinking was: 'how much money could I get for this lot of rubbish?'"

"Always the thief, eh?"

"I am rather fond of my little extras."

"Nonsense. You live more sparsely than a hermit. I almost think you might be better serving as a monk or one of those acolytes who whip themselves."

Aberdin was taken back by this. It was true but how did he know? The rich swag-about-town was one of the parts he played. It wasn't any more real than Korquit or any other number of fake identities he had.

"How do I know? You are wondering," interrupted the fat man. "The way I know everything I know. I saw it—here—in a crystal."

"I would be better pleased if you left my private affairs—private," said Aberdin. The tone was cold. There was a threat there, not too far below the surface.

"Fear not, good Vol. I had no desire to know all your secrets. Only enough to know you are here with sincere intent. We are about to face a most terrible danger—and you sir, will be at the very front line —my sword arm if you will."

"Sounds like a job for an idiot. I am not arrow fodder."

"It is not that kind of battle, sir, calm yourself. This is magic we face, the darkest, the most insidious. I don't need a legion of sharp blades but one man, one smart, quick of wit, and devious. I need you."

"Now you are trying flattery."

"Not at all. Deny it if you like but you are that person. Your personal demons are your own. I don't need to know what makes you what you are—just to know that you are such a man. Come, sit down, refresh yourself." Emmerant waved Vol towards a small alcove off from his crystal room. There was a chair, a table and a lunch of cold chicken, cheese, bread and wine.

"Thank you. I had forgotten this was a lunch invitation."

Aberdin sat, ate the majority of the meat and cheese but only sparingly of the bread. He was a thin, waspish man and he planned to stay that way. He finished by sipping his wine and watching his host stare into his crystal. After a while, the large man picked up the sphere and exchanged it for another, less round, less polished. He gazed into that for a while. Aberdin cleaned his fingernails with his dagger.

"Exciting, old boy," Vol finally said. "But I've got a horse to return."

"Fear not. The owner of your horse is dead. Killed in his own room last night. The young girl he was bedding had another agenda than his sweaty, hairy arms."

Vol thought about this for a second before replying. "Why didn't she steal the horse, too?"

"She works at the inn. She and her lover. They had planned to sell it this morning but you stole it about an hour before they came for it."

"Humh, no hurry then, I guess."

"No, none."

Aberdin went back to picking his nails. "Anybody ever tell you you're pretty much a bust as a host?"

"Nonsense."

"Focus your rock, because you'll want to see me walking out the door."

"I think not. That door won't open until I command it to do so."

"Can you see the dagger I'm holding right now?"

"Yes."

"Can your crystal predict the future? Can it tell you that you're about to have it shoved into your back?"

"That would be foolish. You'd never leave this tower. You'd starve in less than a month. The door will only open if I tell it to. I think you'd best humor me for a minute longer—yes, there it is. Now I know *what you need to know.*"

With that Emmerant rose from his crystal and invited Aberdin to follow him to another short set of stairs that led to another small chamber furnished with rugs and cushions.

"We can talk here."

Vol propped a few cushions under his back, made sure his dagger handle was handy, and relaxed—a little.

"So talk."

"What do you know about history, Mr. Vol?"

"Please, call me Aberdin, or Falcon if you like."

"Alright, Aberdin."

"Not much. I know what old things are worth stealing, a bit about where treasure can be found, and mostly, I don't care."

"Well, today you should."

"Why?"

"Because something very old has come back to haunt us here in Stormcock. You, no doubt, made some investigations in the city. All the magicians are missing, gone."

"Yes, either run off or just plain missing."

"The few who are smart enough to flee have. The rest I fear have fallen to *It*, become party to *It*. Starting with that fool, Turgin. That will be your first job, I think, but more of that later."

"A job without recompense, I fear."

"Yes, perhaps for both of us. But if I know you at all, Aberdin, you'll find some way to fill your purse out of it."

"We'll see. Get on with the history lesson. My arse's falling asleep."

"This age we live in is a distant one. There have been many ages before us, each unique in its own way. One of these was the time of the demon-kings."

"Lovely, demons."

"Not exactly. These demon-kings were actually men, sorcerers who became avatars for powerful beings, strange ones who dwelt outside our world. Great battles between them scarred the earth."

"What happened to them?"

"They all died in a great war. Their arrogance grew so fierce that they challenged the very gods. And lost."

"The gods? Tortrosh or Valhallan?"

"No, not the childish spirits we worship today. The old gods, terrible figures of power, whom no man can name or summon."

"That's handy."

"Be glad of it. Such beings are not friends to humankind."

"Anyway, the demon-kings—"

"Yes, when they lost this war, they were all captured, trapped in the fiery depths of the planet to suffer for all time."

"I see what you mean."

"Only one of them has escaped. Somehow. I have yet to figure out the details. Somehow Turgin freed it, or happened upon it, I don't know which. And you must find out. Take up his trail. Find out what he did. But be careful. If Turgin or one of his new clan finds you – I shudder to think."

"And I don't get paid for having my nuts blasted off by crazy wizards. Why did you think I was the one stupid enough for this job?"

Emmerant stopped for a second and asked, "Why all the faces, Mr. Vol? What is it you desire more than anything in the entire world?"

"I told you to stay out of my private affairs—"

"Calm yourself. I ask not out of some secret exposed but as a genuine question."

"I—"

"Yes?"

"I would like to know who I am. Who my parents were."

"You were an orphan, weren't you?"

"Yes."

"I held in this hand a red stone given me by Turgin. If I had been holding it when he took over the others, I too would be a mindless automaton under his control. But I did not – for when his spell began it started by playing images in my mind, quick pictures of my life in reverse. Then my father's and his father's."

"But you dropped the stone?"

"Yes, for the vision served to analyze the person I was so that it could erase it. But if I could find another of these stones, and change the spell that activates it, I could use it to replay your life, your predecessor's lives without draining you of anything. And then you'd know."

"Damn," said Aberdin, not because he was impressed with the idea, tempting as it was, but at Emmerant's skill at finding the one and only thing in the whole world that could motivate him to join up on this suicide pact of a quest.

"Are you in, Mr. Vol?"

"Yes, but stop calling me Mr. Vol. It's not my real name. I just made it up."

"Of course, you have no idea what your real name is. I understand. But I have to call you something."

"Aberdin will do."

"Yes, of course."

"So I begin with Turgin the bumbler?"

"Yes, find out everything you can about him, his movements over the last month. Especially a little event that took place in the Conclave of Wizards a fortnight ago. That seems to me where it began."

"Alright. When do we meet again?"

"I will be in *The Pregnant Virgin* every night after the sun sets, except tomorrow. When you feel you know enough, meet me there. If it's an emergency, then come here. Alright?"

"Yah, sure."

"I will open that door now." Emmerant waved his hand dramatically. Aberdin could hear the door below snap open.

"Thanks for the lunch."

"My pleasure," said the large wizard who did not rise. He didn't want to embarrass himself in front of his guest.

"*Pregnant Virgin*," said Aberdin as he disappeared, then he was gone, back down the thousand steps for the chair was at the bottom and he didn't know how to summon it. The horse waited outside the tower; the front door gave him no guff. Aberdin mounted, and looked at the city of Stormcock stretching out below him, its opal towers, its stews along the river.

"Home, Crystal," he said, giving the mare a name. He laughed at his own joke, bad as it was. "Crystal *grazing*." And laughed again.

vi

THE SEARCH for Turgin the bumbler was surprisingly easy. Putting on a disguise of Mammon Plenk, tax collector, Aberdin began a quick search of the cheaper boarding houses. Each matron wanted to be rid of him so fast he was soon on the doorstep of Madame Bouw-fronk, a middle-aged widow who kept six rooms over an apocathery shop. Small, dirty and cold, these rooms rented for about the price of a good mug of ale.

"Your accounts seem to be in order," Vol said coldly, after scrutinizing Bow-fronk's previous tax order. "But I have a question about this last one—the man who still owes you two weeks rent—Turgin."

"Yes, he's taken a runner, I fear. Thinks of himself as a magician but most of his money came from mucking out stables, if you ask me."

"I did not, in fact, ask you," returned the false taxmonger. He let her stew for a moment. "Show me his room."

"There's no money there, I can assure you," sniped the older woman, then regretting her words she said, "Right this way."

Once at the open door to Turgin's room, Aberdin dismissed the landlady. "I don't think I will require anything else of you—" He let it hang there like a threat and she took the bait and ran.

He entered slowly, taking time to look up and down for traps, hiding spots and spiders. He found only the latter. A careful survey of the bed, the small chest and empty closet produced a few rags, more spiders and in the chest, a scrap of paper. Vol examined this chunk of filthy vellum and the charcoal lines written upon it. It appeared to say: "Tramminimm--" Whatever that was? Perhaps Emmerant would know?

The tax collector left without further discussion with the landlady. A short trip home and he was Aberdin Vol, "The Falcon", once again with his flashy cape, long gray-colored tresses and pointy beard. He knew he had to go where a gallant would be welcome and a taxmonger most certainly would not. He needed information of a scholarly kind. That meant a visit on his good friend Gorstelmach, the bookseller.

The shop was lodged between an Ijuan grocery with its chickens feet in pickling jars and other oddments, and a saddler's stall where long strips of bull hide hung in the sunny portion of the street to dry. Aberdin entered the doorless cubicle and stared at the rows and rolls of books, piles of scrolls, even a few Merkheen story sticks.

"Those are new," he said to the old man who scrounged in the shelves under the front counter.

"Yes, and whole lot of good they'll do you without a stout Merikheen girl to translate them for you. I think most of the people who buy them use them as walking sticks." Gorstelmach looked up from his dusty search and smiled at Aberdin. The old man's bald head shone where it wasn't white with dust.

"Why hasn't Buk dusted this hell-hole?" Vol asked with false annoyance.

"He's left me again."

"He can't leave you. He is a slave."

"Well—" Gorstelmach waved him off with a gesture of resignation.

"More Bastilian courtiers?"

"He loves me. He'll be back."

"Of course he will. He always comes back. With a sore head and a sorer—"

"What do you want, Graylocks?"

Vol shrugged, handed Gorstelmach the scrap. "This word. What does it mean?"

Gorstelmach eyed the letters, thought for a moment. He had once been a Bastilian acolyte, a junior wizard on the road to high-priesthood. Only the celibacy had turned his course. His incomplete studies did not make him a wizard but they proved useful to Aberdin on many occasions.

"Twenty."

"Twenty? That's steep for one stupid—"

"It's special. I want twenty florens. And not a felspick less."

Aberdin thought it over, doing a fair imitation of Gorstelmach only a moment ago, then he gave the man eighteen gold coins. "It's all I've got."

"Bullshit, but I'll take it. I would have settled for ten."

"Rat bastard! Tell me about the word."

"It's a Hadisan spell word."

"A palindrome?"

"Yes, to complete it just add 'A-R-T'."

"Tramminimmart?"

"Careful! Graylocks. I wouldn't go around saying that aloud. If the conditions for the spell are right – then who knows what will happen?"

"Conditions? Like what?"

"Blood spilled, moonlight, a freshly deflowered virgin."

"You made that last one up, you old dog."

"Who knows? Perhaps all three. The spell is very precise. If the conditions are wrong you can yell it until you're blue in the face. But —"

"Yes, I understand. You're sure the word would be complete with those letters?"

"It is possible there is a longer pattern—say Tramminimmanamminimmart, or some such. It's impossible to know. That's the secret to Hadisan magic. It's very personal. Not for half-baked sorcerers or intuitive bumblers."

"Almost scientific."

"Blasphemy."

"I've made no secret of my leanings toward the heresy of Science. It is very useful," admitted Vol.

"And what has it got you? Outlawed."

"No, that was my over-friendly nature."

"Over-friendly with married women."

"I can't help it if I was cast out as a child and have a need to return to the soft breast denied me."

"And you call me an old dog," laughed Gorstelmach, scooping up his coins and secreting them away behind the counter.

"What would you suggest I do with this little scrap of magic?"

"Burn it."

"Is it worth anything to a fellow magister?"

"If you could find one, perhaps, but not much. A few gold coins."

"And there is no way to determine the conditions needed for the spell?"

"None."

"Thanks, Gorstelmach," Vol said as he walked out. His hand quickly claimed one of the Merikheen story sticks.

"Hey, that's extra!"

"I would have settled for thirty," laughed Aberdin as he disappeared down the street.

vii

IT WAS AN entire day too soon to meet up with Emmerant at *The Pregnant Virgin*, so Aberdin wandered from inn to inn, his ear to the ground for any sign of wizards, Hadisan or otherwise. His trail to Turgin had proven short and cold of information. It bothered him that he would not be able to surprise the hefty wizard with some nugget of wisdom, a clue or two, to show he was really the man for the job. Still, he knew patience and he was prepared to keep a watch out for signs.

It was this watchfulness that saved his life. He was coming down the stairs from the massage rooms above *The Bleeding Nun* when he spied four blond heads. Unfortunately they spied him too, pointed and drew their swords.

"Damn, Taavsites!" Aberdin cursed. One of them was Jorn Stepok's surviving son, Yurik. With Emmerant out of his house, Stepok had become less forgiving it seemed. Either that or sonny boy was too drunk to care. Either way Vol made it quickly back up the stairs to one of the massage rooms. There were cries of indignation as he stepped into the space, into the bed and finally out the window.

If he had been in less of a rush he might have enjoyed the scenery a little first, but this was life and death. No time for gawking.

He made the roof and skipped over the cedar shakes to the building beside the inn, a stable, then jumped down to the roof. He thought he had made his escape when he heard shouts from the inn door. The Taavsites hadn't bothered to chase him but had gone outside immediately to watch for him. Aberdin legged it down the street, cut through a laundry, a pig pen and even up and over a few drain pipes to slip into the crowd in the Street of Cloth-dyers. He slunk along; looking ahead to one of his secret roost where he might change his appearance, throw off Vol for an Ijuan watchmaker or a priest of Gordal. More blond hair and horned helms ahead of him. He had to turn away and sneak into a boardinghouse. He shoved his way past the landlady, crying in his loudest voice, "Fire! Fire!" Tenants flooded out while the housekeeper beat at him with a broom. He made the back door and fled along an alley that spilled into a street near the South Gate. Aberdin didn't want to flee the city. His best chance was to stay inside the walls, make it to one of his hideouts and change his identity. But one look over his shoulder told him that wasn't possible. He was headed out the gate with little or no attention from the guards. It was still early and the gates would not close for at least two more hours.

Outside the massive portal, Aberdin looked to the squalid shacks and hovels that leaned against the wall like lean-tos. Every so often the city guard would burn these, displacing the diseased and dying who dwelt here, but for the moment they were safe. Vol dove into one shack, saw a thin woman with five kids and kept going. He weaved between huts, jumped a semi-permanent fence, shared a moment with a half-starved goat before seeing what he was looking for--lepers! The diseased of Stormcock dwelt aside from the other poor. Aberdin knew he was in the right place for the cloaks of the deceased were hung on the fence around their compound for the next unlucky bastard to wear. That person right now was Aberdin Vol. He acquired one of the filthy, soiled blankets and covered himself with it. In a moment of darkness he pulled off his wig and beard and pulled a set of false teeth from his pocket. A little filth and he was one of them. He took a perch on a pile of refuse and watched for the Taavsistes.

A few beggars came to talk to him, poor souls rotting away one piece at a time. A few coppers and they disbanded to spend their coins on drink, medicines or food. Vol thought to himself, Emmerant better have a spell to cure leprosy—or else.

He forgot about the stench and rot as he saw six blond-haired warriors fly past on fine steeds. They were hunting for him. He watched them disappear in the direction of Jorn Stepok's estate. Their dust trails were evident as they went south. Only they did not veer to the east but west. That was odd. What was west of the city except the necropolis? Even the lepers didn't venture there.

Something had changed. Something Emmerant had either not seen or not told him about. He would have to investigate. The leper costume was sufficient for traveling the road. He found an old stick and used it as a cane. He would have preferred a sword and some leather armor but there wasn't time to sneak back into the city. He moved southwest until he came to the first stone of the ruins, old temples and mausoleums used by the rich in another time. More history. Maybe there was something to it after all. He'd have to ask Emmerant to tell him more, perhaps peruse a few of those volumes in Gorstelmach's shop?

The scattered gravestones gave way to what had once been a road running through a street. Aberdin crept from shadow to shadow, looking for any sign of those who had passed this way. He could make out horse hooves in the dust. Why would the Taavsites come here? Why would Stepok dare cross Emmerant after the paying of the weirgild?

The answer came riding down the street. Aberdin watched from his hiding place, holding his breath in case even that should give him away. It was Jorn Stepok's son, Yurik. He sat on a fine gray-speckled charger. On his head was a Taavsite helm but on its band was a glowing red stone.

"I can smell you, Vol. Stand up," said the cold, impersonal voice.

Aberdin did no such thing. He inched away from the spot, trying to move into the darker corners.

"It matters not. I have a message for your master, Emmerant the Farseer."

He stopped and waited. Still Aberdin made no sound, gave no sign of his presence.

"Tell him that I am coming for him. He has been chosen by Nyoglatha. He can not escape." With that Yurik turned and cantered away.

Well, Vol thought, now I have something for Emmerant. I only wonder if the old goat has seen it all in his crystal already? There was only one way to find out. Meet him at *The Pregnant Virgin* on the morrow. In the mean time, a long, long soak in a tub of disinfectant.

viii

"NYOGLATHA, you're sure?" asked the fat wizard, playing with his whiskers.

"Yup. Oh, and I have this too." Aberdin pushed the scrap of paper towards the wizard before returning to his mug of ale.

"Aren't you going to ask me?" said Emmerant coldly.

"Okay, you've seen all this already, haven't you?"

The larger man smiled. "Some of it, but details are important. And some I can not see, for forces keep my sight from places such as the necropolis."

"What about the Hadisan scrap?"

"You've figured that out, haven't you?"

Vol just nodded. "It's an incomplete spell. But is it of any use to us? Does it explain anything about Turgin?"

"What do you know about that night at the Wizard's Conclave?"

"Nothing. There aren't any wizards around to ask or haven't you noticed?"

"Fair enough. Since I already know, I suppose, I should illuminate you."

"Do tell."

"It was four weeks agone, during the Conjunction of the Silver Lady."

"That's the moon?" asked Vol sarcastically.

"Yes, but it is a very special configuration of the Moon with the stars and we don't really need to get into all that. It was four weeks ago and everyone was there. It was a special conclave to honor the moment. And as you may not know, it is usually at such times that wizards and witches make special announcements, marriages, births, declarations of ascension."

Vol laughed at Emmerant's look which said 'Do You Want me To Explain That Last Part"? He waved the wizard on. There was only one thing Aberdin found more boring than wizards and that was the minutia of their wizardry.

"Anyway, it was at this time that Turgin had promised a spectacular show of his new powers. He began by changing a dove into a tiger then into a princess."

"Sounds impressive."

"Yes, except when asked to turned the princess into a salamander, he turned red of face, began stammering and she turned back into the dove. Then the tiger—"

"And then the princess."

"It was a fake. He had bought a recording crystal from some traveling Hadisans and had thought to put one over on us."

"Hadisans, you say."

"Yes, I thought you'd find that interesting."

"This scrap may have been the spell for activating the recording crystal," said Vol, looking at the charcoal letters.

"Let's put it to the test, shall we? Here," Emmerant drew a green stone from his sleeve. "—a stone such as that. If you'd care to try."

"What about a sacrificed virgin or something?"

"I rather doubt the conditions for this spell are that expensive. You might place a drop of your blood on the stone, if you like."

Aberdin nodded, drew his dagger and produced a red drop of liquid. The stone shimmered then dimmed. "Tramminimmart!"

Suddenly a pulsing flash flared inside the stone, and for one second a dove hovered over the table then winked out of existence. Aberdin swore he could feel the breath of wind from the bird's wings.

"Startling, but incomplete," sighed Vol.

"Without the original stone, that is probably the best we can expect. But the mystery is solved," said Emmerant, taking a bite of his dinner.

"Well, half of it," agreed Aberdin. "We still don't know what happened after the flop at the conclave. Where did he go? How did he become Nyoglatha?"

"He is not Nyoglatha, merely his first vessel. Jorn Stepok's son proves that. Those who take the red stone become part of a single consciousness. Their own souls, minds, what have you, are displaced so that Nyoglatha can reside inside them."

"Why did He send that message? Why didn't He kill me?"

"Because He doesn't want me to lose interest. He wants you—and me—to come to Him when we feel ready. He is patient if nothing else."

"Then we simply don't go there. We leave Stormcock. I hear Narhu is nice."

"Bah, steamy jungles and wolf-worshippers, I think not." Emmerant waved away his suggestion. "No, we can not run from this."

"But we don't dare go against Him. Even if we think we can beat Him."

"No, we wait for Him to come to us."

"He is growing more powerful. Not only does he have all the best wizards – yourself excluded—but he now has Jorn Stepok's bully-boys. Who's next? The city guard, the king himself? Can we afford to wait that long?"

"I need time to think. Time to watch," admitted the fat wizard. "I will come up with a plan."

"And in the mean time?"

"Go back to your life, dear Falcon. I will call you when I am ready. But have faith. We are far from beat."

Aberdin Vol left *The Pregnant Virgin* sure he would be bound for Narhu by sunset of the next day. The truth proved to be much different, more sudden and just around the corner.

ix

As Vol made the quiet night street he spied a figure rounding the corner. Tilden Brulslav, a minor wizard of the seer variety. A nice enough fellow and a surprise to Aberdin who thought he had seen the last of the wizarding kind for a time. He leapt in Brulslav's direction, calling out, "Hey, Tilden, a moment!" The man disappeared around the corner into the Avenue of Martyred Saints.

Aberdin ran but he still did not catch his friend. He saw his back as he turned into the next street. Vol hurried but did not get close until a crowd of pilgrims came pouring out of a local church. Aberdin pressed through the flood that flowed in the opposite direction, calling out again. Tilden stopped, looked about him then continued on his way.

Aberdin was not one to give up so easily, so he fought his way through, apologizing to the odd nun on whose foot he trod but made it into the far street as Tilden came to a distant house. Vol stopped and caught his breath. It was Jorn Stepok's manse, where he had rescued Emmerant only four nights ago. The little wizard knocked, then was let in.

Aberdin was soon at the thick door he knew from his last encounter as an Ijuan trinket merchant. He stopped and surveyed the portal, wondering what he was doing here. What could he gain here except hatred and violence? But he had to know. He knocked. The little window opened and a red-rimmed eye surveyed the man. "Aberdin Vol, you got a pair coming here."

"Yes, I seek Tilden Brulslav. He just came here."

"What's it to you?"

"That is my affair but I am prepared to make it worth your while." The swordsman held up a small bag of coin, copper mostly but the doorman didn't know that.

He heard a bolt being drawn back. The large wooden door swung open and Aberdin stepped back in surprise. "Jorn Stepok! Why do you answer your own door?"

The Taavsite lord looked away in embarrassment. "Because I am no longer master here. Run, good Vol. Run while you can."

"But Tilden—"

"A trap. He is one of them—" he whispered behind his hand.

Jorn didn't finish the sentence. Instead he fell on the floor and whimpered like a dog. "No, no, master, don't—"

Aberdin Vol stepped back again, drawing his sword. Standing there before him was Tilden Brulslav, the little wizard playing with the cuff of his sleeve like a bored schoolboy. His voice was flat, not unlike that used by Jorn's son, Yurik.

"Did you deliver my message, Vol? To that fat fakir, Emmerant?"

"I delivered a message. What makes it yours?" demanded the swordsman.

"Fool! You may go—for now." Tilden waved him off, his left hand bearing a flashing red stone.

"I will go since this is not my house—but I take something with me."

The young magician turned and stared at Vol with red eyes. "And what is that?"

"This man. I do not care to see him stay."

"That is not a man. It is a dog. My dog. You would be wise to leave him and go."

Vol shook his head. He was tired of dancing around things and planned to see what steel could do.

"Come, Jorn. You will return with me."

174

"No, no, no...." The Taavsite lord said, obviously wanting to go but too afraid to try.

"Come, are you a man or not? Take this." Vol offered him his dagger.

"It won't help—" Jorn whined, cringing like the dog Tilden called him.

"Come I say!" shouted Aberdin, hoping to push the man out with his very voice.

"No, no, no....."

"Come, Jorn," said Tilden coldly. "Let us leave this fool." With that the door slammed shut of its own accord. For a second Aberdin thought he could hear a man screaming behind the solid wall of oak.

"A trap was it? Not much of one," he said shaking his head. Then he turned around and saw the four Taavsite warriors who had jockeyed into position during his conversation with the master.

"So, that's your game," he sighed, reversing his grip on his dagger.

The first two attackers came at him straight, lunging with the tips of their swords. The Taavsite blade is long and not very pointed, being a swinging weapon. Vol easily deflected these with his rapier. The other two were not far behind, slashing at his head. These were more difficult to avoid, but he did so by dropping lower. This move was countered by the first two raising their blades to pummel the man on the ground. But Vol did not stay there long. He jumped back up, slashing his own blade under their guard, slicing a throat and slashing a cheek.

He bit down on his lip as one blade slid across his rib cage, ruining his shirt and roughing up the skin along his side. He ignored the pain, shoving the dead warrior into his fellows and gaining enough time to slash with his dagger, taking out another man's eyes. He was too busy parrying the last two's blows to attack, each coming from a different side. He was about to work his way past one Taavsite's guard when he heard a voice behind him.

"Such a fool!"

He felt a cold hand on the back of his neck before a million stars began fighting for room inside his skull...

X

EMMERANT the Farseer, student of Ixarenaxis of Bastil, scowerer of stones, magician of the Black Order of B'fnaro and vocator of the Forgotten Tomes of Ivv, missed the fight between his agent and those of Nyoglatha for he remained in *The Pregnant Virgin*, drinking his wine. The truth of the matter was he was waiting for someone else. She showed up about a half hour after Aberdin Vol knocked on Jorn Stepok's door. Her name was Slee, and she was a Merikheen girl of fourteen.

"There you are, tub-of-reindeer-fat."

"A pleasure as always, my dear." Emmerant smiled a genuine smile and offered her a seat. "The usual?"

"Yes, and extra bread."

"Certainly."

"What do you want now? Are you going to use me some more?"

"Yes, indeed, I am."

"You old goat."

"Come, come, we both know it has never been that kind of an arrangement. In fact, the day you engage in such carnal activity, your usefulness will be at an end."

"Only if I am a virgin. I could be making good coin as a whore right now. I'm in my best years, I am."

"Tut, tut, this is another dodge to extort more money from me, isn't it? How much more?"

"What did you pay me last time?"

"Fifty gold florens."

"I want double."

"I will need proof."

"Same as last time?"

"No, much more 'expert' proof."

"What? Looking up my skirt's not enough? You enjoyed that last time, didn't you?"

"Nonsense. Now, produce them."

Slee grinned mischievously. "What makes you think I even got them?"

"You are an able assistant."

"Flattery. More please."

"And I trust my fifty florens weren't wasted."

"Nope." She waved her hands around with a mystical flourish, then each hand bore a large jade-green stone.

"And you say wizards are showy," grumped Emmerant.

"Proof."

"Yes, keep holding the stones as you are and say your name. Your full name."

"Why? It won't turn me into anything, will it?" Slee put the stones down and pulled her hand away from the dirty tabletop.

"No, they will light up if you are untouched. If you've been having it with the stable boys they will remain unlit. Cold, empty, like your purse."

"I never! Stable-boys!" With that Slee slapped her dirty finger-nailed hand onto the two rocks and said, "' Slee'h'eels '". A bright green light appeared in both hands.

"Good," nodded Emmerant. "A hundred gold florens."

"Tonight. I want it now."

"Half now. Half when we are done."

Slee thought about it for a moment. Wiping a strand of dirty-blonde hair behind her ear. "Okay, but it wasn't easy getting these. I had to sneak into Lord Grundlehow's garden after I got hired on in the kitchen. He found me hiding in the roses and wanted—well, you know what he wanted—only he lost interest when he saw I was a girl. I found'em just where you said though. In the eyes of the dragon statue. How did you know? Nobody ever visits Lord Grundlehow."

"I'm not surprised," Emmerant said, raising an eyebrow then passing her a bag of coins the size of a large onion. His brow wrinkled in worry. "Will you be safe with that?"

Slee laughed, held up a sign and a cup. The sign of a beggar, a prostitute out of work because of infection.

"It keeps the boys away, I can tell you."

"You remind me of a friend of mine, a Mister Vol."

"The Falcon?" asked the fourteen year-old, tucking into her dinner, which arrived with a flagon of ale.

"Yes, oddly enough."

"I don't see it, tubby. Me, like that swaggering bravo. I wish I had all his money though."

Emmerant nodded and left it at that.

"Instructions?" asked Slee, her mouth full of bread.

"Simple enough. I need you to come to the necropolis road two nights from now, around moonrise."

"The city of the dead? I don't know—"

"Perhaps you'd like to give me back my down payment—"

"No, no, just that creepy old place. Sounds dangerous."

"It will be. I won't lie."

Slee stopped chewing. "I should have charged you double, triple, what I did."

"Tell you what. If we survive this one, I will buy you a nice pony."

"What do I want with a pony?"

"I thought all girls wanted a pony."

"Not this one. If I do this—and we 'survive this one', I want a letter of recommendation to the Black Order of B'fnaro in Bast-il."

"You would be a magician?"

"Yah, why not? It seems to keep you in gravy. Besides I might meet The Falcon or someone like him and go off and have adventures."

"Yes, I see a pony is quite silly."

"Well, we might!"

"It is a deal. I will recommend you to my old master, Ixarenaxis, but on one condition."

"What's that?"

"You stop making fun of my weight."

"Deal, tubs."

She lifted her hand away from her plate to shake. Emmerant took it with a good-natured grin.

"Let's continue with your instructions," he said. "We will be going to the necropolis and I will need you to be –uh-hum—in the condition--"

"Got it."

"—plus I will need you to bring these two stones with you. To prove your condition.

"Anything else?"

"Dress simply, cleanly."

"Wash behind my ears, clean my nails, yah, yah."

"This is important, Slee—"

"Slee'h'eels, since we are being formal," the girl said, pretending at being a lady.

"Ssh, let's keep that name between us, alright?"

"Whatever you say, fatt—sir."

"I must be going now. Two nights at moonrise on the necropolis road. Don't be late." With that Emmerant rose, trying to suck his gut in as best as he could as he slid out from behind the table. Slee kept her laughter to herself, finishing her first serving of bread and starting on the next.

xi

WHEN HE woke he was firstly surprised he wasn't in one of the nine hells, roasting over a river of burning bile or screaming in a vat of poisonous blood. Instead he was tied up with rope and lying on the cold floor of a dark chamber. He knew he was inside for he could hear only very muffled sounds. He sat up carefully to make sure he wasn't inside a coffin. The darkness felt roomier as he reached outward. Cold stone, long slab-like box. There was the coffin but he wasn't inside it.

He shook his head and applied a little logic. His hands were tied so escape was possible, and somebody didn't want him dead yet. Or else he would be already. Good, these facts were reassuring. He rose. His feet were not tied so he could move about, feeling all around the chamber he was in. A small opening in the far wall let in just a hint of starlight. It was night and he was inside a square stone box. The necropolis—he'd bet anything he was in one of the mausoleums. The smell, the stone boxes, the lack of windows all made sense.

Where was the door? He found it without difficulty. An exploratory shove said it was locked from the outside. Again, a mausoleum. You wouldn't lock it from inside, would you?

He sat and thought some more. His weapons were gone. He wanted badly to untie his hands. He might have a small chance of escape if not too many bully-boys came to collect him. With his hands free, he might overcome one or two.

His original search had not produced any objects of use. Knowing he was in a room filled with dead bodies, he thought to look there. Where there was dead, there were funereal accoutrements, like the favorite weapons of the dead.

With awkward shoves, his hands before him in a knot of cord, he pushed at a tomb cover. The heavy stone would require his full strength to move. Subtlety was out of the question. He got his hands under the lid and pushed with all his might. The lid groaned with protest, being over a hundred years old, but in the end it ground along for a few inches before stopping. Aberdin tried again, opening the hole a little more before sticking his hands blindly into the aperture.

He felt bones, ashy, dusty things that collapsed at his touch, probably cloth at one time. Then something metal. He retrieved it with much difficulty but wedged it between two captive fingers. It was a buckle. He put it down carefully at his feet. Back the hand-ball went into the coffin. More bones, then he felt a ring or brooch, he wasn't sure. A woman's grave he had invaded. Still, anyone can use a blade.

His search proved unsuccessful in the end. And the other three coffins would not budge to his shovings. In the end he settled for a last desperate choice. He pulled a long leg bone from the open casket. He placed this under his foot and stomped down. The bone shattered under the pressure, leaving him with two broken ends and a number of fragments. Testing the cracked section, he smiled when he found the bone had separated in a sharp fashion. Placing the shard between his feet, he sawed at his rope for what felt like all night. As the starlight began to fade in the little window above, he felt the ropes snap apart.

He was free. Well, of the ropes anyway. But having both hands and a bone pry-bar he was able to open the next coffin. Inside he found a man's bones, still housed in rusted armor. He ignored this and located the long, flat sword that rested beside him. Antique, cumbersome and rusty as hell but it was a blade. He almost felt sorry for whoever came to the door. He stopped and had a terrible thought. If anyone ever came...

But he had a sword now. Aberdin took the blade to the doorframe, looked about the portal for any gap between lintel and panel. He was able to jam the point of the blade into a crack between the two and slowly begin opening the door. He stopped, listened for footsteps. Nothing. He continued until his hand held the edge of the door and he yanked it open with one good pull. The simple lock fell away with an unavoidable tinkle.

"Come, Vol," said a flat-toned voice. "Come join me."

Aberdin said nothing, not wanting to give himself away. He crept forward, looking to flee in the opposite direction. Another step and he saw this wasn't possible. He was surrounded by dozens of figures, most in wizardly garb but a few in the livery and armor of Jorn Stepok. Aberdin could see Yurik Stepok with his helmet and flashing red stone.

"Come, I have a job for you."

"Go to whichever of the nine hells you wish." He raised the sword point in defiance.

"That won't be necessary," Yurik said, raising his hand.

A flame burned on Aberdin's neck. His hand involuntarily reached back and felt the stone attached there. The flashes of red light told him it was active, burning.

"Skelq scoruscorum sheek shek Nyoglatha —" said Yurik and all the others in unison.

Aberdin screamed then fell to his knees. Pictures were flashing before his eyes. Last week, a month ago, two years, ten years, twenty-thirty—and then a blinding flash...

xii

EMMERANT stopped at the door of his tower and said, "Let me in you god-damned fool of a sentry!"

"Yes, master," said the door. "If I can open wide enough."

"Watch it, or you'll be kindling tomorrow."

"Of course, master," purred the door, slamming behind him with extra vigor. Sometimes, Emmerant missed a simple lock and key.

He sat down on the chair next to the table and the wicker device whisked him quickly up the thousand steps to the top, where he placed his hand on the metal plate. The door opened instantly with a whisper.

He had a bag of food items in one hand. Invisible servants took these from him along with his cloak and walking stick. He stumbled tired and sore to his stool and gazed into the green crystal sitting before him. He began to form an image when a loud voice yelled, "Someone at the door."

"Who is it?"

"Aberdin Vol."

"Send him up."

"He says he is wounded unto death."

Emmerant cursed, waved his hand over the green crystal and saw Vol staggering, clutching a bloody stomach. "He's been stabbed." The man in the vision collapsed before the door and didn't move.

Emmerant cursed again, got off his stool and headed for the door. The magic chair met him at the top of the stairs, taking him down quickly. The fat wizard was at the man's side in a second. He reached for Aberdin's shoulder to roll him over, his body wrapped up in a wet cloak. As Vol rolled his hand came up, clutching a red stone. The ruby connected with Emmerant's own hand, attaching itself with a flash of light. Vol rose. The two men looked at each other with bright red eyes. "I am complete," both said at the same time.

xiii

The road was cold and dark. Slee looked up one way then the other. Small creatures skittered in the brambles, making her jump. Where was Emmerant? She wanted the rest of her money and to be in bed. His words about if we 'survive this one' came back to haunt her. Only the cold weight of the two stones in her sash made her feel any better.

Suddenly she wasn't alone. Two figures came from the darkness, lumbering upon silent feet.

"Emmerant! It's about time!" hissed the girl.

The fat wizard and the man next to him—who bore an uncanny resemblance to The Falcon—said nothing, moving on with the same uncaring speed.

"Hey! Fat ass! I want my gold!"

Seeing that neither man was stopping, Slee ran up and poked Emmerant in the back. This got a response. The wizard spun suddenly, grabbing her wrist. Red light flared from his eyes.

"Hey! Let go, tubby!"

The other man turned to look at her as well. Ruby light glowed in his eyes too.

Slee began to thrash, trying to break Emmerant's painful grip. She kicked him on the shin but he did not let go.

"Okay, okay," Slee begged with fright creeping into her voice. "I'll go. Just let me go. I did everything you said. I brought the stones." Her hand went into her sash and brought forth one of the green stones. It exploded with emerald beams. "See, untouched. I never—"

Emmerant reacted by dropping Slee's wrist. His mouth opened and an unearthly hiss issued from between frozen lips. The other man did likewise, backing away.

Slee, not understanding, thrust the stone closer, while the other hand retrieved the stone in her sash. With two bright stones she walked towards the men. "Here, you said to bring these to you."

Emmerant took one slow swipe at the offered stones before falling to the ground. The other man stumbled off but Slee began to understand and chased him. "Hey, are you the Falcon?" she asked. The green stones lit up his graylocks and mustachios. He soon joined the fat wizard on the ground. She stooped to see a small red stone fall from the man's neck. She extended a finger towards the gem --which would fetch her a few gold coins in the market—when she heard Emmerant say, "Leave that. You'll never sell it. You'll become like we were." The fat wizard pointed to another red gem lying beside his hand.

"What the hell is going on, Emmerant? And when do I get my money?"

"Come, Slee, let's help Mr. Vol to his feet. I think we should all go right away to my tower, where I can explain everything. And we can get your gold."

"What about those?" Slee pointed at Aberdin's red stone.

"Leave them. Now quickly before we are discovered."

xiv

"SO I WAS your insurance policy?" said Slee, now comfortably positioned on a pillow with a glass of wine in her hand.

"Yes, I saw certain events unfolding and I knew there was a good chance both Aberdin and I would be captured."

"You saw the future!"

"Nonsense, I merely deduced a likelihood. Even with all my crystals I can not—with a hundred percent certainty—see what will happen."

"What do we do now?" asked Aberdin who sprawled on a cushion but looked like he'd have preferred a chair. "I'll never understand your penchance for Merikheen furniture."

"Please, Aberdin, we have more to worry about than furnishings," admonished Emmerant, stroking his beard. "We are now ready to move against Nyoglatha."

"We are. Well, let's go," cheered Vol sarcastically.

"I take your meaning, good Aberdin, but the last piece of the puzzle is now before us. How Turgin released Nyoglatha."

"I don't see it."

"What do you remember, when the stone was placed on your neck?"

"I saw my life then a brilliant flash after that. It all went so fast I can remember little of it. And it made no real sense."

"And at the end. Where did it stop?"

"In a hole, filled with darkness."

"Yes, the hole that is Nyoglatha the devourer."

"You know where that place was?"

"Yes, in the necropolis, there is a building that was once a temple. A temple to dark gods. Somehow Turgin wandered there and opened

the hole. A hole most likely stopped with a stone like this."
Emmerant held up one of the two green stones Slee had stolen from
Lord Grundlehow.

"You have such a stone?"

"Two. Thanks to our good Slee here."

"So what's the plan then? How do we get Nyoglatha back in his
hole?"

"Leave that to me."

Aberdin laughed. "Damn you wizards and your dramatics. You
can't just tell me. You have to make a show of it."

Emmerant harrumphed. "Nonsense. If I told you the plan you'd try
to run some other scheme and louse it all up. No, it's best if you
leave the thinking to me."

Slee giggled deliciously. "I like when you guys fight."

"Fight?" they both demanded together. "Who's fighting?"

"Leave the discussions to the grown-ups," said Emmerant coldly.

Aberdin gave her a mischievous wink that made her blush.

"What's first in this brilliant plan of yours?" asked Vol after
another drink of wine.

"You will go to Jorn Stepok's house."

"Interesting. And do what?"

"Find every uncontrolled man there, even if it is only master
Stepok and bring them to the necropolis with swords."

"And how will I ever get inside that house?"

"Our good Slee will take care of that."

The girl gave a flourishing wave of her hand.

"And you?"

"I will be in the necropolis, finding that temple. We have to know
where Nyoglatha came from. Without that, we can only hold him off.
We need to finish him for good."

"I like the sound of that. What do you figure are our chances of
success, oh gazer-of-crystals?"

"Harrumph," said Emmerant, dismissing Vol's irreverent question.

"That good, eh? Come on, Slee. Let's see if we can improve the
odds a little."

"One other thing," said Emmerant as they approached the door.
"Aberdin, take this. Use it only in direst need." The wizard handed
the swordsman a small pouch. Aberdin took it, pocketed and slapped
the fat wizard on the shoulder. "It's been an adventure, Emmerant."

"Harrumph," said Emmemrant again, waving away Aberdin's
sentimentality. "Come back alive. I have more work for you."

Aberdin laughed one last short burst then left. "Come on, Slee."

XV

ABERDIN led his young charge to a secret place he kept near the wharf. Disguised as a storage locker for nets, Slee found it held much more.

"Wow," said the girl, looking at his collection of costumes, weapons and other gear.

"Don't touch anything."

Aberdin selected a few items then said, "Stand up tall." Slee followed the order as he pulled a light shirt of mail over her thin frame. She leaned in as he did it, catching his neck with her arms. She kissed him for several seconds before she realized he wasn't kissing her back.

"No silliness now, Slee," he scolded. He pushed her up straight, adjusted the armor at the back. There were leather straps for tightening the fit. He pulled these hard, shortened the mail.

"I don't like this," pouted the girl. "It will slow me down. And it's noisy."

"And it will keep you safe."

"You do care, Aberdin," she teased.

Vol stopped for a second, annoyed at the girl's playing. "Close your eyes."

"What? You're going to deflower me here and now?" Slee put a dramatic hand to her forehead.

"No, close your eyes."

She did, for a second then peeked.

"Do it."

She complied at last. She heard him moving around a bit. "Okay, open them."

What she saw when she looked was a man who looked younger but had no hair on his head or his face. He expected her to laugh or shriek. Instead she calmed, realizing she was seeing something very secret, very private. Her hand rose slowly, felt his head.

"Do you shave it?"

"Yes, and my face, then I apply the juice of a flower that slows the growth."

"Why?"

"When you have to change your face six times a day, you don't have time to shave."

"What color is your hair, when you don't?"

"Red."

"But your eyebrows are gray."

"I dye them. Grey goes with everything."

Slee smiled, a nice smile that said she accepted all this. She looked closely at his eyes. "You're not even old. How old are you?"

"How old are you?"

"Since we're telling secret—I'm actually seventeen."

"You say that like it's embarrassing."

"It is! Seventeen, and a virgin!"

"I don't—"

"You're not Merihkeen. All the girls I knew back in the tents are mothers now. Only the very ugly or the deformed—" She caught herself about to cry.

"You're not deformed. You're actually—"

She put her hands on his mouth to stop him. "How old are you?" she countered, no longer wanting to talk about herself.

"I don't know, being an orphan. Except when that stone took me I saw things—" he stumbled now, pushing her back gently.

"It's not easy being the Falcon, is it?"

"No, but it isn't any easier being a wizard. Emmerant told me. You're going to Bast-il."

"Yes, that was part of the deal. You could come with me? When this is all over."

"Good. Take this." He handed her a long dagger in a beautiful black leather scabbard.

Slee drew the blade and gasped at the quality of the steel. No rusty pig-sticker.

"I can't—" said the girl. "It's so beautiful."

"You'll need it. I want you to go to Bast-il. And take this too." He handed her a doeskin bag. Inside were six quarrels and a small, collapsible crossbow.

Slee examined the weapon as Vol dressed himself in a suit of leather armor stitched with mail rings. He picked through his collection of weapons, looking at swords and daggers but finally selecting a deadly ax, a Narahbezan weapon that offered both the chopping blade as well as a point for stabbing. To finish the ensemble he put on his wig of graylocks and his moustache and beard.

"Ready?" asked Aberdin.

Slee came closer and gave him another long kiss. "Now I'm ready."

Aberdin gave her a grin. That time she might not have been doing all the kissing.

xvi

THE PLAN was simple so it couldn't fail. That didn't make it any safer. Aberdin was to go to the door and bang on it until someone came. That someone would die with a blade in the guts if their eyes glowed red. But that was only the distraction. While Vol banged away, making as much noise as possible, Slee would sneak up the wall in the back to a short balcony and open a window there. It was her job to find and rescue Jorn (and any others who might remain unpossessed.) If Aberdin got past the front door he was to find her as quickly as possible.

Simple, but dangerous. But it was all they had time for. And it went wrong almost instantly. Aberdin walked up to Stepok's front door and banged it three times with the haft of his Narah-bezan ax. Nobody answered. He banged again, this time yelling, "Open up, Jorn Stepok, you son of a trollish whore!"

Still nothing. Not even a stone dropped on his head from above. No boiling oil, not a single arrow. Was there really no one here?

Well, he said to himself, I'm the distraction so I'll distract. He raised the ax and slammed the wicked blade against the oak beams. It left a nice white streak in the yellow wood. I'll chop my way in if I have to, he resolved. He raised the blade and struck again. This time he noticed something odd about the door. It moved outward, only slightly.

He stopped, put a hand against the wood and pushed. It bounced back then opened an inch. Is this door even locked? he wondered. Placing the point of his weapon into the crack he pried. The heavy oak and steel barricade opened with a slow, ominous creak. Shock and surprise wrestled inside him but it was fear and logic that won out. It was a trap! And Slee was walking right into it!

He shoved the door open the rest of the way and leapt through. The same hallway met him, this time empty of guards. In the passage, mere steps away he found a grisly surprise. A body, one of the house slaves, his heart cut out. The ragged wound suggested it had not been done with a knife. The sight sent another thrill of alarm through him.

He threw caution to the wind and yelled at the top of his lungs, "Slee! Watch out!"

"You watch out. And shut up!" hissed the girl from the staircase above the hall. She came down and looked at the dead man in the hall. "There's two more like that upstairs. Killed the same way. No sign of Jorn though. What do we do?"

"The smart money is walk out of here as fast as we can."

"And the stupid money?"

"Follow me."

Aberdin took the lead. They crept into the hall where the Falcon had met Emmerant only five days ago. The throne-like chair was still there and Jorn Stepok sat in it. He writhed and groaned in ropes that held him down both about the chest and the arms. His legs kicked left and right as he curled in pain.

"Jorn," said Aberdin, "what ails you, man?"

The Taavsite lord rolled from one side to the other, thick spit falling from his clenched teeth. He gurgled lost words.

Aberdin leaned in closer to try and make out what tormented the man. With the tip of his ax he pulled back the shirt that bulged below his bonds. There, Vol saw a collection of human hearts, pulsing in some weird syncopation, beating with purple evil.

Jorn's lips opened with agonizing pain. One word made it out of his frantic moaning. "R-r-run."

Aberdin did not stop to consider the word, nor to try and free the man. Instead he dropped his ax and rolled away. He pulled Slee down at the last second, shielding her with his body.

Jorn Stepok, lord of the manor, exploded in a shower of purple flesh, his bones and brains flying in a shower of death, only sorcery could have concocted. The spray of flying flesh tore at Aberdin's cloak, ripping the cloth and stopping only at his leather armor. He waited a few more seconds then looked up. The chair contained nothing but bloody syrup that dripped on the tile floor.

"That was close," Slee said, sitting up. "What happened?"

"Magic. Yurik and his pals have gone, but they left us a little present in case we came back. We'll find no one here to rescue. The servants died to enspell the master."

"Yuck, you're covered in it. Get off me." With a playful shove, Slee freed herself and stood up.

Aberdin followed, examining his back. His cloak was ruined. He took the time to pluck a piece of bone from his leather coverlet.

"That was a little too close. Let's get out of here."

"Let's go out the back. No point in any more people seeing us coming and going," added the girl.

"You think like a thief. You sure you want to be a sorceress?"

"I like the hours better. Thieves work at night."

"What so important you have to save your nights for?" he asked grinning.

She just smiled back.

The pair was about to leave when Aberdin spied something sitting on the gore-spattered floor. He picked it up, wiped it off on his ruined cloak, then pocketed it.

"I have an idea. Come on."

"No, Aberdin. You'll have to go without me. Emmerant gave me instructions. After we freed the house I was to go—"

"Okay, okay, do what he told you to do. But be careful."

"Where are you going?"

"To finish the job we failed to do here. I will meet you at the necropolis with help. Now, get going." With that she was gone from his mind. Slee headed for the back door, turning just once to see if he watched her go. He wasn't. He was attending to his weapons. She sighed once, then ran out into the street beyond.

xvii

EMMERANT had his own part in the plan to execute. First he spent an hour gazing into a crystal with a pinkish haze. With this he found the necropolis near Stormcock. He could not see what his enemies were doing. The stone grew dark whenever he ventured too close. But what he wanted to find wasn't where they were, quite the opposite. Using their dark cloud of influence he worked his way away from them. Nyoglatha won't want to go anywhere near the hole from which it came, he reasoned.

Another hour and he had found it. A remote weed-covered shrine once devoted to faun-like women spirits. Despite his encyclopedic knowledge of magic, Emmerant did not know the name of this particular set of deities. Old, he realized. So very old.

The prison chamber, he could see, was nothing too grand. Just a block of stone with a well-like hole in it. Around this he saw evidence of more recent activity. Turgin's digging and scrapings, no doubt. The foppish git had discovered the hole cover, with its missing center stone. That stone was the green gem that Aberdin had

189

held in *The Pregnant Virgin* or one like it. Turgin had thought it only powerful enough for the merest magical recording, a parlor trick, when in truth the stone had held a monster at bay. And would once again if Emmerant's trap worked. Where was Slee? He needed her if this was all going to work.

An immaterial voice declared, "Mistress Slee is at the door."

"Good. Tell her I will be right down."

Emmerant was a good as his word. Less than two minutes later he was closing the front door, a tall staff of rowan in his left hand. In his right he carried a small pack of magical spell components and the green stone he had shown Aberdin.

"You got them?" he asked without a hello.

"Right here." Slee produced the other two stones and began juggling them.

"None of that now. They are far too precious—"

"Relax, Graybeard." She stowed them away again.

"Graybeard, is it?"

"I promised you I'd stop commenting on your weight."

"Fair enough. Let's go."

xviii

KNOWING that the shrine of the deer-women was on the outskirts of the necropolis, Emmerant lead Slee on a circuitous route around the city of the dead. Rank hedges and brambles tore at them mercilessly, but they moved slowly onward. As the sun set behind them, the wizard spied the over-grown thicket that housed the forgotten temple. "Here it is. Help me with this." He pointed at an old altar that had fallen on one side.

Together they lifted the stone top. Slee held her end with her knee as she piled broken rocks under the fallen slab. Soon the little shrine was horizontal. Emmerant began placing items on the table, centermost a small cauldron of bronze. Slee watched him work with evident interest. As a student of magic, she admired how his hands moved with practiced precision, measuring exactly the right amount of powder, then whisk, lighting it while singing a short incantation. He stopped, turned his head. "Cover your eyes, Slee."

She complied. A second later a dull heat like that of hot summer sunshine coursed over her face and hands, then it cooled and darkened. She opened her eyes. A beam of magical light shot up

190

from the bronze bowl straight into the air for a thousand feet. "Wow, that'll bring them running," she quipped.

"That is the idea—that and to bring the good Mr. Vol and any help he can muster," said Emmerant with a slight dimming of his manner. The spell had cost him physically as well as mentally. He reached for a small flask on his belt.

"Now what?" asked Slee, beginning to get bored already.

"Simple enough. Stand over here. Do you see the opening over there on the ground?" Emmerant pointed to a circular stone lid that looked to cover the hole. There was a dimple in the top of the flat cover. "See here? That is where Turgin pried off the green stone." The wizard reached into his pouch then produced one of the rocks. He slipped it back into the small crevice it had come from. He spoke a few arcane words and the green gem became part of the lid again. Emmerant took the side of the cover and tugged, flipping the cap over. "No point in Nyoglatha seeing that." He kicked some stray leaves and grass over the top.

"And what do I do?"

"You stand here by the hole." The wizard pointed to a spot before the opening. "Now listen carefully. You need to say this word for word: *'Skelqi sorrisucoral shek sheek Nyoglatha—'* Try it."

"Skeeki catcha shek—"

"No, no, concentrate, Slee. There isn't much time. *'Skelqi sorrisucoral shek sheek Nyoglatha —'"*

"Graybeard, I can't—" Slee never finished telling him what she could not do. There was a ring of figures surrounding the deer-women's temple. No escape, she realized, as they all moved in slowly with glowing red eyes.

xix

ABERDIN'S horse made good time once he left the gates of the city. Jorn Stepok's estate soon loomed up on a slightly rising hill. The rider had no idea what to expect. Would Yurik and his red-eyed devils be there? Were all the soldiers of Stepok's *comitatas* taken by Nyoglatha? He did not know but he would soon find out.

The wooden gates, a mere barrier without men to guard it, was open and abandoned. Aberdin was glad he would not be skewered on a pike by a guardsman but the empty look of the lands beyond the gate did not breed good feelings either. Was everybody gone? Dead?

He decided to throw caution to the winds—every second he wasted could mean death for Emmerant and Slee—and yelled towards the log-style buildings that were Stepok's Taavsite version of a mansion with its massive drinking hall. "Hail! Is anyone there?"

He waited only a second before dismounting. He tied his horse to a hitching rail by a water trough and approached the main doors of the hall. The front doors were locked. He thumped his sword pommel against the panel, yelling the same four words. It was this action that masked the approach of feet. Only as he turned away did he see them. Four war hounds from the kennels of Taavst or the dark forests of the Gelt. Unlike most dogs, these did not snarl, only watched with red-glowing eyes, a light that was repeated in the jewels attached to their foreheads.

"So, you are here, Red-Eye. And I see you're closer to your true self," said Aberdin in a low voice. His right hand still held his sword so he lowered it cautiously, ready for their attack. The hounds snarled in unison, acting as one. Their attack came the same way. Aberdin met it with a desperate slash of his sword but before it could connect he felt someone behind him pulling. The hall door was open and a young blond girl was tugging at his cloak. As the perfectly coordinated attack of four jaws bit at the swordsman, he was no longer there. A second slash and the door was slammed shut and locked with a long bar.

Aberdin leaned against the door and caught his breath. "That was close. I doubt I could have fought all four of them at once."

The blond girl was not alone he saw. Behind her stood six adults, four men and two women. All bore the iron ring of thralldom about their necks. Except for the girl. She bore something else, a strong resemblance to Jorn Stepok.

"Who are you?" demanded the girl with practiced defiance.

"I am Aberdin Vol. Is this all who remain here?"

The girl wrinkled her nose as if she had stepped in manure. "You're the one who bedded my sister." The statement was matter of fact. "Helgas always was a slut."

This was Jorn Stepok's youngest daughter. He saw the resemblance now. Fourteen instead of twenty, yet to fill out as Helgas had so charmingly done. Her older sister had mentioned her only briefly, equating her with a toad. What was her name? Tama—Tana—Talla. That was it.

"Talla, I need every able-bodied man to come with me. I ride to save your father—" He knew it was a lie but it was easier than "Your father exploded like a ripe melon."

"I think not, churl. I should have my slaves kill you." She crossed her arms and waited for him to reply.

"If you do that, we'll never get away from here. And those dogs--"

"What makes you think you can save us? We just saved you."

"Granted, but that was before I knew what I was up against. With a good plan—"

"I think not. You are a rapist and a thief."

"Hey, I resent that. I'm no rapist."

"But you are a thief. I should have your hand cut off."

"Enough of this, we are losing time. And your father's life is in peril." Aberdin drew from his pocket the object he had taken from Jorn Stepok's floor. His hand held a gold ring, the lord's sigil. "He sent me to bring as many swords as possible." To finish his play he added, "And any who ride with me now will be freed from their thralldom. They ride free men."

"What about the women?" asked one of the female slaves.

"Silence!" shrieked Talla, holding up her hand imperiously.

The slave ignored her. "Well?"

"Can you hold a sword? Are you willing to die?"

The woman nodded her assent. The other agreed as well.

"I forbid it! Come back here!" shrieked Talla, hitting those around her with fists used to striking without fear of reprisal. One of the slaves shoved her over as they stepped up to take their place around Aberdin. She screamed, cried, then quieted when she saw no one cared.

"You will all die when father comes back," she said in a hissing voice before she fled for her room off the main hall. Aberdin ignored her. She was safe enough if she stayed inside the hall.

"Weapons," said Aberdin. "Get them. Bring a shield too." He pointed at the walls of the hall that bore shields, drinking horns, harps as well as an assortment of weapons. The men came back bearing swords. The two women had spears. Each carried a thick wooden shield.

"The plan is simple. Once we're outside, form a circle. Protect the man to your left and strike to kill." Everyone nodded in agreement.

Aberdin took the bar down slowly, trying to avoid any noise. He opened the door only an inch and looked out. No sign of the dogs. He looked to the hitching rail to see if his horse was still there. A broken strap told him that the animal had either fled or been killed and dragged off. He closed it again. He turned back to the people behind him. "Which way to the stable?"

"It's to the right, two buildings over," said a male slave who looked older than the rest.

"What's our name?"

"Neb."

"Okay, Neb, I'll go first, you follow. We will use our shields to guard the door while the others come out. If we meet no resistance, we go single file towards the stable. Alright?"

Neb nodded.

Aberdin peered out again then opened the door all the way. He held his shield up to protect Neb as he came out and did the same. Soon all eight of them were on the front steps. The last slave pulled the door shut behind them. A loud thunk was heard afterward.

"That little bitch! She's locked us out," said one of the women.

"Forget it, we're not going back," said Aberdin. "To the stables."

The line of armed slaves made it from the hall to the next outbuilding and at last to the stable. It was here the dogs waited with human cunning. As Aberdin made for the stable door, a large black shape lunged from the shadows. He raised his shield and slammed it with malicious zeal into the dog-shaped body. His sword slashed and stabbed the black fur. "Circle!" he called out as he slew the first dog.

The slaves were used to following orders but they weren't trained or drilled soldiers. They tried to bring their shields around but a dog leapt in, tearing out a woman's calf before she could bring her spear up. Soon afterward she was on the ground, screaming her last. Neb came too late, stabbing the wolfish attacker between the ribs before it could flee to strike again.

"Keep that circle together!" barked Aberdin as hard as any sergeant in the army of Stormcock. Though he had never followed a soldier's calling he had spent a few weeks in the ranks, pretending to be a subaltern. It had been enough of a taste to last him a lifetime.

The remaining two black shapes retreated, slunk about looking for a chink in the shield wall. Finding none, they changed their tactics. They split up and seemed to disappear. Aberdin waited a good four minutes before he told the slaves to make for the stable door. It was only as they opened the door that Aberdin realized what the dogs were doing. They were attacking the horses inside! If they couldn't kill the slaves they could at least slow them down.

"Quick! Inside!" he yelled as he charged in.

This was good advice. The stable held twenty horses though only half that number was there. Each large white nag was frightened as it saw the two hounds attacking one of their numbers. Hooves flew in all directions as fangs snapped at flank and fetlock.

Aberdin took the spear from the remaining woman slave and cast it with deadly precision, pinning one of the dogs to the wooden fencing around the horse's stall. One of the male slaves rushed in to stab at the other dog but received a kick to his head that sent him to the ground. Neb moved in to shield the fallen man. He left him a second later. "Dead," was all he said.

"Forget about this last one. Calm those horses," said Aberdin, wishing he had another spear.

The slaves all headed for other stalls to tend to the mares that whinnied in fear, snorting their unease. Only Neb stayed. He said, "You might need some help."

"Grab that pitchfork there." Aberdin pointed to a fork resting against the wall. Neb retrieved the tool then looked to Aberdin.

"Hold it up. I'll drive him out and you get him."

Neb nodded his agreement to the plan.

Aberdin drew his sword and held his shield lower than he would with a human opponent. The dog would not try to slash his throat but would come for his lower body. Or would it? This was no dog but a demon-thing with a man's intelligence. Still, it had a dog's body and would attack like one.

He moved in slowly. The horse lie on the straw of the stall, wounded unto death, whimpering like a sick child. The dog stood up, no longer interested in the mare. It would not hold a rider so the beast's work was done. Instead the dog surveyed Aberdin coldly. It opened its bloody jaws but without the savage animal hate he expected. The creature did not growl or make any dog-like noises. It's a machine, Aberdin thought, cold, deadly. A machine he would stop.

Aberdin lunged with his sword point. The dog wasn't there when the blow landed. The jaws came at him over his weapon. Only the shield saved him from being bitten. Aberdin slammed the wood and leather surface into the dog's face, pressing forward, reducing the amount of room for the dog to move in. The sword went up and down in a chop but again he missed. Aberdin spun, keeping the shield between them. The dog turned to bite and the swordsman yelled, "Now, Neb!"

The slave jumped into the fray. The pitchfork's tines caught the dog in the side and blood flew as he pressed them home. The dog gave no howl or squeal. Instead it tried to bite the fork entering its body. This gave Aberdin the opening he need. His sword came down with a final chop that left the dog's head lying in a pile of straw.

"Well done, Neb," Aberdin said. "See how many horses we have. I have an unpleasant job here." He nodded towards the mare. Neb abandoned his pitchfork and headed into the barn. Aberdin lifted his sword by the handle and stepped up to the mare that shook and quivered in agony. One swift plunge and a few seconds of thrashing and it was over. Aberdin cleaned his blade on a handful of straw before looking to Neb coming with two horses, one for the Falcon.

xx

Yurik, son of Jorn Stepok, stepped out of the ring of shadowy figures. His flaming red eyes burned at Emmerant, while they ignored Slee. "You've come to rejoin us, Emmerant," said the warrior without joy at the news. "We've missed you."

"Of course, what else could I do?" lied the fat wizard.

"Come, receive the stone," said Yurik, holding up a pulsing red gem.

"I am old. Come here and place it upon me," said Emmerant with an innocent face. Slee gave him a look of disbelief but a covert wink told her to follow his play.

"Step away from there, Emmerant. I have not forgotten so easily. Not after millennia, eons in the cold ground."

"I have no idea what you're talking about," purred the fat man. "Step closer and I will do the same."

Yurik moved closer on high leather boots. Emmerant passed the well, holding out a hand. The red gem hovered before his pudgy hand when Emmerant said, "Now Slee! Say it now!" With these words Emmerant's out-raised hand became a claw that grabbed Yurik's wrist, well away from the ruby gem. Emmerant's hand was filled suddenly with a flashing green stone. "Now Slee!"

"Skeeki catcha sheck, no, that's not it. Skeeki—I can't, Emmerant. There just wasn't time!"

Yurik and the rest of the circle let up a shriek of terror in unison. The warrior drew his long sword and slashed at Emmerant's arm that held him close to the green glow. Emmerant let go and ducked out of the way in time, but looked up to see Yurik wasn't backing away but raising his blade to press his attack.

"Skelqi sorrisucoral shek sheek Nyoglatha —" shouted the fat wizard, raising his stone.

Yurik screamed again, but this time the others did not join him. Instead they said: *"Skelq, Nyoglatha, skelq—"*

Emmerant chanted his phrase while backing up. A quick jump saved him from falling into the well. Yurik slashed at his head but refused to come any closer.

"Emmerant, you've got him!" cheered Slee from behind him.

"It's no good, Slee. It has to be you."

The girl thought about this for a second. "Damn, this is that stupid virginity thing, ain't it?"

"Concentrate, Slee, and take this stone." Emmerant handed her the green gem. *"Skelqi sorrisucoral shek sheek Nyoglatha —"*

"I can't do it, Emmerant. I can't—"

"Try. You must—"

The circle of figures was shrinking. Emmerant could make out the faces of many friends and acquaintances, wizards and magic-casters, all in the thrall of the red stone. They began to raise their hands to join Yurik, who raised his sword for another strike. A shrilling noise was building in a hundred throats. Red eyes and gems glowed more intensely.

"I can't—" Slee begged a last time.

"Then hang onto me tight," said Emmerant with grave finality. He grabbed the gem in her hands along with her slender, clever fingers. "Forgive me," he whispered once before a torrent of alien syllables flew from his mouth. The effect on Yurik and the others was instantaneous, sending up an unearthly scream from many dozen throats. For a moment those surrounding them faltered in their steps, Yurik most of all. Under their screams was another voice, Slee's, that wailed as if her very soul was burning her from the inside out.

Yurik recovered a minute later. He pointed a finger at Emmerant and all the magicians and witches around them raised their hands likewise to deal death. Voices rose all about them, as did the feel of energy in the air. A spell of a more mundane nature than Nyoglatha's arcane sorcery was brewing. Emmerant stared deep into the green gem in both their hands. A bolt of fiery lightning came from the darkness and lashed both the fat man and the girl, making them both yell with pain. But the fire all went into the green gem and left the pair frazzled but alive.

"Harrumph," said the fat man as if he were dealing with a foolish novice or a washerwoman. The wizard knew—as did Nyoglatha now did—that all spells coming from the joined beings which comprised itself would fail as long as Emmerant held the green stone.

Nyoglatha snarled its displeasure through many mouths but Yurik's first and foremost. His sword came up. He and the rest of Jorn Stepok's warriors marched on the wizard and his assistant. Nyoglatha burned its hatred from a hundred eyes and what it could not achieve through magic it could through force. Yurik being closest was first to swing his sword at Emmerant. The wizard dodged the blow by backing over the small collapsed shrine of the deer-goddess, but this only brought him closer to other assailants. Slee motioned to her dagger but Emmerant shook his head no. "We must stay together. That is what it wants."

A Taavsite warrior behind them raised his ax and leapt forward. The blade peaked but never arrived. A spear appeared in the man's throat, sending him back. Emmerant turned and saw several horses breaking the line of the circle about them. Aberdin! And he had help. So few but if Emmerant hurried—

"Skelqi sorrisucoral shek sheek Nyoglatha —" he bellowed, raising his and Slee's hands.

Yurik and the rest screamed as Aberdin and his slaves cut down and trampled wizards and warriors alike. The respite was short-lived as a warrior recovered, stabbing his longsword through the chest of the woman who had hurled the spear. Her horse up-ended, landing on another wizard. Aberdin was powerless to help. He cut down a magister who tried to burn him with a flaming hand, while another sent yellow bolts of fire at his head. These dissipated harmlessly. Aberdin wasn't sure why and didn't have time to figure it out. His sword fell again and his horse's hooves likewise.

Emmerant saw another slave die with a dagger in his back, wielded by a hedge wizard who snuck up while his opponent killed another. Emmerant spoke the arcane words again and watched all those like Yurik stumble—but only for a second. The fat wizard wanted to see how Slee was doing but he didn't have time. If he was going to defeat Nyoglatha, it must be now.

"Skelqi sorrisucoral shek sheek Nyoglatha tonkin sklek soril!" With these words Slee let out a scream so dire it could be heard over all the rest. Yurik fell to the ground, his minions all around them likewise. A weird red smoke seemed to leak out his eyes then return.

"Not enough," cursed the fat man. "Gods, you can not have any more."

Yurik stood up, his wide mouth bent in a smile. The usual emotion-less voice was replaced by one of burning vileness and hatred. "Emmeranttttt—" it beckoned. Yurik raised his sword and stepped over the hole. The blade came down with sickening power for Emmerant could not block the descent.

Again it was Aberdin who saved his life. The Falcon took the sword stroke on his hand guard, deflecting the thrust. Pressing forward he formed a wall between the magician and Yurik. He had to use some tricky swordplay to keep from falling back into the hole as Yurik pressed him. Despite being on the defensive he did manage to cut the Taavsite once on the wrist. The man ignored the wound and pressed harder. But they didn't call him The Falcon for nothing. His sword-cuts were deft, slippery and often blinding. With one good feint followed by a lunge, he had Yurik's blade on the ground.

"Yield," said Aberdin, waving his sword point at Yurik's chest level.

Yurik snarled and raised his hand with the red stone buried in it. A whip of red flame flew into Aberdin's face, a blast that should have blinded him, but did not. Yurik snarled again.

"It's the stone," said Emmerant. "The one I gave you."

Aberdin drew the green stone from his pouch and saw that it glowed with a deep light of its own. "Yield," he said again, offering both weapons.

Yurik barked something incomprehensible and a dozen bodies were on Aberdin. The Falcon's blade danced a twisting spiral to deflect sharp points and flung stones. He felt someone at his back, almost turn to stab when he saw it was Neb. "The others?" Aberdin asked. A simple shake of the head told him they were the only two left. "No quarter then," he said with grim determination. Neb agreed and the fighting continued.

Ten men threw themselves at the two warriors, trying to stab them but if not able kill them then to foul their blades. The next ten attackers found Aberdin and Neb chopping and hacking but slowly being mired down in dead flesh.

Emmerant watched this and knew he must act or die. "Come, Nyoglatha, and may you rot in hell," said Emmerant knowing he too would be paying the price for his next actions.

" *Nyoglatha tonkin sklek soril!*" The fat wizard hurled the words at the swordsman as he tore into Slee's hands with his fingernails. At first this did little but eventually the man's hands drew blood and the red drops struck the stone as arcane words flew from Emmerant's mouth. Slee gave one last shriek and it was over.

The red smoke came out of Yurik's and all the other bodies in one great stream, flying into the hole like a crimson snake. Emmerant yelled more arcane words down into the pit as the final wisps of mist disappeared. With a deft foot he turned the lid over in one kick and then silence reigned.

The bodies of the magicians and warriors all stopped moving, then began to move again, each of its own accord. Aberdin and Neb saw their chance to act and raised their weapons for a final assault. Only Emmerant's loud baritone stayed their hands. "Enough! Aberdin! Enough!" And that was enough. The Falcon and his friend saw that the many live bodies around them were not attacking but asking questions like, "Where am I? What's happened?" None of which were answered. The swords came down and no more died that day. Almost.

Pushing a pile of corpses off him, Aberdin shoved his way over to the fat wizard who was gently laying Slee down onto the ground. Even from there Aberdin could see she was mortally wounded. He dropped his blade and leaned in close to her. She was saying something.

"Can I have my pony now?"

Aberdin nearly choked on the words, fighting back tears. "Just rest, Slee. Our good Emmerant will have you better in no time."

One look at the fat wizard shaking his head to the contrary told him there was no point in pursuing the idea.

"I would have liked you to ride with me on that pony, Aberdin," said Slee in a whisper.

"Yes, I would have liked that too." He ignored the ridiculousness of the image of them riding on a small pony. "We could go and have those adventures, eh?"

"I think I've had enough of adventures for now. Maybe tomorrow —"

Aberdin fought back the tears. "Yes, of course."

"And we could have finally got around to that other thing. But I guess I'll never —" and with that Slee passed from the world.

Aberdin rose, looked all around him. The collective wizards and witches who remained alive were all moaning and crying out for succor. Many of them had not eaten or drank, let alone slept, since Nyoglatha had taken them. Aberdin ignored them all.

"Was it worth it?" asked Emmerant.

"How can you ask me that?" demanded the swordsman, his hand flashing to his scabbard, which was empty.

"You saw your father, you grandfather. Was it worth it?"

"No! It damn well isn't! Slee!"

"I will be asking myself the same question tonight and for many nights. Was Slee's life worth all these we have saved and all those who would have suffered under Nyoglatha, maybe everyone?"

"She is only one girl but I would trade her life for a thousand others," admitted Aberdin, picking up his sword and sheathing it.

"And that is why the gods do not let us choose."

"Fuck the gods!" With that Aberdin stalked off through the necropolis, looking for a horse.

"Harrumph," said Emmerant after he left. "Good people!" he called out in his deep, commanding voice. "Gather here and I will help you all to get home quickly and in a better state than you are now." The stunned and wounded about him all turned and looked.

"Come, let me explain first, then I will show you all to food and water, bandages—" Jorn Stepok's manor was not far and Emmerant would take them all there first. "Come, sit here and I will tell you of a fool—"

One man stood up from the crowd. It was Turgin. "I resent that."

"Harrumph," coughed Emmerant, "Now, quiet and I will tell you —"

xxi

TWO WEEKS later, as Emmerant sat to a tea with butter sandwiches and small purple dates, the magical voice shouted out, "Aberdin Vol to see you."

"Send him right up," said the fat man without surprise. For a wizard who can scry the universe with crystals should know when company is coming.

The tall swordsman came up the stairs, having ridden the chair instead of the one thousand laborious steps of his first visit. His head was covered in graylocks and beard.

"Ah, Falcon, come join me," said Emmerant from his cushioned perch.

"Pillows again," was all he said as Aberdin sat with a flounce.

"What can I do for you, my good man?"

"Well, you had offered to show me my parentage, once—" Aberdin stumbled and left it hanging there.

"Yes, but first you must explain what you saw when the stone took you. I had thought my assistance wasn't necessary."

"That's just it, Emmerant. I never saw anyone. I saw my life rushing backward then, at the moment of my birth, a flash of light and nothing. What does that mean?"

Emmerant did not respond immediately. He sat back and thought. Aberdin waited patiently, watching the big man's lips move in and out in concentration.

Emmerant opened his eyes suddenly. "I don't know."

"Then look in one of your crystals and find out."

"You do not understand the use of crystals, obviously, my friend. First, I need to know where –and even when—I am to look. Can you give me some hint? Where was the last place you remember before the flash?"

"A battlefield. I was maybe seventeen, just a kid really, stupid, scared."

"Which battlefield? Who was fighting? Damn it, man, give me something!"

"I don't know."

Emmerant threw his hands up in defeat. "I can't help you, my friend."

Aberdin didn't say anything for a while, then he looked up at the fat man. "Maybe with time—"

"Perhaps, but until then?"

"You said you needed a man with my talents—"

"Yes, but the crisis has passed. Now what I need is about a week more of good meals and soft baths and some time to gaze in my favorite—"

"Yes, but after that. You'll see. You're going to need me. And I'll be around. *The Pregnant Virgin* most nights of the week."

"Fair enough, but am surprised you'd want anything to do with me. I mean after Slee—"

"Slee's death wasn't your fault."

"I beg to differ. If I had prepared her for the rite she would have survived it. It was only because I had to use her as a kind of magical siphon. If I had had time—"

"She might have been shot by a stray arrow or stabbed while you weren't there. We all took the chance and she died."

"You tell yourself that if it helps but I can not. I failed her. I might fail you. Or have to sacrifice you to save the city--"

"And I trust you to make that decision. You wouldn't make it callously, or casually or foolishly—"

"Enough with the adverbs—I take your point."

"Then it's a partnership?"

"That might be laying it on a little thick. Let us say we have an understanding."

Aberdin shook the large man's hand then dismissed himself. It was only after Aberdin left that Emmerant went to his crystal room and took down a dusty old rock he did not often use, for its amber-colored stains within spoke of strange magicks. He waved his hand over the stone and peered deeply into the smoky interior. What he saw there he did not put into words, merely looked away and wondered about his friend, Mr. Aberdin Vol.

Other Books by
RAGE m a c h i n e Books:

The Book of the Black Sun by G. W. Thomas
The Book of the Black Sun II: The Book Collector by G. W. Thomas
Debt's Pledge by Jack Mackenzie
Debt's Honor by Jack Mackenzie
Dragontongue & Other Stories by G. W. Thomas
Ghoultide Greetings: Horror Stories For Christmas by G. W. Thomas
Heralded By Blood by Jack Mackenzie
The Judas Gift & Other Tales of Mystery by G. W. Thomas
The Mask of Eternity by Jack Mackenzie
The Paradigm Trap by Jack Mackenzie
Shards of Time by Jack Mackenzie
The Star-Studded Plain: Space Westerns by G. W. Thomas
Swords of Fire by David A. Hardy, C. J. Burch, Jack Mackenzie and G. W. Thomas
Wild Inc.: The Shattered Men by Jack Mackenzie

... and more to come for the reader of Science Fiction, Fantasy, Horror, Mystery and Adventure. Check out our website at www.gwthomas.org.